And Your Byrd Can Sing

And Your Byrd Can Sing

Jim Roberts

ISBNs: 979-8-9933935-0-6 (paperback); 979-8-9933935-1-3 (ebook)

Library of Congress Control Number: 2026930260

First Printing: 2026

Printed in the United States of America

Published by Silent Clamor Press, Los Angeles CA

Cover photograph of vintage prosthetic arm courtesy of Enemy Prey Ignore Museum Gallery, Toronto, Canada. Used with permission.

Chapter 2, "Good Day Sunshine," was previously published, in altered form, as a short story titled "An Arm and a Prayer" in the short story collection *Of Fathers & Gods* by Jim Roberts (Belle Point Press, 2024).

Praise for Jim Roberts

In *And Your Byrd Can Sing*, Jim Roberts conjures a world so instantly evocative that, from the novel's very first page, readers are privy to and invested in the intimate pain and passion of Billy Balstrop—a boy who's lost his mother, sister, and arm to tragedy and is hell-bent on tracking down his absent father, no matter the cost. From Texas to Ohio to Mexico, and through both unspeakable violence, desperate choices, and palpable shame, *And Your Byrd Can Sing* is a deeply moving, transfixing story full of hard, brave truths that underscore our universal longing for answers, redemption, and belonging.

—WHITNEY COLLINS, AUTHOR OF *BIG BAD* AND
RICKY & OTHER LOVE STORIES

In the tradition of Southern Gothic, Roberts brandishes Flannery O'Connor grotesqueness to bring something akin to Cormac McCarthy's *Outer Dark* into the sixties and seventies. Billy Bastrop has one arm, a handful of wits, and a whole lot of pain to drive him and his tail-finned Cadillac through the "collective smallness" of Korvus, Texas and Cincinnati, Ohio on his hunt for salvation. But this book knows that if a person like Billy deserves salvation for his sins (even if they have roots in the sins of another) it is a burden of proof. The atmospheric writing of this novel illustrates how the smallest towns can hold the biggest atrocities. Roberts will leave you bruised and battered. And he only needs one arm to do it.

—TOBY LEBLANC, AUTHOR OF *SOAKED* AND *DARK ROUX*

An outstanding debut novel with brilliantly rendered story-telling and steeped in the essence of a place. Billy Bastrop will capture your heart, break it, and then capture it again.

—JOHN MATTHEW FOX, FOUNDER OF BOOKFOX AND AUTHOR OF
I WILL SHOUT YOUR NAME

From the little East Texas town of Korvus to Cincinnati, Ohio's Little Appalachia, Jim Roberts puts the dirty realism of U.S. poverty on a pedestal, not to worship, but to always keep in mind. *And Your Byrd Can Sing* is a bit of everything: bildungsroman, road story, action, mystery, but empathy and discovery are at its heart. Out of a long legacy of grit lit, Jim Roberts rises to the top. His writing doesn't stay mired in cycles of poverty and violence; he offers the reader a little bit of faith, a load of compassion, and a glimmer of hope.

—NICK REES GARDNER, AUTHOR OF
DELINQUENTS AND OTHER ESCAPE ATTEMPTS

Jim Roberts' debut novel sings with vulnerability in the tradition of Flannery O'Connor's "Good Country People," complete with its own prosthetic limb. Southern quirkiness and coming of age meet in this study of contrasts: title word play, religion as comfort and manipulation, a boy with one-too-few arms and Hindu Shiva with many, Southern drawls and Indian accents, exotic spices and Camel smoke. *And Your Byrd Can Sing* is an unflinching look at blood and gained family, tempered by often-dark humor and its music backdrop - the Beatles, Patsy Cline, Hendrix, Merle Haggard, and a reindeer Christmas chorus.

—AMY CIPOLLA BARNES, AUTHOR OF *CHILD CRAFT, AMBROTYPES, AND MOTHER FIGURES*

For Donna.
Thanks for the journey
full of love, laughter, and light.

Chapter 1
Carry That Weight

I've killed three men, but I'm not a murderer. Really, I'm not. The King James Bible—the official user's manual of Korvus, Texas, where I grew up in the 60s and 70s—says, "Thou shalt not kill." Many scholars interpret that to mean "Thou shalt not *murder*."

Killing ... well, it depends. I'm sticking with the scholars.

Whether God or law considers me a murderer, those three men are still my burden, my doom. They circle and hover, standing in my yard as I wash the car on a quiet Sunday afternoon. They move in and out of my dreams and bolt me awake, damp and dazed. Hang around when I'm alone, watching me eat or shave or take a piss.

For better or worse, they are gone from this world because of me and are as irretrievable as my right arm. The arm I lost when I was four years old.

Are their deaths forgivable? I tell myself yes, but honestly, I'm beyond knowing; you will have to be the judge.

But not before you know the whole story.

Chapter 2
Good Day Sunshine

It was a Hindu, not a Christian, who gave me a new arm. This happened despite the best efforts of my aunt, Sunshine Bastrop. I called her Sunny. She fought hard for my new arm to be a miracle from Jesus. If I had been lame or blind, or even comatose, her efforts might have worked. At least according to the Sunday morning TV preachers she sent money to, money we couldn't spare. But a new arm? Their weepy donation-driven miracles couldn't conjure that level of magic.

I was in third grade when she invited Brother Howard Granger for a visit. No, he wasn't a TV preacher. I doubt he even owned a television.

I knew something was up when Sunny opened the door after he knocked. Our usual reaction to people at the door was to hide in her bedroom closet and attempt to pray the intruders away, usually Jehovah's Witnesses or smarmy life insurance salesmen.

"I'm here to help you pray for the boy," he said, a dusty black Stetson in hand, loose turkey skin jangling around his Adam's apple.

He was thin, stern-faced with salt-and-pepper hair cut unevenly, like he'd run out of money halfway through. He said he was starting a new church in Korvus, the little East Texas town down the road from where we lived on a lonely stretch of US Highway 271, our only neighbors being a tattered weekend drive-in movie theatre, scattered stands of loblolly pines, and forlorn cattle.

The preacher and I sat alone in our tiny living room while Sunny got Cokes. He didn't speak while she was in the kitchen but focused intently on the empty right sleeve of my sweatshirt, where Sunny had folded it over and pinned it. It was typical for people to stare for a few seconds, then avert their eyes. Brother Granger gawped at my emptiness. A long, hard, hungry stare.

"Jesus Christ can give the boy his arm back," he said, and slurped the Coke. Sunny sat on the opposite end of the couch from him, her heft pressing a mournful croak from the springs and frame. Had the couch been a seesaw, she would have popped Granger into the air. She lit a Camel and studied the man.

"If you truly believe, anything is possible," he said. "Have you accepted Christ, Mizz Bastrop?" He fixed his small, dark eyes on her, unblinking and merciless. A challenge.

"You think Ah'm a goddamn atheist? Shiiiiiit," she said, twisting her head sideways, blowing smoke. "Nobody loves the Good Lord more than Ah do. You can bet your lily-white ass on that."

"Praise be, Mizz Bastrop. Praise be." He trained his snakish eyes on me.

"Boy, take that shirt off. Let's see what the Devil's done."

I turned to Sunny, and she nodded. She grabbed my left sleeve and pulled the shirt off. Granger reached for my scars, but I twisted away impulsively, violently, as if escaping a scorpion or big hairy spider.

"Don't you believe, boy? Or not?" His words boomed at me.

"Yes. No. What?" I said, wanting desperately to run out the door and down the highway. "Billy Wayne Bastrop!" Sunny shouted and stubbed out her Camel. She glared at me.

I was embarrassing her in front of the holy man.

I couldn't help it. I felt completely naked in front of the rough, grizzled stranger. No one other than Sunny had seen the truth of me. The scars at the top of my right shoulder, the scars that marked where my arm departed this world, were the most intimate, shameful, and sacred part of me. Much more so than my genitals. I sobbed and sank to the floor.

"Shit fire, Billy," Sunny said. "Git your ass up off the rug and let this man help you. Let the power and love of Jesus come into you." There was no stopping it. The two of them were a team now.

"Let me lay the healing hands on you, Billy." This time his voice was as inviting as he could make it but still held a whiff of menace—scary-sweet—like syrup flowing across shards of glass.

He put both hands around the top of my right arm socket. The coldness of his hands cut through my body, the chill shooting down my spine and into my toes. And as he prayed to Jesus to grow me another arm, his acrid breath wormed down my throat.

He laid on the hands a few moments at a time, almost knocking me to the floor, then broke away, mumbling to himself and slouching as if exhausted. He did this three times, led us in a long, rambling prayer, and finally announced he had to go to prepare a sermon.

"Bring the boy to services Sunday," he said to Sunny as they stood on the porch.

"Y'all handle?" she asked.

Granger brightened and cockeyed her, gave a brief, faint smile, and said, "Oh my yes, Mizz Bastrop. Just like the Good Book says, Mark 16: 'they shall take up serpents.'" Sunny almost beamed, a rare and curious expression for her.

"Are you that strong of faith, ma'am? Do you handle?"

"Ain't done it in forever. But Ah can take it back up. If you think it'll help the boy."

Granger clasped his hands and did a victorious pump. "It always helps to be of strong faith, Mizz Bastrop. Always."

As he left, she gave him fifty dollars for his ministry, which meant nothing but beans and cornbread for us that week. And never mind ice cream. Thankfully, we didn't go to his Sunday services because

Sunny said she couldn't stand to be around a bunch of holy rollers for two hours. Besides, she said, the assholes don't allow smoking.

For the next couple of months, the preacher stopped by on random afternoons. During these visits, he admonished her for not coming to his new church, The Church of All Truth. Then he repeated the laying-on-of-hands ceremony to grow me a new arm.

When it was apparent nothing much was happening, Sunny got tighter with the money until one day Brother Granger pointed at some scar tissue and convinced her the smooth, shiny bumps of skin were the beginnings of new fingers protruding from the top of my shoulder. He scored a healthy donation that day, but still eventually stopped coming, either disgusted by my lack of faith, or maybe just knew when to drop a scam that had run its course. I knew the man liked snakes. I think they were his kin.

It must have been tiresome for Sunny—a never-married, childless, fiftyish woman—thrust into reluctant motherhood. In those first couple of years—she took me in when I was four—I pestered her constantly about my missing family. It wasn't that I enjoyed hearing about my family's ruin, like a kid transfixed by the umpteenth reading of *Green Eggs and Ham*; I just kept hoping the story of Billy and his lost family, in at least one of the recitations, would have a different ending.

But the story never changed: car wreck, sister Lucy dead, arm gone. A family blinked away by fate on a blacktop road. My mother, Julia, a budding poet, foreshadowed Sylvia Plath and poured her blood down a rusty bathtub drain, unable to cope with Lucy's death and my mutilation. My father, Cecil—Sunshine's brother—apparently less courageous than my mother, loaded a pickup with the tools of his mechanic's trade and vanished into distant memory, erasing me from his life.

. . .

I constantly thought of my family, my missing pieces. Drew a hundred crayon pictures, Sunny sitting on the floor with me at the coffee table—a daring feat given her size—holding the paper because I couldn't steady the page and color with only one hand. She'd bring in Fritos and queso and giant slices of pecan pie and watch me color away at Mama's dress, Lucy's long hair, Daddy waving from his truck.

"They're not gone forever," Sunny kept telling me, taping my best work to the fridge. "You'll see them when you get to heaven."

"My arm too?"

She groaned, pondering the question.

"Ah don't know why not. The Lord probably ain't got nothing against your arm."

If prayer couldn't give me my arm back, I reasoned, there was certainly no retrieving the dead. But my father Cecil was another matter. He was alive somewhere, as far as we knew, but there were never any cards or letters. Or phone calls.

I decided he wanted to come back, but couldn't, because he was being held in an enemy prison, captured as a spy. Or hit his head and had amnesia and was stranded on a South Pacific island. I imagined him as a covert astronaut on his way to Jupiter, part of a top-secret U.N. mission to save the world. Could it be he was a time traveler? Chained in the dungeon of a medieval castle?

I built an ever-growing wall of movie-trope explanations around my heart to block out the darker, more venomous possibilities:

He didn't want me.

He never wanted me.

He especially didn't want the one-armed me.

———

The Hindu I spoke of was Dr. Vijay Chaudry, a pediatric prosthetics specialist in Dallas, who ran a clinic named New Limbs. Sunny and I left for our appointment at New Limbs shortly after sunrise on an overcast day in late November, three days before my ninth birthday. It was a long drive. About two packs of Camels long.

Sunny was against it. Mrs. Finch, my school nurse, who after much cursing (Sunny), name-calling (again, Sunny), and tears (me and Mrs. Finch), convinced her to take me to New Limbs. Finch called to make the appointment so Sunny could be spared talking to anyone and drew us a map with the clinic's address and phone number written across the top. The nurse also made a brilliant but risky move: She listed the doctor's name only as V.J. (not Vijay and omitting the "Chaudry") and made no mention to Sunny that he was Indian.

To find Dallas, we just pointed Sunny's boneshaker 1950 Ford pickup—inherited from her daddy, Turner Bastrop—west on I-30, listening to the radio reception improve from hiss-and-crackle to mildly audible as we got closer to the city, the country songs sounding more and more like actual music, reports of the President's planned visit that day cutting in from time to time.

Once in the city, however, we got lost three times before locating Dr. Chaudry's office two blocks north of downtown, between Big D Used Cars and Lester's Mustang Lounge. Chaudry's office was in what appeared to be a former gas station, or possibly a muffler shop, with the reception area located in the cash-register part of the building, and the examining rooms, X-ray equipment, and prosthesis display rooms in what used to be the garage bays.

There was no one in the waiting room. No patients, no receptionist behind the small battleship-gray metal desk. Sunny forced her ample butt into a green vinyl chair and poked another Camel between her lips. I sat beside her, thrilled by a stack of National Geographics a foot high on the side table.

Sunny had the room well smoked when a perfectly proportioned, obsidian-haired, caramel-skinned woman swept in. Her gorgeous hair was long and twirled and folded up on the back of her head, every strand precisely placed. She wore an ankle-length dress of shiny burnt-orange cloth, expertly wrapped around her classic figure: delicate shoulders, moderate bust, narrow waist, graceful hips, long slim legs. A red dot rested between her black eyebrows. You always remember a moment like this, the exact moment you fall in love for the first time.

The woman floated over to her ugly metal desk, an incredibly unfitting place for her to be, like a swan assigned to a rusted washtub.

"Be-lee Bahs-troop," she said melodically, addressing me and smiling. Drilling deeper into my heart.

"Yes, ma'am," I responded. Should I call her ma'am? That didn't seem quite adequate.

"The name's Bastrop, not Bahs-troop." Sunny's stone-tongue drawl came through a haze of smoke and startled me.

"Quite sorry," the Indian lady said to Sunny, "I must tell Dr. Chaudry you are here." She vanished in a swish of cloth and a hint of spice. I liked it here. I liked it here a lot.

"Now wouldn't that frost your balls!" Sunny folded both meaty arms across the barrels of her breasts, loose flesh hanging from her armpits almost to her elbows. She leaned her head back and exhaled enough smoke to finish filling the room with a stinking cloud.

"GD foreigners! And that stupid shit-for-brains, stupid-ass school nurse. Why didn't she tell us? Tears welled in Sunny's eyes. She gave me a pitying look, a look asking me to forgive her for leading us into some kind of trap. With genuine fear, she leaned over to me and whisper-shouted, "They're spies, you know they're spies!"

"Be-lee! Be-lee!" Dr. Vijay Chaudry burst into the room, followed by the graceful receptionist, so easy in her movements, effortlessly matching the doctor's rapid pace. The doctor was small and lithe, no taller than Sunny. He moved everywhere in a hurry and talked faster than anyone I had ever met, always using more words than necessary to make his point.

"Please now, Be-lee, please now, you and your mother come back to room number three. Yes, room number three it shall be." He waved his hands, as if he could create a current strong enough to sweep us into the correct room.

"Ah'm not his mama. Ah'm his aint," Sunny announced as we entered the exam room. She was almost shouting—which amped up her drawl—as if Dr. Chaudry was deaf and mentally challenged.

"I am so sorry, Mrs. Bash-trap, but please forgive me for not maybe understanding you, but … " his eyes shot back and forth at Sunny and me, clearly embarrassed, "… but you are saying you are a saint?"

He squinted, his smile forced and nervous. Sunny sneered and moved back two steps, curling her upper fluorescent lip. She raised her voice even more.

"Holy hell! Shit no, Ah'm no goddamn Catholic. Ah'm the boy's aint, Ah'm telling you Billy's my nephew. NAY-FEW."

With this, Sunny skulked to the window, exhaling smoke at shafts of sunlight that briefly crossed her broad face. She muttered something unintelligible—but you can bet hot and nasty—toward the glass.

"Yes, yes, of course. I see now. Be-lee, this is your aunt. You are the nephew. Very good."

"Yessir." I was terrified Sunny would gather me up and bolt from Chaudry's office in a snit. If I was lucky, maybe he would send her back to the front, to keep the pretty woman company. I couldn't leave Dallas without an arm. I was desperate for it, to take a first step toward normalcy. To move away from the otherness I felt everywhere and every day. But most importantly, I needed it to get my daddy back.

"Be-lee, please take off your blouse. I will return soon. Blouse and under garment off, OK?" He darted out like a cat. Sunny dropped her gaze-out-the-window ruse and shut the door behind him.

"Dr. Whatzit there must think you're a girl. Take off your *blouse*, Billy," she mocked him, but didn't attempt the accent.

"Some people call shirts blouses, Sunny. He didn't mean anything by it. I read that in my geography book." I unbuttoned my shirt as I spoke, and as I reached the last button, Sunny helped pull it off. It was unseasonably warm for late fall. I shivered anyway.

The doctor reappeared with a black bag. At his first touch, I withdrew, just like with Granger. I couldn't help it. Every time anyone or anything touched me there, something yanked me back. He was not surprised and spoke to comfort me.

"Oh, Be-lee. I am all about new arms and new legs, new feet and new hands. An arm to make you a whole boy again, no? An arm to make you very, very normal! Now, please, don't be holding back from the doctor. Let the doctor see!"

I forced myself to relax, and he examined my shoulder. He pushed his fingers firmly against the scar tissue until he found the flatness on one bone, the tip of another one. He inspected my ribs and my collarbone on the right side. Then he checked all the same places on my good side.

"Does any of this hurt, my child?"

"No," I said. The only pain being that of shame and longing.

"Such good news," he said to Sunny. "I can help your son—sorry —nephew. Definitely yes! It will not be a functional prosthetic, of course. Purely cosmetic. But these things can help with self-esteem. With psychological healing."

Sunny sighed and mumbled something under her breath. Please God, not a slur.

"Yes, Mrs. Bay-torp?" Dr. Chaudry inquired, trying to be polite, thinking she had said something meant to be heard.

"It's Bastrop."

"Of course. My apologies." Vijay smiled and bowed. She snarled. Pursed her lips. I thought she might spit into his gleaming hair as he bowed. I closed my eyes, scared. So close, so close.

The receptionist entered with a saucer in her outstretched hand.

"Please, Mrs. Bar-stroop. If you please, no smoking."

Sunny moaned and slammed her cigarette into it. "Worse than a GD church around here."

"Veda," Dr. Chaudry said to the receptionist, "perhaps our guests would like some refreshments?" He made a mock drinking motion.

"Do you have Cokes?" I asked. Veda nodded, then turned to Sunny.

"And for the lady?" she asked sweetly.

Sunny said nothing at first, still eyeing that last, half-smoked Camel Veda had confiscated from her.

"Ah'll have some ahs tee, if you got it," Sunny said.

Veda's eyes widened, she blinked rapidly at Sunny, then at Chaudry. The doctor and Veda moved to the door, their voices low and quiet. He handed her some cash. Not three minutes later, I saw Veda pass by the window, headed into Lester's Mustang Lounge, money in hand.

"Be-lee, now we must take some X-rays," Dr. Chaudry said, drawing my attention back to him. "Have you had X-rays before?"

"No, sir."

"Well then, it is nothing to pain you. We take pictures of your bones, that is all. This way, please."

I sat motionless on the X-ray table, as instructed, and stared out the window. Veda passed by, headed back from Lester's Mustang Lounge with our drinks.

I waited for the giant insect-looking machine to pulse, or stream some lights, or at least hum into my shoulder. Nothing. And before the machine could make a peep, Sunny crashed through the door, holding what appeared to be a small bottle of champagne.

"Git off that table, Billy. We're going home."

Here it was, the crash-and-burn I'd feared all morning. My face warped into an airless, tearless cry at first, then went full motor. A runaway, stuttering wail.

Sunny pulled me from beneath the X-ray machine with one hand and flung the little bottle of champagne on the table with the other. Between drooling sobs, I saw the label. It read: Asti Spumante.

"Communiss spy bastards!" Sunny dragged me down the hall toward the front door. Dr. Chaudry was on our heels, trying one more time to reason with her.

"A terrible mistake on our part, Mrs. Bat-soup. Of course, of course! Your religion forbids alcohol. How could we know? We thought it was what you wanted. A thousand—no—a million apologies!"

Veda was near tears, still holding my bottle of Coke.

"But the boy! He is so disappointed," the doctor implored. "Let us give the boy an arm today. He is so sad. Please, we meant no insult. An unfortunate misunderstanding."

"Goddamn heathens! Ahs tee. TEEEE! Don't y'all know plain English?"

"Please, Sunny," I stammered, and dropped to the floor, wrapping myself around a leg of Veda's desk. "Please," I begged. I knew there was only one chance at this. We'd never come back if we left.

She said nothing, just looked down at me disgustedly, mouth agape that I would betray her with these strangers. Then she dug through her massive patent-leather purse, scratching and pawing until she found a previously lost, stale Camel, bent almost at a right angle.

"Hell. Ah'll be in the car." She raised the aged cigarette overhead like an extended middle finger to the world and rolled out the front door.

After the X-rays, they moved me back to exam room three for the actual fitting, where I sat alone a while, wrapped in an elephant-patterned blanket and listening to violin music on the radio, and then the news, talking about a parade for the President later that morning.

When the door opened, it was Veda flowing into the room, cradling my new arm against her bosom, as she would cradle a newborn. Veda, beautiful Veda, my angel of restoration, delivering another unforgettable moment for me—rare and precious—the moment of the second chance. I ogled the arm. I ogled her, too, trying to breathe in her perfume without her noticing.

"Go ahead," she said. "Touch it. Hold it. Get familiar." She placed it gently in my lap.

My first thought was, it feels like a log. Close your eyes and it's a log. Open your eyes and it's a hard plastic log covered in weirdly pinkish, spongy rubber "skin."

Dr. Chaudry arrived to do the actual fitting, carrying an octopus contraption of straps, buckles, and brass buttons that snapped everything into place. He looped one canvas belt around the upper part of my chest, did some adjusting and tugging, then positioned two other straps across the collarbone and around my neck. With each step of the process to attach it to my body, the arm lost more and more luster in my eyes. Sunny will shit, I thought, when she sees how complicated this is.

It was much heavier than I imagined, hot, totally useless, and had to be worn over a T-shirt to keep from chafing my skin. Although my outer shirt was supposed to hide the straps, one strap always showed in front unless I buttoned my shirt all the way up. Which choked. Not to mention making me look more freakish. What a letdown. All the angst and struggle of the morning for this unwieldy thing? No way it would impress anybody and would be of no help in luring my Daddy back. It seemed all we'd managed to accomplish was to put lipstick on my pig of a problem.

Veda managed to cajole Sunny back into the building to pay the bill, and while Sunny paid Veda, I walked over to get a closer look at a tall bronze statue in the lobby. A dancing Indian man with four arms. He stood in a circle that looped from beneath his feet up and over his head, around all his outstretched arms. The man held a small drum in one of his four hands, a flame in another. I'd seen a picture of this guy somewhere before. He gets four arms. I get one. Shit.

Sunny went to the bathroom, and I examined the statue's metallic hair. It held a skull and a moon. I swept my finger over the moon, then let it slide toward the skull, enthralled. Veda came up close behind me.

"That is Shiva," she said, her breath tickling my neck. "He is Lord of the Dance."

"More like Lord of the Arms," I said. Veda smiled and touched me lightly on my good shoulder.

"See, Shiva's dance is the dance of all things, the very motion of the universe. He dances inside the circle. This shows that beginning and end have no meaning. Something ends, another begins. Death becomes life and life becomes death, over and over."

I really wanted to hug her—she had been so kind—but I knew better. Instead, I blurted out something I'd never told anyone, especially Sunny.

"I can feel it, you know. I can still feel my arm sometimes, just like nothing happened. It hurts, it burns. It even itches. In the dark, before I fall asleep, I'd swear it's back." I stared at the floor, embarrassed at what I'd just confessed, afraid she would think less of me. Afraid she'd think I was crazy.

"Sweet boy," she said, bending down, bringing her face close to mine. "People often feel things that cannot be seen."

Veda stood so close, soft-eyed and smiling. A warmth wafted from her to me. A connection. I could see us married one day. Owning a coconut farm. Riding elephants at sunset.

"C'mon Billy. Time to git the hell outta Dallas!" Sunny said as she emerged amid flushing noises from the bathroom, shattering my daydream.

On my way out, Veda stopped me at the door and slipped a small cloth Shiva into my shirt pocket. It was as beautiful as she was. Hand-sewn in gold, red, black, and blue silk. "For good luck," she said.

While Sunny searched for Stemmons Freeway, making a wrong turn every other block, I took Shiva from my pocket. I propped my fake arm across one leg, and wedged Shiva between a couple of fingers on my new hand, so I could stroke all four silken arms and name each one: Arm of the Dance, Arm of the Moon, Arm of the Skull, Arm of Asti Spumante.

We were cruising south on Stemmons, searching for I-30, when we heard the sirens. The wave of noise came toward us, northbound. Sunny slowed, and a half-dozen police motorcycles screamed past, escorting a motorcade of large, dark convertible limos. Everybody in those cars was hunkered down except for the drivers. In one car, a man in a suit—his necktie flapping in the wind—lay across people cowering in the back. A human shield.

We had no idea what we'd seen, the whole stream of vehicles flashing by in a long black blur. Soon after, at a Dairy Queen in Mesquite, we heard that somebody had killed President Kennedy. Sunny, Shiva, and I had passed through the tail of his surging comet.

We set our corn dogs aside, and Sunny led a prayer for his soul, asking that it be taken directly into the heart of Jesus. As we drove home, there were more radio reports of the assassination. I took Shiva from my pocket. I touched the skull. I traced my finger around from top to bottom, bottom to top, hoping Veda was right about the circle.

———

Three days later, on my ninth birthday, we watched JFK's funeral on television. Well, I watched. Sunny lapsed into a fit of wet, flappy snores on the couch. There was a half-eaten cake on the coffee table, and alongside the cake, my new arm. Red gift bow attached.

Even to a nine-year-old, the images were overpowering: a flag-draped coffin, rolling caisson, riderless black horse. Flames on a grave. John Jr.'s heartbreaking salute.

I, too, will salute my father, I vowed. If I ever see him again.

Chapter 3
Blackbird

My new arm immediately drew unwanted attention from a kid named Ricky Vander, a year older than me. The Vanders bought a large tract of land directly across the highway from us when I was in first grade and turned it into their weekend ranch, where they occasionally came to ride horses, hunt, fish, or host pool parties connected to local politics in some way. A.W. "Arch" Vander, Ricky's father, was the Knope County Judge, and they were rich as fuck.

A county judge in Texas is not a "wear-a-black-robe-and-preside-over-court-cases" judge. Most don't even have law degrees. They are more like CEOs, presiding over the County Commissioners Court, the body that basically controls all the county's money. In other words, the power brokers.

My introduction to Ricky was as a sniper. He'd lie in the grass beneath a long fence row across Highway 271 from our house and plink at us with his BB gun. At first, he'd ding shots off the tin carport roof while we were unloading groceries. After two or three dings, Sunny would tromp around the front yard in a paranoid fit, cussing and searching the sky for Japanese Zeros. Over time, we figured out it was Ricky shooting at us, but not before he had taken out a taillight on the pickup and punctured a half gallon of milk as Sunny lifted it from the truck bed. That's when Sunny called his mother, and the harassment stopped. Well—paused. Ricky kept shooting, only now his aim shifted a little farther from our bodies. Some days from my bedroom window, I would watch puffs of red dirt rise from the driveway, and occasionally a BB would pop off the window glass as I looked out, leaving a dark chink.

Although we played together as kids, we were never really friends. I was just another one of Ricky's toys, invited over to the ranch to alleviate his boredom on long weekends or provide him with an audience for all sorts of boyhood malfeasance, serving as his lookout while he tormented cows or chickens on the ranch.

I longed for companionship and distraction from Sunny's lunacy, so I was willing to tolerate a lot to keep getting invited to hang out on the Vander ranch. True, Ricky was hard to take, but it was worth it to be somewhere *else* for a while, someplace where you didn't drink rusty tap water, the toilets flushed first-time-every-time, and trucks didn't rattle the windows in their frames at each passing. And color television. With a clear signal. Heaven.

My new arm fascinated Ricky.

"It looks so creepy," he said. "You can't feel nothing with it?"

"Just where it touches the top of my shoulder."

He punched it.

"Oww."

"You said you can't feel it."

"I feel it hitting my ribs when you punch it."

"What about this?" Ricky opened his pocketknife and stabbed my fake bicep.

I just looked him in the eye and shook my head.

"Damn, that's cool. Nothing at all?" He pulled the knife out and sliced it across my rubberized hand.

"Shit! Stop it. Please. Sunny's gonna kill me. This thing cost a lot of money."

"Take it off. Let me wear it."

"Three arms?"

"Sure. It'll be like Halloween. Oh, oh, let me have it on Halloween!"

"I got to go."

"Wait. I have an idea." He ran into the house and came back with a Sharpie.

"Tattoo!"

"No. No." I backed up, but he grabbed me. I slapped at him and broke away and ran toward the highway. But Ricky was always bigger and faster than me. He caught me on the shoulder of 271 and wrestled me to the pavement. Two eighteen-wheelers roared by, spraying us with dust and dried grass. I struggled beneath his weight but there was no escape. He held me down and wrote his initials—RAV—in squiggly letters on my brand new arm.

———

Sunny burst through my bedroom door one spring Saturday morning with newly washed and sun-dried clothes for me: a pair of almost new, still too stiff Levis, white Fruit-Of-The-Loom underwear, white socks, and a blue T-shirt. I got dressed and slipped my feet into black Keds while she poofed up her perm and coated her wide, flatworm lips with brilliant red lipstick. We were going somewhere—a rare event, other than our trip to Dallas and the New Limbs clinic almost a year earlier. Sunny almost never left the house, except to work half-day shifts at the DQ while I played in the car, or to shop at Piggly Wiggly.

I walked to the bathroom for Sunny to tie my shoes—as a one-armed boy, it took me until fifth grade to completely master shoelaces one-handed. She knelt to tie my sneakers, and I looked down her nose at those shining lips. I rarely saw her with bright red lips, and it disturbed me for some unclear reason, the same way it would have disturbed me to see Mr. Garth—our pig farming neighbor to the south —spray-paint a fluorescent smile on one of his boars. Shoes tied, we grappled with my arm and harness, as we always did, but finally managed to hang it like a misplaced stalactite from my shoulder tip. Sunny ran her fingers across the slice to my hand, then pointed at the RAV initials further up.

"Goddamn brat. Ah ought to kick his ass. But then the Judge would own mine."

In the kitchen, I helped her pack six cases of home-canned vegetables, two each of string beans, green tomato relish, and mixed tomatoes and okra. We loaded the vegetables into the old Ford pickup, asked Jesus to crank it for us, and when He did, headed for town.

Korvus, like most small towns in East Texas, is built around a courthouse square. Many neighboring towns have beautiful granite or limestone Victorian courthouses on their squares, surrounded by trees and grass and flowers, but Korvus has a concrete, almost windowless bunker on a treeless square, encircled by native asphalt. At three stories, it's the tallest building in Knope County, a stack of three gray blocks, each successively smaller, like a set of porch steps left behind after a tornado has blown your house away. *Forever Texas Magazine* once voted it the ugliest courthouse in the state.

But the courthouse wasn't the only ugliness. One of the first things I learned to read was the billboard—soon to be demolished— we passed every time we ventured into town:

Welcome To Korvus
Home of the Blackest Oil
And The Whitest People in Texas

Crude pumped from beneath the woods and creek bottoms around Knope County was low quality—heavy, dark, and sulfurous—better suited to making roofing tar and asphalt than gasoline. Over time, tiny Korvus laid claim to the title "Asphalt Capital of the World." A Pentameter Petroleum Corporation refinery and asphalt plant built in the early 1950s provided income to half the families in town, but came with a steep price: cursing Korvus with a vile stench, an almost daily assault of rotten eggs, scorched sulfur, and eye-watering refinery-generated flatulence that draped across downtown and many residential areas east and north.

We were infamous for the odor. Rival football fans arriving on Friday nights mocked us with clothespins on their noses and hand-written signs held high during the game: *Korvus—Deep In The Fart of Texas.*

Looking back on that day, our trip into town should have been a simple errand but ended up leading to an encounter with a boy destined to be my first haunter.

We were in town to deliver a partial payment to George Byrd—known by all as the Tamale Man—for mowing our property and plowing a half-acre for Sunny's vegetable garden. She hired him every year because he was honest, reliable, and willing to barter his services for her home-canned food.

George was a short black man, not much taller than Sunny. He was about fifty, thin but muscular, with a patchwork of silver woven through his hair and long sideburns. Round, wire-rimmed bifocals magnified his bright, kind eyes. George's tamales were the best, freshly steamed and plump with chicken or pork, fillings darkened with spices and chopped chiles. Sunny, of course, called him Blackbird, but never to his face.

He sold tamales on Friday nights and all day on Saturdays, but otherwise fed his wife Bitty and their eight kids by doing odd jobs, including auto repair. George was a great shade-tree mechanic, even selling a used car occasionally, usually a clunker he'd bought for next to nothing and restored to running condition, fixing only the mechanicals, not bothering with body or paint work, to keep his prices low. He called them "uggers" (ugly good runners)—ugly skins with good guts.

George's tamale cart stood in its usual spot on the square, beneath the statue of Colonel John Nathan West, the town's memorial to the Confederate War dead. The Colonel faced south, everyone said, so his ass would be in the face of any future invading armies that might descend upon us from the rest of America.

Sunny parked her father's old pickup nearby, and George walked over to the truck when he saw us.

"Morning, Mizz Sunshine. How's that, Billyboy?" George smiled at me and tipped his cap.

"Mornin', Mr. Byrd," Sunny said. I snickered inwardly, hearing her call him Mr. Byrd instead of Blackbird.

"Billy and I brought you a payment."

"Very nice, very nice," he said, and picked up two cases of vegetables at once to put in his pickup. When he came back for the tomatoes and pickled okra, he asked Sunshine, "This here the truck you want to trade?"

"Sure do. Ah never know when it'll start."

"Now, Mizz Sunshine," he said, eyeing the old Ford as he spoke and running his hand along the rust-streaked hood, "y'all come over to the house and look at a fine car I been fixing up. I'll do you a sweet deal on it."

"What make?" she asked.

"Cadillac," the Tamale Man said. "Fifty-nine. Got them big, tall tailfins." He illustrated by holding his hand flat out and about chest high.

Did George Byrd see the same explosion in Sunny's eyes that I saw? If he did, the Cadillac's price shot up a few hundred dollars. She believed, largely because her father had believed, that Cadillacs were the only cars worth owning. They were the cars of recognition and respect, the cars of oil and oil men. A status now extinct among the Bastrops.

"Would you take this truck and my old DeSoto both in trade?" she asked.

"That old black car you got in your yard? The one's been waterlogged?"

Sunny nodded.

"Sure thing, Mizz Sunshine. I'd take it too. I can make almost anything run. I'd need some cash in addition, though. We can talk about how much after you look over the Caddy."

I didn't know what a Cadillac was, but I knew that as we ran our other errands in town that day, Sunny was consumed by the idea of trading her glitchy pickup and the broken-down, stinking DeSoto for a real car, a car even Turner Bastrop never had.

After Turner's attempts at sharecropping cotton failed, he took work as a roughneck for Texaco. Texaco was generous with its oil-field workers in those days, giving each man a share or two of stock along with his weekly paycheck. Turner never sold a single share of it. As the decades passed, his nest egg grew impressively for a blue-collar man.

He was nearing retirement from Texaco as a tool pusher (drilling foreman) when he died. His handwritten will gave all the stock to Sunny, with the stipulation that she never sell any of it. He figured she'd never marry, so his plan was for the stock dividends to provide her a steady, if moderate, income.

She wouldn't be wealthy and would need to work, but she wouldn't struggle or starve. Sunny also inherited his small house on five acres across the highway from what was to become the sprawling Vander Ranch. My father, Cecil, got nothing.

Now she had me under her roof, a twist Turner Bastrop never saw coming.

———

We headed to the Byrd household late Sunday afternoon. It was beyond the double row of railroad tracks on the far western edge of town, between the fetid oil refinery and the chicken processing plant, almost constantly cloaked in the stench of one or both. There were several modest, livable homes very similar to Sunny's house. But, for every livable house, there were at least two or three that were little more than rotted shacks made of bare, gray-weathered plywood, some with rusted tin roofs, many with tar-paper roofs. Kids and dogs—lots of dogs—ran up and down a sidewalk, chasing a bicycle tire they continuously kept in motion.

The Byrds' house was larger than most other houses on their block, blond brick with a stony, raked-dirt front yard. George had cars in various stages of repair parked in neat rows on either side of the house, and car parts organized expertly in a nearby shed.

We immediately spotted the Cadillac. George had showcased it under an impressive live oak tree in the front yard. He and his wife, Bitty, shot out the door as soon as we arrived.

"Welcome, Mizz Sunshine," Bitty said. "So nice to meet you."

As they stood and made small talk about the weather, it struck me how similar the two women were in stature and bearing. Both about the same size with pumpkin-round faces, one ashen-pale, the other deep ebony. Sunny was taller than Bitty, but Bitty had a larger, more blubbery bust than my aunt. Both looked uncomfortable in the presence of strangers, especially with strangers in a mixed-race group.

Where Bitty spoke eloquently with only a tinge of accent, Sunny spoke ... like Sunny. Later, Sunny would tell me how Bitty had been too fancy and "put on airs" while we were there. I had no idea what that meant.

George yelled at some of the kids playing the bicycle tire game to be more careful with the younger children. Several children answered, some calling him Daddy and others calling him Mallyman.

He showed us to the car, a well-used and battered pale-green Cadillac Sedan DeVille, one of the largest cars ever made. It was produced in 1959, the high-water mark for the size of tail fins in

Detroit. And because Cadillac was the best of all cars, it had to have the tallest of all fins.

It was a fitting car for Sunny. It matched her scale and provided a persona and bravado she could never muster without the aid of GM heavy metal. Even in its tattered state, the car's brazen ostentatiousness provided more than workable transportation from Points A to B in daily life; it came with an illusion of respect. And maybe a means of escape—no matter how momentary in a run for groceries or gossip rags—escape from a Dairy Queen life, from a lonely, decaying house on the edge of a great pine isolation. It was all self-delusion, of course, but you can't hear people laughing at you with Patsy Cline belting out "Crazy" on a Cadillac radio.

"She's got some rough spots on the body, Mizz Bastrop. You can see this window here's a little cracked. And that left back door only opens partway. But I got her running real nice."

"Ever been wrecked?"

"Truth is, ma'am, it was in a little tussle. Now, let me ask you, you don't drive much over sixty, do you?"

"Not less Ah'm being chased." Sunny's rare attempt at humor stunned me.

"That's good, 'cause I wouldn't recommend pushing her over sixty. Faster, and things could go whopper-jawed. But if you go easy on the gas, then this pretty little lady will take you anywhere you need to go. Here ..." George handed her the keys. "Why don't y'all take her out for a spin? See for yourself."

In the car, Sunny seemed a half-acre from me across the vast bench seat. We drove out of town on a blacktop road, past the chicken-processing plant, through thick groves of pines to Monty Lake.

We found Hank Williams on the radio and ran all the electric windows up and down—neither of us having ever seen such magic before. Sunny moved the power seat into every possible position, and I screamed with laughter when she tilted the seat too far back, lost control of the wheel, and nearly veered us into the water.

We drove all the way around the lake, staying out until dusk. Somewhere on the return trip to tell the Tamale Man she would indeed buy his patchwork Cadillac, we named it The Green Lizard.

———

Near sunset, as Sunny and George negotiated the final price of the car, traffic increased on the Byrds' street. Cars full of white people crept down the street, slowing down almost to a stop as they passed in front of George and Bitty's home.

George glared over his shoulder at the passing cars. I turned and saw an older boy—about thirteen—staring out at us from inside the house, from the Byrds' living room window.

"You can go on outside, honey," Bitty's voice rang out from somewhere deeper inside the house. "I believe it's dark enough now."

The boy stepped out of the house with the deliberate, cautious steps of a cat in a dog park and sat on the front porch swing.

I knew it was impolite to stare, but I couldn't help myself. The boy was clearly black, with classic black features, but he was white. I don't mean with skin the color of a Caucasian, I mean his skin was the color of pearls, looking as fragile and translucent as bone china. He had tightly wound snowy hair, packed close to the scalp. We locked eyes for a second or two, then I looked away, chilled as the full weight of his gaze met mine. His pupils were black, but the irises were barely distinguishable from the whites of his eyes, save for an infusion of creamy pink, like drops of blood mixed in a glass of milk.

"Wonderful, are you feeling alright, baby?" Bitty's voice floated from the house.

"Yessum."

Bitty came out and stood on the porch near her pale child. She looked favorably at the sky, now devoid of the sun, a force—we later learned—that made the photophobic Wonderful sick.

"Billy, this here is my oldest boy, Wonderful," she called out to me.

I lifted my hand in acknowledgment, and Wonderful did the same, then I looked quickly away again, shamefully, wishing Sunny and George would hurry and strike a deal for the Green Lizard.

The cars full of white voyeurs made a final run down the street. I understood their circular cruising. They were waiting for nightfall and the emergence of Wonderful Byrd, Korvus's only tourist attraction. They slowed and gawked, and Bitty dashed toward the sidewalk from time to time to angrily wave them away with her dish towel.

George brought Sunny over to introduce her to Wonderful, but she just nodded her head a half nod in greeting. Bitty sent her son to the backyard and out of view of the unwelcome drivers-by, and George went inside to get the car title.

"Looks like we both have special boys," Bitty said to Sunny.

"What do you mean, special?"

"That they'll both be having a hard time in the world, you know, because of their differences."

Sunny stared at her blankly.

Bitty continued, "And it's not bad enough for my boy to look the way he does. That poor child's got a simple mind. A real simple mind. He's nearly fourteen, and it's like he's about four or five. They say it could've been caused when he was birthing. Not enough oxygen to his brain."

"Some young'uns just come out half-witted like that, I guess. Probably ain't your fault."

Bitty's brow crinkled, and she pulled her head back. "That boy's got a heavy burden. You saw them vultures driving by, ogling him. They were pretty quiet tonight, but sometimes they catcall. Holler out the meanest kinds of things. Happens almost every night during the summer."

"They likely never seen a fella odd as him."

"I prayed to Jesus all day long and into the night right after Wonderful was born. And you know what He told me?"

Sunny picked something from between her teeth with the edge of a fingernail.

"Jesus told me to name my boy 'Wonderful,' so every time his name was spoken, it would make people smile, and it would make him feel like he was somebody special, but a good special, not a freaky kind of special. You know what I mean?"

"If that's what He tole you, then Ah'd say you done the right thing. Ah sure wouldn't buck the Good Lord."

George arrived with the pink car title. Sunny wrote him a check for the Green Lizard and gave him the keys to the two vehicles she had promised in trade.

"Come on over and get that DeSoto off my property soon as you can," she said as we headed to our new car.

"Yes, ma'am. The one's got all that water damage. Was it in a flood or something?"

Sunny didn't answer. She cranked the Caddy. Let it roar.

"Haul it off. Ah cain't wait to be shed of it."

As we drove away—passing yet another car of whites headed towards the Byrds—I looked back and saw Wonderful's head rise above the backyard fence, haloed by a yellowish streetlight just then flickering on. He waved at us—a slow, childlike goodbye. Something I'd never forget, not because of the circumstances of that first meeting or because of his wraithlike appearance, but because in barely a handful of years I would be the instrument of his death.

Chapter 4
Piggies

I could have used a real family all my life; of course, I could have used their love and teaching and guidance. But I could have used a father most of all as I ventured clueless and anchorless into the testosterone crossfire of Korvus High School in the fall of 1969.

"What do you think happened to Daddy?" I asked Sunny this as she watched a rerun of *Wagon Train,* and I lay on the floor, puzzling over my ninth-grade algebra homework. "You think he's still alive?"

Sunny sucked her cigarette long and hard, as if to draw all the nicotine out in one pull, and was silent for a moment. Shot a long trail of stink out the side of her mouth.

"If Ah know your daddy, he's still a-kickin. Out there somewhere." She stood and waved a hand at the smoke and went to her bedroom, soon to return with a small box of photographs.

"This here's a box of stuff your mama had. Ah got it from y'all's house in Angelina before it got emptied out. After you was hurt. There's a picture of your daddy in here somewhere." She pulled pictures out two and three at a time and laid them out across a scratched black Naugahyde ottoman.

"See this picture here? That's your mama and daddy, taken right after they married. And this one was probably taken over at Houston." She pointed at a photo of my mother holding me as an infant in one of those coin-operated photo booths that stream out six pictures for fifty cents.

"Here's another one of your daddy and some men working." A dozen men turned sullen, weary faces to the camera. They stood shoulder to shoulder, grimy and sopped in sweat. Sunny pointed Cecil out to me, the tallest of the bunch, shirtless, cowboy hat in one hand and machete in the other. He was lean and muscled with short-stubble hair ringing his head below a giant dome of bald scalp.

"Are they in a jungle?"

"Cane fields. You know, ribbon cane. *Sugar* cane."

"I thought Daddy worked on cars?"

"He mainly did. Helluva fine mechanic. But come harvest time, he cut cane for extra money. Lots of men down that way did it. Damn hot hard work."

"Who's the baby?" I said, picking up another picture.

"That's Lucy on her first birthday."

"Looks like a party."

"Yeah, a couple your mama's friends and their kids was there, and Ah drove down to Angelina in my old DeSoto, when it still ran."

"I bet Daddy could've fixed it."

"Sure. Ah used to pay him to work on it now and then. Ah'd drive it down to y'all's place and leave it for him, then ride the Greyhound back to Korvus. After a week or two, he'd call me, and Ah'd take the bus back down to Angelina to get it." She swept the pictures back into the box and handed it to me, saying, "You ought to keep these."

I sat on the couch with the box in my lap and gently lifted one picture after another in random order, hoping some deeply buried but sweet memory would come forth. In one shot, Lucy and I played tug-of-war with a scruffy stuffed rabbit, me with two arms. Did I remember the bunny or its name? No. Did I remember having two arms? No. The faces of my parents were the faces of strangers from another world, a world that somewhere held my lost arm. I tossed all the photos back where they belonged—into my little cache of missing pieces.

During a break in the *Wagon Train* action, I opened a topic with Sunny that I'd been avoiding.

"Ricky invited me to spend the night over at the ranch and go dove hunting with him and his daddy tomorrow morning."

"You?" Sunny scoffed. "You never been hunting. They might just want you for target practice. Or to run and fetch the birds."

"You care if I go?"

"If you wanna hang out with assholes, then gwon. And don't wear your arm over there." She still held a grudge over Ricky mutilating my first arm when we were kids. She didn't need to say it. I was wearing it less and less anyway. "And just so you know, they don't give a rat's ass about you," she warned again.

She was probably right, but I knew I would go anyway because that's how pathetic I was, willing to overlook Ricky's twisted approach to companionship in exchange for a break in monotony, to escape Sunny's dark cloud for a few hours. With Ricky and me, our relationship clearly went only one way. His way. I was never invited to their fancy house in town, and Ricky rarely acknowledged me in the hallways of our high school. He was a rising-star linebacker for the Korvus Lobos and didn't like being seen in public with a stray cat like me.

"Ah ever tell you about the boar your daddy killed when he was, I guess, eleven or twelve?"

"Not that I remember."

"Our Papa made us tough, Billy. That's why Ah say Cecil's still out there. He can take care of hisself. Just like with that boar.

"Papa took us deep into a cypress bottom that day. Trees and thicket so tight daylight'd hardly pass through. It was fall, but the weather ain't cooled off yet. We were riding on horseback, me and Papa together, on his ole black horse and Cecil on a mule. Papa killed many a wild hog in that bottom. A couple winters that was about all we had to eat.

"We'd stopped at a clearing where hogs'd been wallowing, right by the river. Papa took the horse and mule down to drink, and me and Cecil walked around the edge of the wallow. Big ole spiky needles cut us up, and skeeters the size of blue jays tried to eat us alive. Ah just knew some kinda booger would pounce any minute.

"Cecil spotted a tunnel through the vines and underbrush, and since Ah was the oldest, Ah went in first. So, there was some grunting and snorting and then Ah came face-to-face with a hairy, stinking sow. Ah about trampled your daddy in the mud trying to reverse my ass back out into the open, that sow right on my tail. She had a buncha babies up in that thicket, and a wild sow with babies will sure as hell kill you. She'll kill you dead as shit." Sunny paused and guzzled her Coke, glanced at the TV, where Apaches were attacking a stagecoach.

"How'd y'all get away?" I asked.

"Papa shot the sow. Cecil had helped me up a live oak, and the sow fell dead a few yards in fronta him 'fore he got up the tree."

"I thought you said *Cecil* killed the hog. And it was a boar, not a sow."

"Ain't finished the story yet.

"Both Papa and Cecil had twelve-gauge shotguns. Single shot. Before Papa could reload, a huge razorback boar came stomping up and froze right between Papa and Cecil. The boar rooted the ground a time or two, then made a beeline for Cecil on a dead run. I could see Papa grabbing and patting hisself all over, like he couldn't find another buckshot for his gun.

"Cecil slung his gun down in the mud and started up a tree. But Papa would have none of that. He hollered at him to stand his ground: 'Git your gun outta the fucking mud, BOY, and git ready!'

"Cecil was shaking and crying, and too nervous to get up the tree anyway, so he did as Papa said, and pointed the gun at the charging boar. That boar came right at him, gnashing and chomping. Long ole nasty tusks. Cecil's gun was swaying all over the place. He was barely twelve, mind you; that goddamn gun was way too big and heavy for him.

"Ah screamed and hid my face. Papa kept hollering at him. 'Stand yore ground! Stand yore ground!' Poor Cecil. Papa was always yelling something at him.

"Next thing was, Papa yelled, 'Shoot! Shoot!' The blast about scared me off my perch. When Ah finally peeked through my fingers, Cecil was flat on his butt, his back up against the tree.

"When the boar fell, its ole wiry flea-ridden head landed in Cecil's lap. The hog was dead, but Cecil'd been cut. Way the hell up high." Sunny unconsciously touched herself on the inside of her right thigh, very near her crotch.

"Cut almost to his ... well ... almost to his balls. Cut him bad. Papa laughed at first, but Cecil kept bleedin' and bleedin' till his overalls was soaked. That boy went white as a summer cloud and passed out. Papa finally stripped Cecil's clothes off and used his pocketknife to cut some bandage strips. Poor kid shoulda had stitches, but Papa didn't believe in doctors. Your daddy ended up with a bad scar on his thigh, long as your hand. Thick and hard and shaped just like a crescent moon."

"I bet Granddaddy Turner wished he'd brought some extra shells," I said. She stood and gathered our two empty Coke bottles.

"That's the hell of it, Billy. Papa did have one. Right in the breach of his GD gun. Ah saw it when I put the guns up back at the house. He just wanted to test Cecil. See if he'd stand up to the boar. I'm pretty sure Papa'd shot it if Cecil hadn't braved up."

She headed into the kitchen to trash the empties and clean her ashtray.

"Pretty sure," she mumbled on her way.

———

As a teen, there were times when I hated them all for leaving me behind, and more than once did I strike a match and hold it close to the box of old family photos Sunny had given me, then lose my nerve, and singe the few precious fingers I owned rather than burn the only bridges to my past.

I hated my mother, Julia, for being so beautiful and leaving me behind to live with Sunny. I hated Lucy for being such a sweet ghost, for not allowing me to know her, for being more shadow than substance. Julia had chosen to leave me, that was true, but her decision was irrevocable. I convinced myself she would come back if she could.

But during intermittent bouts of wallowing in love, longing, and hate, blaring *Sgt. Pepper's* or *Electric Ladyland*, I found an acute—but complicated—emotion for Cecil. Something that wasn't fixed, but vibrated, waved, mixing and remixing, at times equal parts loathing, hope, a peculiar admiration, and rage. All because Cecil lived. Lived willfully out there somewhere without me, unknown, undefined. A gaping absence. The nine-hundred-pound enigma in the room.

I'll find you, I vowed to the absence. I'll find you and tell you how much I wanted to know you. Tell you how much it hurts. How much I hated you in the dark of night. And how much I wanted you to rescue me by sunrise.

Chapter 5
Think For Yourself

The main gate to the expansive Vander ranch was directly across Highway 271 from Sunny's house. Past the front gate and across the cattle guard, it was about a quarter mile of gravel road to the main house on the property. I walked in fading daylight down the long path to the Vanders' main ranch house, carrying a change of clothes and a toothbrush in my Army surplus backpack. In my hand, I carried my new, unopened *White Album*.

Ricky sat on one of several lounge-type lawn chairs by the swimming pool, bugs swarming all around the floodlights. He had a gallon of Jack Daniels next to his chair—half full—and was sipping it from a coffee mug. I knew immediately that Judge Vander was not around, although his truck was parked in the driveway.

"Where's your dad?"

"Mama got him. They went to play bridge in town, said they'd be back about midnight. Want some Jack?"

I looked around to make sure we were out of sight of Sunny's house and let Ricky pour me a full mug of whiskey. He and I had sneaked a sip from several bottles in the ranch house bar over the years, but this was the first time we had been there without one of his parents around.

"That's too much. Your dad will know!"

"Don't turn chickenshit on me, Bastrop. He's got a case of the stuff in the stables. We could drink this whole bottle and he'd never notice."

"We drink all that and nobody's getting up at six to go hunting. You told me your daddy said six a.m. Sharp."

"Piss on him. Hey, I know. We could ride Daddy's new bull, Buckshot." Ricky grinned and punched me, knowing I was as likely to ride a bull as I was to fly to Mars.

"I'd rather just drink and listen to this." I held up the *White Album*.

"Pussy music. Let's see if we can get Merle on the radio."

Ricky was way ahead of me with the Jack, but I could catch up fast, since I'd never had much booze and my tolerance was low. Every sip snaked into my brain, and soon my teeth and lips vibrated.

Gnats were thick, attracted by all the light. Ricky stumbled up to the house to turn off the floodlight and came back with magazines and a flashlight.

"Sumpin to read?" I slurred.

"Oui," he drawled a poor French accent. "Oui, oui."

He plopped down a half-dozen *Oui* magazines, each cover featuring what at first appeared to be the same buxom, blond, almost naked girl, but on closer inspection, they were actually different girls. Different and the same. I took another slurp of Jack, and this time it surged into my dick, making it roil and buzz.

After a few more gulps, Ricky decided to unzip his pants and point his dick at the stars. He started to stroke himself, sank lower in the reclining lawn chair and wedged the flashlight into the plastic webbing of the chair so the light would shine on the magazine, which he opened to the centerfold, and spread it across the empty chair between us.

"Jack-off party!" he said.

"Oui," I said. I was two places at once, both on the lawn chair and floating above it, hot honey oozing through my veins in place of blood, cheeks flushed. I ignored the *Oui* girl and let Rita Burke come to mind, a girl I'd been obsessed with since junior high but never spoken to. I was sure she didn't know I was alive. She wore swishy skirts that zipped up the back, and I imagined myself in her room in her glitzy house—her dad was a doctor in town—with *Sgt. Pepper's* playing and her laughing and me unzipping her skirt with my teeth. But the image dissolved as suddenly as it appeared. I had one arm, and I needed two for Rita. Jack was pretty good, but not that good.

The whole enterprise began to fizzle for me until Ricky said, "You know what they say? Some other guy lopes your mule, it feels just like you're with a real girl. Wanna try it?"

I drained the last of my whiskey.

"I dunno. Sounds kinda weird."

"Come on, don't be such a dud about every damn thing. You do me first, then I'll do you. Let's see if it's true. I'll close my eyes."

As I considered the concept—strange boy hand equals imaginary girl hand—the whiskey spoke to me, hot whispers in my ear, "It's fine … why's it matter? … who's gonna know?"

While I floated there trying to decide, Rita reappeared, skirt unzipped. I leaned to get a better look at the *Oui* girl. Too beautiful to be real, legs too long and nipples too hard in the golden flashlight glow.

Black Jack and Rita and the *Oui* girl coalesced and overwhelmed the last of my normal senses. I would indeed, indeed, yes indeed, like to know what a real girl feels like. I moved off my chair toward Ricky.

As I reached for his dick, floodlight exploded across us. We drowned in a lake of sudden, frightening light, jumping and tripping over each other, scrambling to get to our feet and get our pants up. I stomped down on one of the lawn chairs and my foot punched through the webbing. No amount of shaking and kicking dislodged the chair as I hopped around in a circle, clawing to get my jeans up, the lawn chair-turned-snowshoe stuck on one foot. Ricky kicked wildly at the whiskey bottle, trying to send it into cover in the high weeds. But there was no chance of hiding the stack of magazines.

I had my pants up and buckled when the sliding glass patio door squeaked open, and the wide shadow of Arch Vander's cowboy hat fell across our little slapstick show. Ricky managed to get his pants up only as high as his butt cheeks before his father got through the door and onto the lawn, quick-stepping right at us.

"The hell's going on out here?" He scowled at Ricky, then gave me a death stare, his face full of disgust, as if about to spit.

"Daddy. Nothing. We ... uh ... we were looking at these magazines."

Vander stepped to the edge of the pool toward the stack of *Ouis*. I bent to retrieve my backpack and the *White Album*, thinking I might slip away in the dark, but the whiskey had a different plan. I stumbled to my knees and belly flopped in the grass.

"Y'all are drunk as shit, aren't you?" He lifted Ricky's coffee cup to his nose. "Get your goddamn pants up, boy."

Ricky stood and wobbled and pulled at his jeans until they were back in place. He pinched his shoulders inward and lowered his head, eyes glued to the ground. I struggled to my feet, a first hint of vomit forming in my throat.

Vander picked up a magazine. Held it to the light and thumbed through it.

"Would either of you numbnuts know what to do if you got your hands on one of these?" He unfurled a centerfold and shook it in Ricky's face. Ricky didn't move. I swayed and watched a moth crawl across my shoe.

Vander pointed at me. "I'm awful goddamn sure you wouldn't! Y'all weren't touching each other, were you?" He squinted at me and set his jaw.

I doubled over and puked.

"No, sir, no, sir," Ricky said.

Vander rolled up the magazine and whacked Ricky twice in the face with it. "I should hope the fuck not. 'Cause I guarn-damn-tee you I'll put your nuts in a jar and keep them on the mantle."

I gathered my stuff and headed around the opposite side of the pool.

"Where you going?" The judge asked.

"Home?"

"Oh hell no. That loony aunt of yours is jumpy as a cat. Liable to shoot you at this hour. I don't want you staggering in over there full of liquor. Not from my house. You two get inside. Sleep it off."

Chapter 6
Happiness is a Warm Gun

At six the next morning, I woke on the floor next to the bed I should've been in, struggled to my feet, and dragged a head-full-of-rocks hangover down a hallway toward a hazy light. The light came from the kitchen, where Judge Vander sat alone in a cane-back chair pulling on heavily scarred cowboy boots, once dark brown but now faded to an oddly pinkish color, with rock-hard cow-manure barnacles crusted on the heels.

The whiskey was mostly—but not entirely—gone from my system, and I swooned a bit in the doorway. When I saw him alone there, without Ricky, I paused, and on impulse, tried to turn back down the hall, hoping he hadn't seen me.

"Coffee?" He asked before my slow-as-syrup brain could shift my body into reverse.

"No sir."

He poured me an extra-large mug.

I blinked at him dully.

"Is Ricky still asleep?"

"I sent him down to Mr. Garth's place to borrow some bird shot. We're running low."

I sat at the table and watched my reflection ripple in the steaming blackness of the coffee, the mug almost too hot to touch.

"Well, answer me this, Bastrop. Are you some kinda damn queer or something? 'Cause I'm pretty sure I saw you trying to grab my son's pecker."

I couldn't speak. I averted my eyes and stared into my undrinkable coffee, looking for some words there. I felt a tremble in my elbow and it moved to my hand. I set the practically boiling coffee down on the table and gave serious thought to declaring myself sick and bolting out.

"We were pretty drunk, sir," I squeaked out, not much above a whimper.

His crisp blue eyes took me in carefully, shoes to cap, and when he was done looking me over, he said, "Well, I hope to fuck that's not what I saw. Keep your goddamn hands to yourself around here. Hear me?"

"Yes, sir."

"'Cause you know what? It's not common but hunting accidents do happen from time to time. Trust me, nobody looks good with a hide full of birdshot."

Knots took hold in my bowels and chest. He peered out the little window over the kitchen sink at a pair of headlights making the turn onto the main ranch road.

"That's Ricky," he announced.

Thank God.

As the truck made its way up the quarter-mile approach, Vander began to hum. His hum turned into singing, and he watched the truck approach and sang softly, in a smooth baritone:

I went to the cellar to get some cider
And there sat a cockroach jackin' off a spider
I went to the attic to get some gin
And there sat the sumbitch doin' it again

Ricky came through the door with a case of birdshot, and the singing stopped.

Vander looked at his watch and said, "Boys, it's quite unlikely the doves will commit suicide. We're going to have to shoot them ourselves. Let's saddle up."

———

The three of us rode single file through the gathering light—Judge Vander on War Eagle, Ricky on Falcon, and me on Abbey.

War Eagle was a towering, bad-tempered Appaloosa who nobody but Arch Vander could ride. All the Mexican ranch hands gave War Eagle a wide berth, and Vander always strutted more than usual when he had a reason to saddle up the big stallion and stick twelve hundred pounds of barely controllable muscle between his legs.

I had long been envious of Ricky's horse, Falcon, a bronze Remington sculpture come to life. Even standing dead-still in his stall, his mane had a sense of flow and speed, as if he was leading a renegade pack of mavericks to freedom, all muscle wrapped in a silky coat. Falcon was a shiny, deep chestnut color, tinged with black on his legs and taut belly. Some mornings right after daybreak, I'd hear him whinny and snort in the pasture across the highway from our house. I'd stand in the window, naked except for my underwear and fully visible to all the wild-ass truckers on 271, and watch Falcon sprint like a demon, breath streaming behind him in the cold air like the contrail of a sleek fighter jet.

My horse for the hunt would be Abbey. She was old, tired, sweet, agreeable and about as dangerous and exciting as a golf cart. I didn't really need to hold her reins because she was programmed to follow the other horses wherever they went. It made sense, I guess. I'd never been invited to ride at the ranch. Had never been on a horse at all.

We left the house and headed east into a hazy sun with War Eagle in the lead, Falcon behind him, and Abbey and me brown-nosing Falcon. About a mile out, we stopped atop a low ridge above a dusty, rocky gully. Judge Vander pulled half a dozen tin cans from his saddlebags and scattered them on the ground around us.

"Let's take a little target practice, boys."

Vander and Ricky dismounted in one smooth motion. I dropped Abbey's reins and tried to maneuver my right leg up and over the back of the saddle, but caught my pant leg and tumbled to the ground. Ricky gave me a hand up while his father packed the cans full of gravel.

"Him first," the Judge said, tipping his head toward me. "Ricky, you throw. When I say pull."

I opened the breach of the single-shot .410 they'd assigned to me —generally considered a child's gun—held it between my legs, and inserted a long, thin shell into the breach, a toy-like shell compared to the thick, lethal rounds Vander and his son plopped into their guns. They each carried an Italian-made Benelli over-under twelve-gauge, the combined cost of which—I was sure—would buy Sunny a brand new non-whopper jawed Cadillac.

"Pull!"

Ricky threw the can underhanded in a steep trajectory out over the ravine, giving it plenty of hang time. I jerked the gun to my shoulder, pointed it vaguely in the direction of the rapidly descending tin can, and pulled the trigger.

There was no "bam!," only the thud of the can landing untouched at the bottom of the gully, and the sounds of the Vanders chuckling.

"Now that's what I call going off halfcocked," Vander smirked.

The .410 I had was a single-action gun, meaning it had to first be manually cocked before it would fire. Learn something new every day.

"Stand back and let Ricky show you how it's done at the Vanders'." Ricky stood expertly with one foot forward, gun barrel at a forty-five-degree angle.

"Pull!"

Judge Vander flung a hard, fast one into the sky. Ricky's shot splintered the can into a shower of dirt and aluminum shards that caught the rising sun and fluttered like glitter.

"Throw me two, Rick." He positioned himself.

"Pull!"

Ricky pitched two cans in quick succession, and they moved together as if connected by an invisible string. Vander blasted them both at the top of their arc.

War Eagle jumped and tugged at the mesquite bush where he was tied. Falcon pawed the ground. Abbey nibbled at a tuft of buffalograss.

"That's enough of this. Let's not waste our shells. We're hot today," Vander said.

"Listen, son, I got a little business to take care of over at Boxcar City. I'm going to see a Mexican named Jorge Tico. Put these in your game pocket." He picked up two of the unused target cans and handed them to his son.

"And listen carefully to what I say when we get over there. When I say 'pull,' you throw them high as you can. Got it?"

"Yes sir, but ..."

"No buts, you just do it now, you hear?"

Ricky nodded, face full of confusion and concern.

I shivered and shook, partly because of the hangover and the weird spider-cockroach song, and partly because I was nervous about the idea of riding into Boxcar City. But then again, we were with Judge Vander. He owned the place after all.

———

I'd overheard things about Boxcar City from teachers and kids at school, and Sunny had told some tales. I didn't believe much of it. Until I went there with the Vanders.

Many area ranchers and farmers wanted to hire cheap Mexican laborers, but few were willing to provide them housing. Vander saw that as a business opportunity, since he knew no one in town would rent to the Mexicans, even if there was enough space available for all of them, which there wasn't.

Vander found a way to do it fast and cheap. He bought up old box cars from the Southern Pacific railroad freight yard in Dallas and set them up tract-house style on the outer reaches of his ranch, near the bottomlands.

All the tenants were men. If they were married, their families usually stayed behind in Mexico, so Vander could put eight or ten or maybe even twelve men in one boxcar, dormitory style, with cots and wood-burning stoves. Ricky said he charged fifty dollars a week per man. "And that includes free firewood."

The workers were willing to pay because a month of twelve-hour days here equaled a year's wages back home. Occasionally, the Knope County sheriff would raid the place and arrest anybody without documentation. Sometimes, he only arrested those who were owed back wages by a rancher having a hard time making his payroll that month.

———

We followed the Judge, and he led us toward the lone muddy street of his makeshift village, a street that bisected two rows of metal dormitories, ten on either side. As we approached the boxcars, War Eagle's odd violet eyes batted against the stench of an open sewer flowing south into Cypress Creek.

"You boys sit tight." Vander dismounted and pulled his Benelli from a holster strapped alongside War Eagle. He loaded his shotgun and handed his reins over to Ricky—who held them as I imagined you'd hold a tiger's tail. Vander nestled the Benelli across the crook of his left arm and fingered the handle of the .45 revolver in his belt holster before walking along a line of boxcars that had been numbered "1" to "20" with a can of spray paint. He walked toward a group of men standing around a burn barrel.

Five skinny young Mexican men, most with droopy mustaches or ear-to-chin, wispy sideburns—wearing Saturday-go-to-town laundered blue jeans and brightly colored discount mart sweatshirts—stood around a fifty-five-gallon drum that produced more smoke than warmth. From my angle, heat waves wafting from the fire distorted their facial features, each face a melting shapeshifting carnival mask.

A dirt-colored dog with matted hair and scattered bare spots across its back trotted from the nearby woods, pulled its tail aside, and shot out a long, spiraling, yellow turd. The dog plopped its rectum into the muddy street and dragged itself toward Judge Vander, an expression of dog ecstasy on its face. When the dog tried to mount his leg, he knocked it aside with the barrel of his Benelli, careful not to dip the business end of the fancy double-barrel in the mud.

Ricky and I exchanged anxious glances, but decided not to speak, hoping to remain as invisible as possible in this hidden place. Vander spoke in a low voice to the men around the fire, some Spanish mixed with English and hand signals. One of the men pointed at boxcar number three.

Judge Vander walked there, signaling us to ride down. He walked to the open door of boxcar number three and shouted inside for Jorge Tico. He shouted again, his voice reverberating in the crude metal house, sounding like God with a drawl. Eventually, a short Mexican came out, so short I at first mistook him for a young boy. He stood shirtless in a cheap straw cowboy hat with a cyan bandanna circling the crown. As I got a better look at his face, and the obligatory mustache, I could see he was no boy, about twenty years old, and moved with surety at first, then trepidation, wisely frightened of the well-armed Arch Vander.

"Habla English?" Vander asked.

"Si, uh, yes," said the Mexican, "little bit." He held a finger and thumb a fraction apart.

"Your name Jorge Tico?"

"Si."

"Jorge, I'm Judge Vander, and I own this land you're on and that house there you're living in." He pointed at the boxcar with his shotgun.

"Si, Señor Vander." He looked back at the cold, dank metal box and beamed a smile befitting someone just emerging from a palace. "This very fine ranchero here. Muy bueno."

"Well, I'm glad as hell you like it here, Jorge. You want to stay a spell longer and earn you some more of that good American dollar?"

"Si. Yes. Of course, Señor, Mr. Vander." Jorge's eyes widened, and he frowned with concern. Vander was upset about something. I could see Jorge squinting, as if searching his mind, maybe going over the events of the past work week. Had he broken something? Maybe he had driven a tractor too fast? Too slow?

"You like white girls, Jorge?"

Jorge looked puzzled by this question, and I silently tried to guess the right answer for him. Would "no" be an insult? Would "yes" get him a belly full of birdshot?

Vander didn't wait for an answer. "If you do, Jorge, stick to the white girls in town. I don't want to catch you birddoggin' after one of my girls like you did up at the main house last week. Any girls you see up there are my daughters. You don't look at em. You don't talk to em. Not if you want to work around here. Comprende?"

Jorge looked more confused than ever. The wheels spun faster and harder.

Vander turned his back to Jorge and pointed toward the tree line that ran along the sewage ditch.

"PULL!"

Ricky flung the two cans his father had given him, up and out against the sky. They reached their apogee about fifteen yards from the flaming barrel. Vander annihilated each target in turn, as they hung momentarily at the point where gravity began to pull them back to earth.

He never looked back at Jorge or the others. He mounted War Eagle and pointed the ornery Appaloosa down the mud street out of Boxcar City, toward a placid little pond far from the stench of the bleak little hamlet he'd created, ready now to spend the rest of the morning dropping doves from a brilliant sky.

Chapter 7
Dig a Pony

The next few hours were spent blasting mourning doves as they circled a small pond at the farthest eastern point of the Vander ranch. Ricky and his father brought down all the birds. After several attempts, I was able do a half-ass, one-armed, shoulder-cock-fire of the little single-shot .410 shotgun they'd assigned me. And once or twice, I might have even had my eyes fully open. But of course, I was too unpracticed to hit anything as small and fast as a mourning dove in flight. After the first five or six attempts, I pretended to hunt from that point on, pulling the trigger now and again at empty sky, hoping I wouldn't actually kill anything.

"Looks like I beat you today, son. Ten to nine," Vander said. "They've stopped flying this way, so let's head to the house."

The Judge rode out a few yards ahead of Ricky and me, and sang out:

Oh, I'm talking 'bout a monkey and a baboon
Sittin' in the grass
Monkey stuck his finger up the baboon's ass
Baboon said, "Now that ain't fair,

You stuck your finger where there ain't no hair.

Shit almighty. I gave Ricky a wide-eyed, sidelong glance. *What's up with this?* Ricky refused to look my way and nudged Falcon into a trot to put some more distance between himself and me.

We topped the ridge near the spot where we'd started the day with target practice. Vander stopped War Eagle and looked across panoramic pastures, broken here and there by a clump of post oaks or cottonwoods ready to drop their leaves, or a scattered strand of loblolly pines and scrub cedar, impervious to the coming winter.

"Son, I don't believe your friend's nicked a bird all day. Maybe he should take another crack at it." He pointed at the beer can I'd missed early that morning, lying inert in the wash below, leaning against a rusted-out stock tank.

"Want another try?" Ricky asked.

"Why not," I sighed.

Ricky leaned to dismount Falcon, presumably to throw the can for me.

"Stay on your horse, son. Let him shoot at it there on the ground. That can's not in much danger either way."

I looked at Ricky with a "what-the-hell" face, but he looked away. It was true, I had no one to teach me hunting ethics or protocol. But I'd read plenty of gun and hunting magazines at the barber shop. I knew honorable hunters never shoot birds at rest, only on the wing. The Judge was going out of his way to mock me. Was I the monkey? Or the baboon?

I moved to climb down from Abbey and shoot the GD can.

"Just tell him to shoot it from where he sits. Abbey don't care," Vander said.

I gave up worrying what he might think of me and instead throbbed with humiliation. Anger. I'd show him.

I reached to whip the .410 from its scabbard, movie-cowboy style. When I jerked at the gun, it fired, still halfway in the holster. Some pellets took a swath of skin off Abbey's lower leg and peppered the ground, kicking up swirls of red dirt around us. I'd forgotten to unload the gun before we remounted to ride out. But much worse, I'd left it cocked.

Abbey—the notoriously mild and sweet Abbey—bleeding, stung by pellets, and terrified at the inept shooter atop her, reared and pawed the air with her front legs. I flung the gun to the ground and took a hang-on-or-die grip on the saddle horn, but she still threw me off with two bucks. Falcon bolted down the steep slant into the gully, and War Eagle slung his head side to side, snot flying, and launched into a rodeo show of frantic bucking. Judge Vander scolded his horse with a harsh, hung-spit growl: "Steady Eagle. Steaaaaady Eagle. Waaaaaaar Eagle. Steaaaaddy!"

I landed in the dust and bull nettles and immediately focused my full attention on War Eagle, thinking him the most dangerous. Vander remained mounted and masterfully brought the big Appaloosa under control; the horse's snowy white eyebrows twitched, and its head jerked, its strange violet eyes locked on me the entire time.

Falcon was down on his side in the gully. Moaning and sluggishly kicking one front leg at the sky. Ricky struggled upright in the gravel beside him, dazed and groggy, the game pocket of his hunting vest ripped loose, bloody birds dropping out and thumping to earth.

"God fucking damn!" Vander barked as he scrambled off War Eagle and dropped the reins. He slid and stutter-stepped down the loose sand and rocks to get to Ricky and his injured horse. War Eagle trotted off toward the house. Abbey followed.

"You alright?" Vander asked. He told Ricky to stay down, grabbed one of his arms, cautiously moved it around, then the other. Then both legs. Does this hurt? Does that hurt? Any pain? Ricky was okay. He got up, almost every inch of him heavy with red dust. They both turned to Falcon.

Ricky patted and easy-talked Falcon until he was calm enough for the two of them to steady the horse's wayward leg. Ricky gripped the leg in his armpit while his father ran his hands slowly and methodically from hoof to shoulder.

"I bet it's not broken," Ricky said. "He'll get up. Let's back away and give him a minute. I bet he can get up on his own."

Vander shook his head and kicked the ground.

"It's not broken. Is it Daddy?"

"I'm afraid it is. Sure as fuck. Right above the fetlock. The cannon bone is cracked. Probably a spiral."

I looked down on them from the ridgetop, every cell in my body thumping. I tried to will myself invisible.

What's the right thing to do after wounding someone's horse? And after causing a prize quarter horse to spook and break a leg? Help dust Ricky off? Bring the water bottles down? Or reload the .410 and put it to my head?

Falcon's sides heaved under the hazy sky. He lay quiet now, waiting. Once, he tried to roll and rise, but fell back with a whoosh of air from his black nostrils.

Judge Vander took his .45 Smith & Wesson revolver from its holster—the snake charmer Ricky told me he always wears when hunting—and handed it to Ricky.

"I can't do it, Daddy."

"You gotta be a man about this, Ricky. There's nothing we can do for this animal."

"Let me run to the house and call the vet. There's got to be something they can do." Ricky's voice broke. He fisted tears from both eyes, the moisture and thick dust muddying his face.

"Take the gun, son. Man up. A man doesn't do what's easy. He does what's right."

The Judge brought back that phlegm-edged growl to his voice. Not as harsh as when he scolded War Eagle back from his flailing panic. But enough.

Ricky took the pistol. Said nothing else. Just stepped over to Falcon and never paused, and shot him twice in the head.

They climbed out of the ravine to where I stood impotent and guilty. My wish for invisibility came partially true; Arch Vander walked past without a word or a glance. Ricky—puffs of dust lifting from his body with every step and silent tears tracking down his filthy face—shoved me to the ground with both hands.

"Pussy!" he screamed.

The Judge whistled for Abbey, who was still grazing within sight, and she dutifully came. He and Ricky rode her slowly back to the house. I retrieved the .410 from the edge of the gully that was now a grave for Falcon and Ricky's nine doves and followed the horses back to the house.

Ricky would forever hate me for Falcon's death. But I didn't return the hate. Not then anyway. Not until after Wonderful Byrd died.

Chapter 8
I'm Down

After Falcon, there was an almost daily posting of signs on my locker door, all by Ricky and his posse:
PUSSY
FAGGOT
NEED YOUR MONKEY SLAPPED?
SEE BILLY WAYNE AFTER SCHOOL

And once, a round, dried, crumbly horse turd taped to the handle.

Before the signs, I had mistakenly thought I could slip through Korvus High School over the next four years essentially invisible and ignored. There had been several factors in my favor:

- I was an outsider living in the sticks whose only family member appeared to be a sideshow escapee driving an ugger.
- Some days, I had a useless plastic log hanging from my shoulder. You'd think that would make me visible as hell, but paradoxically, it did the opposite. It made people

57

avoid me altogether. Some were sympathetic but tongue-tied, others repulsed but ashamed of their repulsion, and some simply hated gimps.

- I was a dedicated scholar with a voracious reading habit—always, always reading. Anything and everything. I wouldn't restrain my bookish nature for the sake of popularity. It was the only way I had of honoring the memory of my mother, the nascent author and stillborn poet.

But the final death blow to my hope for invisibility was Marsha Fergus, one of the faculty advisors for The Akela Club. Miss Fergus taught Advanced Placement History and was the assistant director of the Shewolves drill team. She produced the annual program and skit for the school-wide Christmas Assembly—years later to be renamed the Holiday Assembly—in addition to staging two full-scale plays every year, one drama and one musical comedy.

She was much younger than the other teachers at KHS, and her demeanor and dress made her appear out of place among the faculty —yet just as misplaced with the students, like someone a little too old to be a Shewolf herself but not quite ready to step into adult life.

The Akela Club was an academic honors society for boys at Korvus High School, named after the wolf character in Kipling's *The Jungle Book*. Girls, back then, had a separate honor society, the Athena Club. The new inductees from the freshmen class of Akelas —which included me—were named halfway through the year. In a school district where it was common to budget more for athletic tape than for the entire high school English department, the club's name was more an allusion to our football team, the Lobos, than it was to the literature of Kipling.

The faculty and some enlightened parents considered it a great honor to be named an Akela. And it was true that several four-year Akelas had won National Merit Scholarships. An Akela from the 1920s was on the Texas Supreme Court, and another had served in an unspecified capacity in the CIA before his untimely and unexplained death in Chile in the late sixties.

All incoming Akela Club members were required to entertain the school with a skit of some kind during the traditional Christmas Assembly—essentially as an initiation rite—because it's always fun to laugh at geeks and freshmen.

———

Fergus summoned us to discuss the obligatory skit, and I arrived along with four other 1970-71 Akela inductees at the appointed time and place, the physical sciences lab on the first floor of the main building.

I had known two of them since grade school: Allen Crane and Joe Rand. Of the other two, one was a transfer from a school in Longview and his name was Terry Singer, and the other was a black kid, and although he was from Korvus, I didn't know him because he'd attended Booker T. Washington Jr. High the previous year before the all-black schools were closed and their students bused to the formerly all-white schools. His name was Holly Atwood, but naturally, everyone called him Hollywood.

The skit the five of us would perform that year would turn Allen and me into notorious figures in the long history of the Akela Club, the two of us forever linked in the ribald folklore of KHS. My missing arm and Allen's girth alone would have been enough to draw unwanted attention and ridicule, but because of Marsha Fergus's latent Shakespearean desires, amputation and corpulence were leveraged beyond self-consciousness and into total humiliation.

Allen rivaled Sunny in bulk, although he was a few inches taller than her five feet. He had meaty arms and dual-barrel butt cheeks, but most of his fat was concentrated between the bottom of his rib cage and his crotch, putting great strain on his zippers, which indeed hung open more often than not, usually with a piece of shirt tail escaping. One day before a junior high gym class, an assistant basketball coach had called out: "Hey, Crane! Is that your dick hangin' out, or are you just glad to see me?"

Allen was quiet and shy and rarely spoke in class unless asked a direct question, which he would answer precisely in a honeyed baritone and smooth, measured drawl that generationally linked to the true Deep South, say Georgia or South Carolina, polished and aristocratic, rather than the slurred and sloppy jabberings of those with a long East Texas lineage, East Texas being more the butt end of the South. He sang in the Lobo Chorus and played sousaphone in the Lobo Band and, in the first ten weeks of school that year, demonstrated that he knew more about Algebra than the assistant football coach who was teaching it. Marsha Fergus almost visibly drooled when she heard him speak, having found a new centerpiece for her theatrics.

In that first meeting, Miss Fergus had each of us introduce ourselves and talk about our favorite subjects, our plans for college, and our parents. She passed out some pamphlets on college selection, planning and financial aid sources. She gave each of us a booklet listing all the past and present members of the Akela Club, where they were now and what kinds of careers they had.

She explained that "Akela" means "leader" and that we were expected to be the academic leaders during our high school days and help other students who were struggling. We would also publish four issues of *Wolfen*, the Akela Club newsletter, and organize some money-raising activities for the school district, such as car washes and leaf raking.

When called upon, we would help the Pep Team and the Shewolves write and display motivational banners, and we would paint store window fronts with GO LOBOS messages, and write personal signs for each Lobo and stick them in the players' yards every Thursday night before a game so they would see them first thing in the morning on Friday game days. Next, she explained that since Lobos had to maintain a 60 (out of 100) GPA to be eligible for a game in any given week, Akelas always gave first priority to Lobos when it came to tutoring other students. Any questions?

Marsha told us about the skit freshmen Akelas had performed at last year's Christmas Assembly, a skit based on Dickens' *A Christmas Carol*. In Miss Fergus's adaptation of Dickens' story, Scrooge had locked the Lobo's quarterback in a closet, and three Akelas, each in the form of championships Past, Present, and Future, had to show Scrooge the error of his ways. The quarterback was released just in time for the state championship game.

But Miss Fergus was growing bored with adapting other people's work to one-act plays. This year, she wanted to create some original material. Something she hoped would be livelier and faster, a little more "with it."

"Have any of you ever been in a play before?" she asked.

"In grade school," I answered. "I was a prince."

"Did you have a speaking part?"

"No ma'am."

"So, you sang in the chorus?"

"No ma'am. The boys dressed up like princes. We wore red sashes across our chests, and we danced with the girls, who wore fancy dresses."

"Oh, how perfect! What kind of dance, Billy?"

"A waltz, I think."

"Yes, it was a waltz," Allen added. "Third grade. We did *Cinderella*."

"Were you one of the dancers, too?" she asked Allen.

"I was the King who announced the beginning of the ball. And I danced with the Queen."

"What about the rest of you? Anyone else ever been in a play? No? How about a skit, maybe in Boy Scouts? Church? Summer camp?"

Everyone shook their heads no. Liars. I now envied them their silence and wished I'd kept my mouth shut.

Miss Fergus appeared to be in a daze, her head slanted to one side, staring blankly at Allen and me, imagining us in her play-to-be.

Chapter 9

I Should Have Known Better

I tried to put my bad week of locker door harassment and Miss Fergus's theatrical plans out of my mind by going to Friday night's football game. It was supposed to be a big night for Korvus High School. Turned out, it was also a big night for the Bastrops. And neither fared well.

I sat on the hard, grooved aluminum bleachers at the top edge of Lobo Field and watched the Milton Lions eliminate the Lobos from the first round of the 1970 state playoffs. Milton won by a single point when the Lobo kicker missed a twenty-three-yard field goal in the last seconds of the game.

"Good thing that asshole graduates this year," a big-haired woman in front of me said to her husband, between bites of a Frito pie.

"Pitiful," the man said, on the edge of tears. "That kid ain't worth knocking in the head."

I looked over my shoulder toward the parking lot and saw the Lizard's taillights flick on and off. Sunny was nervously and mindlessly pressing the brakes. Over and over. She'd come to pick me up, and right on time.

When I got to the car, she jangled the keys at me.

"You drive. And go around the courthouse square. Let's see if Blackbird's still there." She moved into the back seat, where she slouched down and donned a pair of almost saucer-sized Jackie O sunglasses she had taken to wearing. Even after dark.

"You want tamales? He's probably gone by now."

"He was still there when Ah came by."

"Sunny, please, can't we just go home?" I was halfway through *Slaughterhouse-Five* and determined to finish it before sunrise.

"Ah, by God, want me some tamales!"

We drove by the square, and as I'd predicted, the Tamale Man was gone.

"How bout the Dairy Queen? Ah bet he moved up there after the game."

The Dairy Queen was a riot of cars. A long line at the drive-through, another dozen scattered around the asphalt parking lot, some parked and others in perpetual motion, circling and dodging potholes, occupants either shouting or honking. Some friendly, some taunting.

There were no Milton fans around; they'd had the good sense to beat it out of town and leave the wounded Lobo fans to feed on each other.

George and Wonderful Byrd had set up business on the far end of the DQ lot. George stood at the tailgate to sell his wares, the tamales hot and plump, packed in foil-wrapped bundles of one or two dozen. Wonderful sat in the back of the truck, up on the side rail against the cab. His job was to drag one of their crumbly Styrofoam coolers down to the tailgate when his father needed more.

If business slowed, George became a mock traffic cop, playfully putting up a hand to slow a carful of Lobo fans circling the lot, waving them over to his truck.

He sang out to hawk his wares.

"I got chicken and they's the best. I got pork you'll swear is blessed. Eat 'em if you win or eat 'em if you lose. They good for your highs and they good for your blues. I got the good ones, yes and by golly! I got the very best dang tamales!"

I parked the Green Lizard a few feet from George's tailgate, and Sunny peeked over the car seat behind me and momentarily pushed the Jackie O sunglasses up to take a better look.

"Jesus God! He got that freaky, milky-skinned boy with him?"

"You mean Wonderful?"

"Was that his name? Son-of-a-bitch if he ain't growed up and made a scary booger-looking thing."

"He can't help how he looks."

Wonderful was about twenty-one by then, tall and lanky with a gaunt face that added to his spectral appearance. I'd seen him only a handful of times since Sunny bought the Lizard—and always at night —aimlessly walking the streets near the courthouse square or wandering between there and his parents' neighborhood.

"He still simple-headed?"

"That kind of thing doesn't change."

"Gwon over there and get us two dozen. Chicken. They's the best."

"But the pork is blessed," I said.

"Naw. Chicken." She gave me some money.

When I handed Sunny the warm, cumin-scented package, she immediately pulled a tamale out and shucked off the corn husk.

"Oh, that's damn good. Want one?"

"Not now, maybe at the house."

"You know, when Ah worked up here at the DQ, Ah'd sometime see that boy walkin the streets at night."

"Wonderful?"

"Yep. He'd show up sometime after dark. People say nighttime's the only time he could be outta the house. Daylight hurt him or made him sick or some such. He'd walk all the way up here. He'd walk around this parking lot, or up and down the street out there. After a while, a car'd come and stop and he'd get in."

Sunny shook her head and peeled another of George's chicken tamales.

"Ah mean a car with white people in it. *White people.*"

"Maybe they were people he knew. Giving him a ride home?" I said this between cringes and turned on the radio, hoping to shut her up. The Temptations came on. "Ball of Confusion."

"It'd happen a time or two a week. Different cars and different people, too. Where you think a car full of white boys was taking a haint-looking creature like that? Craziest damned shit Ah ever saw."

"He's an albino, Sunny. That's how they look. Nobody chooses that. Don't you think he'd change it if he could? It's like me, don't you think I'd choose two arms?"

"You ain't no freak though," Sunny said and dug through her purse for a Camel and a match.

Yeah, tell that to the world.

"One night he came outta that little stand of woods, right over there," she lit her cig and pointed at a thick growth of honeysuckle and cedars behind the DQ dumpsters.

"Me and another woman brought a load of grease out to dump in them grease barrels out back, and here he come outta them bushes. Butt-ass nekkid! Scared the pure-dee shit outta us. He said, 'Call my mama, call my mama.' We spilled grease all over creation and locked ourselves back in the building. Somebody called the sheriff and they come got him. Had blood running all down his ass and back of his legs. Nekkid as a GD jaybird!"

"Why didn't you try to help him? Jesus!"

"Don't use the Lord's name in vain! Ah taught you better."

I turned up the radio and cranked the Caddy to leave, jerked the shifter to "D." James Taylor crooned about fire and rain.

"Wait," she said. "Ah want a chili dog. You want something?"

"What about the tamales?"

"Let's save 'em for tomorrow. Ah'm already tasting a chili dog."

. . .

I killed the engine and headed to the walk-up window of DQ.

"With mayonnaise," Sunny called out behind me. "No mustard."

"Mayo. Got it."

While I waited for the order, someone cruised by and shouted.

"Hey Bastrop! Where's your cow horns? They fall off the front grill on that piece of shit somewhere?" It was Ricky Vander driving a new Trans Am, several other Lobos stuffed inside. A middle-finger saluted me from the backseat as they rolled by.

I got back in the Lizard with the chili dog. Sunny opened it and stiffened. She held the partially unwrapped chili dog up to the car window to catch some of the dim yellow-red neon coming through. She scowled, disgusted.

"Is Helen working tonight?" She spat the words at me.

"Yeah."

"The stupid bitch put mustard on this. You don't feed mustard to a starving rat bastard. And there's no speck of onion. Goddamnalmighty! She knows Ah don't eat mustard. This is a spite!" There was bad blood between Sunny and Helen. I'd heard her say she wouldn't piss on Helen's head if her hair was on fire.

I took the rejected chili dog back to the order window.

"Can I talk to Helen, please?"

"She's gone. Her shift ended." A sullen teenager I recognized from school had taken Helen's place.

"OK, well, I ordered this chili dog with mayonnaise."

"Mayonnaise? Really? No shit? Who eats mayonnaise on a chili dog?"

"Okay, I know it's odd. Just trust me, I need one with mayonnaise."

"Let me check the order. No, it doesn't say mayo. If it doesn't say, we always put mustard on them. Because that's what's *supposed* to go on a chili dog." I wanted to punch the smirk off his face.

"OK, can you please make me one with mayo?"

"That'll be eighty cents."

I walked back to the car and asked Sunny for a dollar. That's when the night went apeshit.

I was of two minds when it came to Sunny. I hated the perpetual cloak of sadness and negativism she held so tightly around her. I thought I wanted to see her come out of her hole and walk among the living. Learn more about the modern world. Interact with people enough to develop some modicum of tact and tolerance. Then, on the rare occasions when she did come out, I regretted it, finding myself forced to grab a chair and a whip and try to herd her back into her cage.

As Sunny stomped toward the DQ, I saw what felt like the entire student body of KHS gathered there—ground zero on late Friday nights after football, especially after the big games, win or lose. I knew the injection of Sunny into the after-game DQ culture would not end well.

People talk about being in car wrecks when time slows down almost to a stop, and they can see individual pieces of glass and steel slowly float by, almost suspended in the air. They talk about moments of truth, of profound happenings, when you gain omnipotent senses, and can see everything in full panorama without moving your head, can hear and remember every word spoken by every speaker, the details of the scene singed directly on the matter of your brain. Almost see atoms vibrate.

When Sunny reached that window, I sensed the cogs of the world slowing. I could see the next few minutes happen before they happened, could see the flying pieces of glass and steel slowly take a bead on my head.

"Did you put mustard on this GD chili dog?" she shouted at the startled window attendant and pushed the Jackie Os to the top of her perm.

"No ma'am."

"Who put mustard on it?" Sunny pushed her short log of an arm past the window attendant and waved the ruined wiener at some of the other workers in the DQ.

"Helen made it," a frightened voice said, from back near the ice cream machine.

"Call her for me. Tell her Ah'm coming to her house, and Ah'm going to ram this crap up her ass!"

"Ohhh-kay."

"Now, one of you geniuses make me another chili dog, with MAYONNAISE. That is if any y'all smart enough to pour piss from a boot."

"Ma'am, we can make you another one, but you'll have to pay for it."

"Like GD hell!" Sunny pounded the window ledge.

"Yes ma'am. The order said mustard. We'll get fired if we give you one for free."

"No goddamn way we ordered mustard! We're not idiots for chrissakes! Now give me a chili dog with MAYONNAISE, or Ah'm coming through this widow!"

"Maybe we should call the police," the voice from the ice cream machine said.

Sunny's conniption fit stopped cars in mid-orbit around the DQ. Scattered clumps of people previously talking or listening to music or conducting shady transactions for pot or beer moved toward us. The Lizard, less than ten feet behind Sunny, became the gathering point, people leaning against it or sitting on the hood or the trunk. One kid tried to get in, but thankfully, that door was stuck.

"Who's this crazy bitch?" somebody asked.

"His mama, I guess," a girl pointed at me. "Figures, huh?"

I was caught in open view, up against the front of the car,

wracking my brain for some way to extract Sunny—and myself—from her earthquake.

"Billy Wayne," someone called to me, a Lobo with three letter stripes on his KHS jacket. "Don't the looney bin close soon? Better get her back before lockdown."

Somebody slammed the window in her face, and she headed to the front door.

"May-Yo! May-Yo! May-Yo!" Ricky Vander yelled, looking to start a chant.

"Stop it!" I shouted. "Stop."

Ricky repeatedly lifted his arms in time with the chant, recruiting the crowd to join in.

A DQ worker leapt over the counter and threw the deadbolt on the glass doors. Sunny shook the handle, leveraging all the heft she could manage, and kicked at the glass.

I grabbed her by the arm. "I bet we got mayo at home. Let's go, Sunny. Please. Please."

She twisted away and headed to the rear door, me trailing behind. Locked. She bulled her way back to the front.

"May-Yo! May-Yo! May-Yo!"

The chant was now full-throated, some thirty voices strong and growing. The crowd—still led by Ricky—whooped and hollered her on.

"You get 'em, lady."

"You're feisty for a fat girl."

"Maybe you already had one chili dog too many?"

Sunny pressed her face against the front window, shouting, "Y'all tell Helen that Sunshine Pearl Bastrop is coming back tomorrow for my refund."

She stepped away from the building—the crowd hooting—cocked her arm quarterback-style and sent the mustard chili dog sailing in a high arc onto the roof of the Korvus DQ.

Horns honked and lights flashed. People screamed the screams they'd been holding in for the winning score that never came against the Milton Lions that night. A group of drunks on the far side of the parking lot, near Dean's Auto Supply, started a disjointed stadium wave.

Sunny plowed past me and climbed into the back of our car. She lay there in the darkness, pressed against the hump of the floorboard. Pulled the big sunglasses back down to the bridge of her nose.

"Get me home!" she hissed.

I drove the getaway car.

In the rearview mirror, I could see dozens of kids jumping and laughing. Throwing all manner of stuff onto the DQ roof: burgers and fries and Cokes, GO LOBOS signs. Beer. A lawn chair.

"May-Yo! May-Yo! May-Yo!"

Chapter 10
I'm Happy Just to Dance with You

The featured sign on my locker door that Monday after the chili dog incident had been "MAYO" and somebody (and by "somebody," I mean Ricky Vander) had stacked a pyramid of mayonnaise jars at the foot of my locker that would have been the envy of any Piggly Wiggly stock boy.

And to top off the beginning of a great week, I soon learned that Marsha Fergus was going out of her way to apply a coating of feathers to the tar Sunny's DQ mustard fit had already lathered on me. When the Akela Club inductees met with her in the library for our first read-through of the Christmas Assembly Akela Club skit she'd written, this is what she handed us:

Rudolph's Wish
by Marsha Fergus

Cast Of Characters
Santa Claus — Allen Crane
Mrs. Santa Claus — Billy Bastrop
Head Elf — Joe Rand

Assistant Head Elf — Terry Singer
Rudolph — Holly Atwood
The Reindeer Chorus — The 1970 Shewolves Drill Team

Scene I: The Living Room of Mr. and Mrs. Claus

(Santa and Mrs. Claus sit by the fireplace, rocking and relaxing after a long day. Santa smokes his pipe and reads the paper. Mrs. Claus knits. The Head Elf and the Assistant Head Elf sit on the floor playing Monopoly.)

Mrs. Claus: Isn't this nice, Santa? Just a quiet evening at home.

Santa: Yes, my lovely. Some peace and quiet at last! Boy, is it nice to take a break from all the noise and hubbub down at the toy factory!

Head Elf: I'll say!

Asst. Head Elf: I work harder than you.

Head Elf: Do not.

Asst. Head Elf: Do too.

Head Elf: Uh huh.

Asst. Head Elf: Unt uh.

Mrs. Claus: Boys!

(Off stage can be heard rock music: "Born To Be Wild" by Steppenwolf. Low at first, but growing progressively louder.)

Santa (dropping the newspaper in disgust): Now what's that?

Mrs. Claus: Rudolph!? Oh no, not again!

Santa (shouting): Rudolph!! Rudolph! Turn that racket down! (Music gets louder and louder)

Mrs. Claus (shouting at Santa): Dear! DEAR!! We'll have to go in there!

HE CAN'T HEAR US.

Santa: What?

Mrs. Claus (rising and signaling for Santa to get up): LET'S GO!

Santa (nodding): Oh, all right.

(Santa and Mrs. Claus exit stage left, headed for Rudolph's room)

Scene II: Rudolph's Room

(As Santa and Mrs. Claus enter, Rudolph dances wildly, oblivious to them, the music growing louder and louder)

Mrs. Claus: Rudolph. Rudolph.

Santa (booming): RUDOLPH! EARTH TO RUDOLPH!

(The music stops. Rudolph stops dead in his tracks, limbs frozen in mid-dance. He looks sheepishly at the audience)

Rudolph (to the audience): Whoops!

Mrs. Claus: Don't your ears hurt?

Rudolph: My ears are OK. My antlers don't feel too good, though. Kinda fuzzy.

(Rudolph reaches up and feels his antlers)

Santa: It's going to be more than his ears hurting if he keeps that racket up!

Rudolph: You don't like my new Steppen***LOBO*** album?

Santa (Shakes his head)

Rudolph: I'm in trouble again, right?

Santa (unrolling a long scroll): Lessee, lessee. R's, r's. Ricky, no, Roland, no, Ross, no. Here we are RUDOLPH.

(Santa moves to the front center stage and reads to the audience)

Santa (reading from scroll): Rudolph didn't come to any pep rallies last year!

(Santa boos and encourages the audience to join in booing Rudolph)

Santa (continues reading): Rudolph didn't help put motivation signs in the Lobos' yards last year! And, Rudolph didn't buy a booster club membership last year!

Santa (To Rudolph): Now, to this list, I'm going to add: Disturbing the peace.

Rudolph: Does all this mean I'm not getting what I want for Christmas?

Santa: Well, I don't know! Let's ask the Lobos!

Santa (To audience): Well, what do you think? Has Rudolph been a good boy?

(Audience answers)

Santa: Does he deserve something?

(Audience answers)

Rudolph (To audience): Wait, wait! You don't know what I was asking for.

I want a STATE CHAMPIONSHIP for the Lobos!!

Santa (To audience): NOW what do you think!

(While the audience answers, The Reindeer Chorus rushes out and takes their places around the back perimeter of the stage)

Mrs. Claus: Now, that makes ME feel like dancing!

(As the Reindeer Chorus sings "Have a Holly Jolly Christmas", Santa and Mrs. Claus do a traditional waltz around the stage. Rudolph and the Head Elf and Assistant Head Elf dance wildly and independently at center stage.)

Principal Upchurch (Backstage, over house PA): Next year! Lobos in 71! Lobos in 71!

(Song over. Curtain)

END

Miss Fergus patiently waited for us to finish our individual, silent read-throughs. Terry and Holly smirked and rocked with laughter. Joe was silent as usual.

Allen squirmed uncomfortably in his chair. He nodded slightly to himself, as if to say, "That's right, make the fat one Santa." Given his great voice and stage presence, he was a natural for the role.

I finished reading the vile thing but couldn't look anybody in the eye. The life force drained from me, puddled on the floor. I've got to get out of this. Somehow someway.

"I can't wait to see y'all kiss," Hollywood said, puckering his lips at me from across the library table.

"I'm thinking you might look really hot in a wig. Your behind is a little curvy, if you don't mind me saying so." Terry winked at me and began to hum "I Saw Her Standing There."

Their ribbing me was all good-natured enough, but Jesus, I didn't need to add this thousand-pound gorilla to the troupe of monkeys already riding my back. My fellow dweebs could laugh at it without malice, but everybody else in that assembly would be laughing with shark's teeth.

"I don't think I can do this, Miss Fergus," I finally spoke up, my voice cracking.

"Oh, sure you can. It'll be fun! A really neat twist that no one will see coming. Can you imagine the laughter we'll get when you step out on stage in costume?"

"Why me for Mrs. Santa? How about one of the others? Maybe we should draw straws or something?"

"You're the best fit for the dress I want to use. And Allen makes the best Santa, and the two of you already know how to waltz."

"We were in third grade! We've forgotten. Allen, haven't you forgotten? Miss Fergus, why couldn't I be another elf? Or how about a reindeer, you know, like Crispin or Blotson or whatever their names are?"

"The script is already approved by Principal Upchurch. He thought it was great. Come on, Billy, can't you be a leader in the spirit of Akelas? Be a good sport?"

"Please find somebody else," I begged.

"Participation is mandatory," she said, unyielding. "No one has ever refused to be in the annual skit. No play, no Akela Club membership."

Arguing was useless. She was clearly dug in. And her strong pride of authorship for this imbecilic piece of crap would not allow changes to the script for the trivial reason that one of her charges wanted to avoid a lifetime of therapy. And Upchurch was backing her. What else could I do? Take it to the school board?

———

Home-Ec students—as part of their midterm sewing exam—fitted me with an ankle-length green taffeta dress covered in leaping reindeer, snowmen, and Christmas trees. Sequins abounded: red on reindeer noses, purple eyes for the snowmen, and a rainbow of colors sprinkled across each tree.

One girl brought in a wig donated by her mother. It had a late '50s Sandra Dee sort of shape to it, big-haired and bulbous with a jaunty flip. The students spray-painted it an unnatural silvery new-tin-roof color.

A pair of round John Lennon glasses from Goodwill—sans glass—and a cane finished off Mrs. Santa's wardrobe. Miss Fergus thought the cane would add to the effect and offer an opportunity for more action if Mrs. Claus would first hobble, then, near the end, throw her cane to the winds in order to joyously dance with Santa.

The Home-Ec seamstresses decided I would look more matronly and grandmotherly if the dress had long sleeves with gathered cuffs at the wrists. I hated the idea because it meant I would have to wear the prosthetic, which I used less and less as I got older.

Fergus avoided the subject of my arm as long as possible, but ultimately pulled me aside one afternoon and pointedly asked if I planned to wear "it." Without stating it outright, she made it clear she wanted Mrs. Santa to appear as whole as possible. And of course, the dress would look even more stupid with the right sleeve pinned up or entirely absent, so I told her I'd be happy to wear my useless albatross.

———

On the big day, the cast of "Rudolph's Wish" stood in costume backstage, wondering how we—allegedly the brightest of the freshmen class—had been suckered into a suicide pact. A Home-Ec attendant made a last-minute adjustment to Allen's patent-leather Santa belt.

Principal Upchurch strode past us with a toothy possum grin, pointed at me, and winked before he stepped out to center stage and called the assembly to order. The upperclassmen Akelas color guard walked in with the flags. A prayer was said.

"Ladies and gentlemen, welcome to the 1970 Korvus High School Christmas Assembly and celebration. Go go Lobos!"

There was wild cheering and flailing, and most everyone sprang to their feet. While Mr. Upchurch spoke, a Home-Ec girl touched up my makeup and refreshed my lipstick. Cranberry Passion.

Allen was already sweat-soaked and had unbuttoned his rather heavy Santa coat, making a deal with his dresser that she could button it back up as soon as the Shewolves—who performed first to warm up the crowd—neared the end of their routine. Allen kept turning his back to the rest of us, futzing with the zipper on his newly sewn Santa pants. He would fix it, and it would push apart again, and then he would turn away and zip it back. And repeat.

His Home-Ec team of novice tailors could have used more practice installing zippers before they started sewing for Allen. Allen's portliness and the overwhelming tendency of his body to push constantly outward in the zipper region, would have been a challenge even to Savile Row.

Principal Upchurch shouted, "Next year, State! Nothing less. Right? Right?"

Deafening roar of cheers, and the chant: STATE, STATE, STATE …

Upchurch let the student body and faculty sound off for a few moments. He signaled for quiet and made several announcements, then called out the Shewolves, wearing clip-on antlers for the occasion, who jumped and twirled and twitched their short-skirted butts to music from the Stones and Chicago, soon moving into a high-kicking Rockettes-style routine.

As the Shewolves wound down their high kicking, Allen's dresser frantically helped him button up his coat, Terry and Joe adjusted their elfin hats and stockings, Hollywood shifted his antlers a little further to the back of his head and tested their stability.

My attendant patted my forehead with yet more makeup to tone down a glare that was bothering her. I pushed my foam-rubber boobs up, which were much too ample and inviting for Mrs. Claus, I thought, but that's what happens when you steal one of Sunny's medieval bras and put a group of teenage boys in charge of stuffing it.

The Shewolves remained on stage—since they would become the singing chorus in the finale—but backed up and formed a semi-circle around where the Akelas would perform.

Mr. Charles—the band director—tinkled the piano keys.

Mr. Upchurch arrived back at center stage. "Ladies and Gentlemen and Lobos, I give you the 1970 Akela inductees performing 'Rudolph's Wish,' a play by Marsha Fergus."

The attendants, Marsha Fergus, and some of the Shewolves rushed our props out on stage and placed them in their appointed spots. As we had practiced, the players trotted out on stage in a particular order, Santa first (much cheering and clapping from the crowd), the elves, Rudolph half trotting, half dancing (surge of laughter, cheering, clapping), then lastly, Mrs. Claus hobbling as fast as possible over to take her seat in the rocking chair.

My sitting was the cue for the show to begin.

I hobble-trotted on from stage right and people screamed with laughter. Piercing wolf whistles and May-Yo, May-Yo, May-Yo. Who's the new chick in town? Can I have your number? Baby baby baby. What's under that dress?

I tried not to look at her, but Rita Burke—as a captain—anchored one end of the Shewolf chorus line and was maybe twelve feet from me, smiling at the crowd, sequins on her short-shorts glinting in the spotlight. *What must she think of me? Fuck. My lips are more sparkly than hers! God damn Marsha Fergus to hell. I've got to move to another town after this. Change my name.*

The Lobos football team—seated together in seats reserved for them in the first three rows—elbowed each other and pointed. I tried not to look anyone in the eyes, as Miss Fergus had taught us. I tried to look over or through the gathered students and teachers, to the very back row of the auditorium, not looking specifically at any one of the four hundred people.

Although I tried to avoid the Lobos most of all, I looked randomly into the first few rows of the Lobo football team, and directly into the eyes of Ricky Vander, who cupped his hands and screamed: "Freak!"

I sat down and rocked and counted to ten as Fergus had instructed. The noise from the audience quieted considerably, as she predicted.

I rocked and recited, "Isn't this nice, Santa, (shouts of May-Yo from the rear) just a quiet evening at home."

I glanced at Allen, whose skin had taken the hue of a giant, steamed lobster, almost matching the red of his Santa suit. Long rivulets of sweat cut down both sides of his face, from behind his ears and down from his temples into his fluffy white collar.

Allen rocked several beats longer than he was supposed to and finally said, "Yes, my lovely ... (raucous laughter at the word 'lovely', several high-pitched whistles, a chorus of foot stomping on bleachers to the right) ... some uh quiet and peace and quiet at last. Boy, it's great to break from all that noise and hullabaloo and uh down at the factory ... toy factory." Allen was blowing his lines, but who the hell cared anymore? Let's just get it over with.

The Akelas pushed bravely on through Fergus's stinking play. We wanted to be good sports. Some of us even believed that our willingness to self-efface would improve our social status a notch or two. We were so ignorant. We were so wrong. No respect was earned, no quarter given. No subtlety registered on the black and white minds of our audience. We may have been laughing at ourselves with the hope that the world laughed with us, but the world we inhabited at that time in that place was far too vicious to give the rabbits a head start. We were shredded.

Mercifully, we reached the end. I stood and delivered the last line, "Now that makes ME feel like dancing," and threw the cane high and to the back.

Santa reached out and took my fake hand and placed it on his shoulder, then put one hand on my waist. I put my good hand in his other hand, and Mr. Charles struck up "Have A Holly Jolly Christmas" on the piano. The Reindeer Chorus (Shewolves) sang out.

Allen and I started waltzing—quickly and with high energy—as Marsha Fergus had directed. Our bodies rotated in a small circle, clumsy but workable footwork, and this rotating pair of Clauses orbited in a larger circle around the stage.

In the center of the action, Rudolph and the elves gyrated rock-and-roll style, completely out of sync with the music. A few Shewolves ad-libbed some choreography of their own. The plan was for Mr. and Mrs. Santa to continue to circle the stage until Mr. Charles and the Shewolves had completed two complete singings of "Holly Jolly Christmas."

To keep my lifeless arm resting on Allen's shoulder during all the twirling and circling of the stage, we had improvised a method of attachment: a bent paper clip taped firmly to my ersatz middle finger. When Allen lifted my prosthetic arm and put it on his shoulder to initiate the dance, he took care to hook the bent paper clip into a small loop sewn into his fluffy white Santa collar. This worked perfectly in rehearsal. It failed miserably live.

Near the middle of our third or fourth full traverse of the stage, the loop on Allen's collar detached, letting my arm flop straight down, with the paper clip snagging some of Santa's shirttail hanging out his splayed zipper, looking like my fake arm had grabbed his crotch. It hooked his shirttail as firmly and irrevocably as Hemingway ever hooked any marlin.

The audience screamed with laughter. They screamed and stomped the wooden bleachers almost into splinters. I heard reports later that two teachers actually peed themselves. Joe and Terry and Hollywood slowed their dancing almost to a stop, confused about what was happening, thinking maybe Allen and I had begun to improvise a new scene.

Allen jumped and twisted and jerked. He grabbed my prosthetic and tried to tear it loose, but his movements set the hook more firmly, through his shirt now and into the elastic leg band of his briefs.

Most of the Shewolves continued to sing, but many stopped and roared with laughter, covered their faces with their hands, peeking through spread fingers, disbelieving.

Mr. Charles, his back to us and largely oblivious to what was happening, played on. Joe and Terry looked offstage at Miss Fergus, who was flailing hand signals and arm gestures no one could interpret. The elves and Rudolph—prisoners to the script—kept dancing their asses off as long as the music continued.

Backstage, Principal Upchurch rocked with laughter, shaking his head, tears streaming down his face.

Mrs. Claus stood very near center stage in front of four hundred screaming teenagers with her hand bare inches from Santa's dick. Allen tried to disconnect the hand by repeatedly jerking his butt backwards or shifting his gigantic hips from side to side. He gathered his strength now and again and laboriously leapt backwards like a great hippo encountering a cobra face to face.

At the same time, I tried to dislodge my arm from Santa's crotch by twisting my upper torso, rotating my body from the waist up, pulling my right shoulder back, thrusting it back violently, trying unsuccessfully again and again to disconnect.

Our wild, desperate maneuvers to break free of one another made it look for all the world like I was giving Santa a very spirited hand job. Stomping and clapping and laughter rocked the auditorium almost to the ground, and Ricky led the Lobos down front in the official Bastrop chant: May-Yo! May-Yo! May-Yo!

Eventually, most of the student body took up the chant. Many didn't know the genesis of the nickname, but they knew it applied to me. And a new twist was added. Two or three voices in random locations shouted "Faggot!" as the curtain fell.

———

Near dusk that day, I sat about fifty yards out in the pasture behind our house, quietly reflecting on how short the trip was from near invisibility to undisputed leader of freakworld.

Tin-haired, one-armed, cross-dressing, Santa-abusing, mayonnaise-eating, white-trash king of freaks.

I skipped school the next week, unwilling to face anyone. Several mornings that week, Sunny and I woke to a dozen or more mayonnaise jars scattered around the front yard, most of them a broken, greasy mess.

Clearly, I had to do something.

I had to learn to kick a football.

Chapter 11
Back in the USSR

How did I learn to kick? The same way I learned everything: by reading.

Day after day, I sat in the school library, drinking in Jan Kubicek's *Kicking and Screaming*—part autobiography, part instruction manual on how to kick an American-style football through the uprights—for fame, adulation, and, in Jan's case, ultimately profit.

Kubicek's book tells of his escape as a young boy from Soviet-era Czechoslovakia and subsequent journey across East Germany, into Estonia, then across the Baltic Sea in a small boat with a dozen other refugees into Norway. He eventually arrived by freighter in the port of Galveston, Texas, in the 1950s.

Kubicek was a master storyteller, and interspersed chapters detailing his escape from Communism with chapters on how to adapt the European side-winder approach of kicking a soccer ball to the American game of football.

Jan was adopted by a Czech family living in the Hill Country of central Texas (many German and Czech immigrants have historically settled there), and as a teenager taught himself to kick field goals and was so accurate that he was recruited to kick for the University of

Texas. He gained national notoriety as the first "soccer-style" kicker in major college football. Jan went on to play several years for the New York Giants, where he became something of a media sensation and occasional talk show guest because of his unorthodox kicking style and adventurous life story.

He was far ahead of history. Even though he was hugely successful at kicking and set several NCAA records during his time as a Longhorn, he was considered an amusing curiosity by the football world at the time. It would be at least another decade before soccer-style placekickers became common at major colleges and the NFL.

Since I already held full freak status at KHS, I had nothing to lose by shamelessly copying Jan's style. Besides, his was the only book I could find on the topic of "how to kick a football," because almost all instructional books on football focused on the glory positions of quarterback, running back, or receiver.

That winter, I kicked incessantly. I used the pasture south of our house as my primary practice field, where I identified a droopy telephone line as a fair approximation for the height of the crossbar on a goal post. It was higher than an actual goal post, which was good since it trained me to keep the ball up as much as possible.

I walked off the distance on a section of the line to represent the location of the upright bars, and I threw a couple of lengths of rope over the phone line in the right places to represent the width of the "window" the ball had to pass through to score. I found a couple of discarded footballs in the trash behind the Lobo's field house and fixed them well enough with duct tape.

In the early going, I recruited Sunny to hold the ball for me, but she bitched and moaned too much about the cold and how GD crazy I was.

"Listen here. Kick me and Ah'll wring your neck," she admonished.

Half the time, she'd keep her eyes closed or jump and let the ball drop just as I kicked, in a perfect imitation of cartoon Lucy taunting Charley Brown, throwing my timing and rhythm off badly.

Sunny's weight and short legs made it difficult for her to take a kneeling position to hold the ball. When she flinched and jerked back from the ball, she'd sometimes lose her balance and tip over Galapagos-turtle style. I eventually replaced her with empty tuna cans. They held the balls in place nicely and were infinitely easier to right when flipped.

Every day after school, I'd rush through whatever homework I had and sometimes kick until after midnight if the sky was clear and the moon full, or until I heard Sunny bawl out across the frozen field. "You plumb gone nuts! Gonna catch pneumonia. How much you think that'll cost?"

———

Every spring, after basketball and track seasons ended, in the few remaining weeks before the end of the school year, the Lobo football coaches conducted Spring Drills.

This was generally a time for conditioning and agility exercises. No pads or helmets were used, only shorts and T-shirts. Lots of running and jumping, screaming and yelling. A and B offensive teams would run plays against their defensive counterparts, all under "touch football" rules. No pads—no contact. Quarterbacks would throw tirelessly to backs and receivers. Place kickers and punters would kick up and down the field. And coaches would put a microscope on everyone.

I decided it was time to move up from tuna cans and telephone lines, and went to see the head coach, Coach Clay, to ask his permission to try out for the team as a placekicker. I met with him and his offensive coordinator, Coach Lee, in Clay's office in the Lobos' field house on a rainy afternoon after they had finished the drills for the day.

I walked around and through mud holes to the field house, a

place I'd never been inside. It was on the edge of one of three practice fields, a couple of hundred yards behind the high school. As I approached the field house, I passed through a throng of freshly showered players headed back to the student parking lot, some I knew from this class or that, many I'd never had a class with or spoken to. Most gave me a perplexed "what's the deal with him" look. There were a few dismissive sneers.

I approached the front door, and for the first time, passed under the sign that made very clear the expectations for all Lobos:
THROUGH THIS DOOR,
NO COWARDS PASS

"What's your name, son?" Coach Lee asked. He stood behind and to the right of Coach Clay, who sat in a well-worn leather chair behind an ornately carved, dark wood desk, most of its surface covered in disheveled piles of papers, 16mm game films, three-ring binders, and dirty coffee mugs and empty pop cans.

"Billy Wayne Bastrop, sir."

"You think you can play football?" Coach Lee asked. Assistant Coach Lee did all the talking while Clay played Sphinx and avoided looking at me directly, or if he did, it was in short, quick glances, as if too long an exposure would burn his eyes. He kept his chin tilted close to his chest, the brim of his Lobos' ballcap blocking any view of his eyes.

"I've been practicing all winter, learning how to kick."

"Punt or placekick?"

"Placekick."

"You played any football before?"

"No, sir."

"Nothing? No junior high, nothing nowhere?"

"That's right."

"Most of these kids been playing since they were in grade school. Son, we're looking for state of Texas playoff and state-championship level play here. How you gonna do that if you've never been on the field before?"

Clay swiveled his chair to one side and rolled his eyes up at me. When I met his gaze, he turned quickly and stared at his telephone, as if willing it to ring.

"I've practiced at least a hundred hours over the winter. I'm just looking for a chance to show you what I can do. I've practically memorized Jan Kubicek's book ..."

"Book?!" Clay spoke at last, head hanging to one side as if too exhausted to raise it. "Son, you can't learn nothing from no book. Football don't come from books. It comes from knocking heads. And getting yours knocked back."

He stood and eased toward me. He poked his index finger into my belly right above the navel. Pushed until I grunted.

"Football comes from your guts. It sure as hell don't come from a damn book."

"A book by Koobla-chevy?" Lee said. "What kind of name is that? Sounds like a communist."

"Field goals won't make us champs. Touchdowns will," Clay said.

Clay looked me in the eyes for the first time. His face was too pale for someone who spent so much time outdoors, and his expression weary and joyless.

"You know as well as I do what the problem is."

"My arm?"

"I'm worried about that." Clay shifted his eyes back and forth between me and Lee.

"I can kick, sir. I don't need two arms for that. Just two strong legs."

"But you see, we don't give special privileges here. Everybody's gotta practice and run through all the drills. Block, tackle, hit and get hit. No quarter is given or expected. I make all my boys play real football—no prima donnas—no one gets to sit anything out. Everybody gets his licks in, and everybody gets his butt leveled to the ground. Keeps you humble. Makes you brave. Quarterbacks as much as linebackers. I'll be just as honest with you as the day is long, you need two arms and two legs to play at the level we expect. Besides, you have to be able to protect yourself out there."

"Everybody's required to have two positions, one offense and one defense," Lee said. "How the hell you gonna tackle somebody? Read any books on that?"

He had me. I hadn't thought beyond kicking.

"Let me show you what I can do. I'm sure I can learn how to, or adapt some way, to play at a second position."

"I'm sorry—what'd you say your name was?—I don't think we're able to use you this year," Lee said and put his hand on my shoulder.

Clay turned and picked up a reel of film and moved to mount it on a projector next to his desk.

I walked out the main door—under the NO COWARDS sign—retraced my steps across the sloppy earth back to the parking lot and waited for Sunny and the Lizard to pick me up.

I spent that time brainstorming. There had to be another way into the Lobo pack.

———

The Intra-Lobo Spring Scrimmage was held on a Saturday at the end of the school year, right after final exams.

For the Spring Scrimmage, players would partially suit up in shoulder pads and helmets on the top half and gym shorts and cleats on the bottom. Hitting was allowed, but only above the waist, and there was no tackling of ball carriers. And don't even think about touching a quarterback.

The A-Team Offense played against the A-Team Defense for a while, then the B teams would have a shot at each other. The event was well attended by parents, students, and townspeople. It was held on the central practice field, where there was limited seating. Once those seats filled, everyone else stood two to three deep around the perimeter of the chain link fence all the way around the field.

Sitting in the Lizard a discreet distance away, I checked the equipment I needed for my plan to work. I needed four balls in total. I had my original two scavenged, duct-taped balls plus one I'd bought with money scammed from Sunny (money to pay late "lab fees"), and a final ball I'd liberated from the edge of someone's lawn near my old grade school. Four footballs, yes. Four empty tuna cans, check.

I walked around to the north end of the central practice field, where the Lobos were engaged in combat, and out into an open pasture that abutted the end zone. I paced off twenty yards from the goalposts and set up one of my tuna cans with a ball. Next, I measured off a location thirty yards out for a second ball.

I could see a few spectators in the bleachers turning my way. Some stood, ignoring the scrimmage to focus on what I was doing in the pasture. I paced off a forty-yard distance from the goalposts and set up my third ball. The fourth ball was set at fifty yards, and I was ready to begin. Now, if only the wind would stay calm ...

At my twenty-yard location, I lined up with the ball, exactly as Jan had taught me, three steps straight back and a side-step and a half to the left.

I held still and waited for a play to move the Lobos down closer to their north goal line. A long pass brought the teams down to the ten-yard line, and as the offense huddled, I kicked a duct-taped ball dead straight through the back of the uprights. It hit the ground before bouncing up and smacking the helmet of Lobo All-State linebacker Jimmy Royce.

I couldn't hear what Jimmy said, but he got everyone's attention, because all twenty-two players and all referees on the field turned and looked at me, many pointing, many throwing their hands up in frustration at the interruption. But most importantly, the crowd and all the coaches looked where the players looked. Right at me.

I sprinted to my thirty-yard position, took my steps, and launched into the kick. Focus, imagine the ball flying, easy first step, smooth swing. Bullseye again. This time, the quarterback caught my ball as it descended after splitting the uprights. About half the crowd clapped and cheered.

I heard someone shout, "Who the hell is that guy?" Another voice yelled, "He's missing an arm!"

I ran to the forty-yard position. My heart did flips, and for the first time, I had second thoughts about my wild-ass plan. Too late now, I thought, and kicked the brand-new ball that Sunny's lab-fee money had bought. This time, the ball flew less straight, veering to the right, but still passed through the uprights for a score.

Lobo parents, fans, and students cheered and clapped. The traditional Lobo victory howl broke out. The coaches and players stood stunned.

Coach Lee jogged toward me, waving his hands and blowing a whistle, but it was too late. He had at least seventy yards to cover across uneven ground, and he wasn't that fast.

There was one ball left. The fifty-yard ball. This time, I didn't hurry—every eye at the scrimmage watched. No one would look away or even blink until they saw if the mystery kicker could hit four in a row, from rough ground in a cow pasture, and make the last one a fifty-yarder. There were only a few high school placekickers in Texas who could hit from fifty yards.

All my focus went to the last ball, the stolen football, sitting pretty on its Starkist perch. I saw nothing else, heard nothing else.

I hit it square and sweet, and it rocketed into a high arc and found the point where propulsion and gravity equalized, floated there a moment. Fell back to earth in slow motion, cutting between the uprights. Plenty of room to spare.

And the crowd went—as they say—wild.

Chapter 12
I Saw Her Standing There

I learned to kick field goals so well that, momentarily, I was celebrated in Korvus and became famous across most of East Texas. My photograph even appeared in a statewide publication in 1971, *Texas Football*, alongside other top high school players, some of whom would go on to become NFL stars.

For a few short months during the fall of '71, total strangers came up to me on the street and shook my hand and slapped my back. They smiled and told their young children who I was, and the kids would look up at me with a perplexed mix of awe, discomfort and aversion. My missing arm never failed to give kids the willies. They just weren't as skilled as adults at hiding it.

My name and picture were featured on a bronze plaque on the "Wall of Fame" in the central hallway of Korvus High School, a spot reserved for those holding district or state records in football, track, baseball and other sports. It was all later expunged in great shame, almost as suddenly as it had appeared.

Some say football builds character. Having played, albeit briefly, I don't think that's true. Football *reveals* character. And while I would never say Coach Clay was right about much, he was onto something when he linked football to your inner self, your gut.

Football has a way of making what's written inside you visible to others. But that revelation of character and spirit is not limited only to those who strap on pads and helmets. The intense passions of the game eventually throw an X-ray on all those bound together by the ritual and spectacle of combat—players, parents, coaches, and fans—and show the bones of their souls to the world.

Against Clay's instincts and druthers, I played on the varsity squad for the 1971 football season. Preparations began in August—two weeks before school started—with the annual demonic torture-fest known as "two-a-days." We practiced twice a day every day until school started, in the mornings and again in the late afternoon. Each session two to three hours.

Two-a-days were designed to cull anyone not fully committed to trading pain, insult, humiliation, and emotional abuse for—what? Glory? Fame? Girls? No, during my season with the Lobos, I learned why the price was paid; it was paid to *prove*. To prove you belonged. To prove you belonged to the pack and had a place at the table where respect was served.

But the road to respect, like any good quest road, is guarded by a malevolent force. An ancient, potent beast that is the wellspring of much war and chaos and mayhem, fed by putting young men, desperate to prove, under the charge of older men, insatiable for proof.

———

Texas in August. Thirst consumed us. Thirst like a scared, trapped animal, trying to claw its way free from a flaming pit deep inside. Coach Clay allowed only one water break halfway through each practice. And even then, the portions were tiny, usually two small Dixie cups per person. It was an era when coaches thought too much water caused cramps or lethargy, or that nothing would be accomplished if players were constantly running off to drink. Indeed, the coaches had discovered the perfect twin engines to propel us to the end of every practice: our maniacal desire to prove ourselves, and our crack-whore lust for water.

Near the end of evening practices, just before we lined up for wind sprints, pickup trucks full of Shewolves and cheerleaders rolled up, leading other trucks brimming with jugs of ice-cold water and tea and Gatorade. The sight of them, the arrival of our curvaceous, pony-tailed rescuers—bearing drink and more drink—was as salvific as spotting an exit sign in hell.

If Clay noticed too many helmets turned toward the trucks and the girls, he blasted his whistle and said something like, "Keep your heads in the game." Or, "Stay focused on business—don't get distracted by any feminine delights."

To which I once heard Jimmy Royce say, to no one in particular, while doubled over trying to catch his breath from a hundred-yard sprint, "Right now ... don't care nothing ... bout no 'feminine delight' ... unless she got a snatch full of Gatorade."

———

On the last day of two-a-days, the post-practice delivery of water and Gatorade morphed into a major party. The Doors and Stones blasted from car stereos, and the Shewolves and cheerleaders were present in full force, dancing, cheering, singing.

Instead of rushing to the showers as usual, we lingered in the twilight, many players stripping off jerseys and helmets out on the field, stripping naked to the waist. They waded into the throngs of girls clustered around the trucks, raking gamy bodies across as many of our pristine, pony-tailed saviors as possible.

A combination of exhilaration and surprise at having survived the passage through two weeks of football hell made everyone high on adrenaline and relief, a high strong enough to temporarily trump our physical exhaustion. Even the coaches seemed relieved it was over, and showed no disapproval of the impromptu party, content to watch the fun from the safety of the field house.

I scored a quart bottle of icy Gatorade and pushed my way through the crowd—past a couple of Lobos dancing and guzzling iced tea from gallon jugs—and sat alone on the turf with my back against a goalpost. My brain steamed. Our black helmets were suffocating in the August temps—absorbing and retaining heat like Satan's buttcrack—but I couldn't get the infernal thing off. The chinstrap was stuck, with no equipment manager in sight to lend a hand.

Sinking fast from heat exhaustion, I tried drinking *through* the facemask. I tilted my head and aimed as much liquid as I could in the general direction of my mouth—at least six inches away behind the grid of my facemask—much of it splashing up my nose and across my cheeks and running wastefully down my chin.

"That's a different way to do it." A girl's voice.

Rita Burke—one of the four captains of the Shewolves—stood over me. She'd been my obsession since junior high. It was her image I'd drunkenly tried to conjure that night by the swimming pool at the Vander's ranch. When all the naked *Oui Magazine* girls failed to keep my wick burning. I'd never been brave enough to talk to her before, but damn did I love watching her gyrations on the field during Lobos halftime shows.

"Can I help you with that?" she asked.

"God, yes. It's stuck."

She knelt on both knees, got a two-handed grip on one side of my chin strap and popped it loose with one jerk, then sat next to me in the parched grass.

I sat my helmet to one side and instinctively tried to smooth my hair and wipe some errant Gatorade from my face and neck.

"Thanks. I'm Billy Bastrop."

"I know who you are, Billy Bastrop. Everyone in Korvus knows who you are by now. I'm Rita Burke."

"Yes, you are. Everybody knows you too, Rita Burke."

Rita's father was a prominent surgeon in town, one of the few surgeons who lived in Korvus, and her mother—a former Miss Texas finalist— owned the largest flower shop and nursery in the region. Chester and Vanessa Burke produced three gorgeous children, all as stunning as diamonds, but Rita was the crown jewel of the set.

The Burkes were town celebrities, our "beautiful people." Everyone talked about them: their house, their clothes, their cars, their vacations. Where Rita's older siblings were headed for college. Would they become doctors like their father, or businesspeople like their mother? Did you hear that Dr. Burke was elected to the Hospital Board? Did you see Vanessa's picture in the newspaper having lunch with the Governor's wife?

"Drink! Drink!" she said. I took a long swig and looked at her dopily, wishing like hell she had been absent from school the day I was Mrs. Santa Claus, the day my lips outsparkled hers.

She sat about a foot from me, and after the first drink or two, I completely forgot about Gatorade and instead drank in Rita, figuring I'd never be this close to her again. I tried to commit the vision to deepest memory: Cocoa skin, royally high cheekbones, plump expressive lips, extra slick and glittery in this moment.

Her lips alone were worth my obsession, and even though she was at that very moment speaking to me with those lips, I was hearing only sounds, not words, satisfied to simply watch as her mouth moved up and down, lips dancing along. McCartney sang out somewhere inside me ... *Lovely Rita.*

"Are you as good as they say?" she asked.

"We're going to find out." I floated back into the here and now—taking a couple more gulps—and slowly rehydrating enough for my senses to sharpen.

"Let's hope so," she said. "We need all the points we can get this year."

Before I could speak again, she popped up, chirping a "see you" over her shoulder and vanished into the crowd almost as quickly as she had appeared, making me doubt for a moment that she had ever really been there at all, sitting next to me on the frazzled turf.

I scrambled to my feet and spotted her climbing into a pickup bed. She was dancing with two other Shewolves to Credence Clearwater's "Fortunate Son," corvine hair pulled up and out the back of a scarlet Lobos cap, her black eyes fiery and mischievous.

"Forget about that one, Bastrop," Coach Lee said and chuckled as he walked past.

"She got herself a college boy."

Chapter 13
Don't Let Me Down

I'd proven I had the skill—indeed, a very critical skill—to contribute to the Lobos football team. And I'd survived the crucible of two-a-days. But mere skill and survival were not enough. I needed to *belong*. Few players talked to me, and as a kicker, I was isolated from most of the rest of the team during practices. Disconnected from combat. I needed to be respected as a comrade, a warrior, not seen as an easily broken curiosity, something to be set aside. Something marginally useful and delicate, in need of constant protection.

My chance to gain a deeper level of respect came one afternoon during the first week of regular (one per day) after-school practices. We were driven indoors by angry, sweeping winds and pulsating lightning. Rain, no matter how heavy, would not stop the Lobos from taking the field. But a lightning storm and tornado warnings would.

The coaches told us to dress in helmets, T-shirts, and practice pants without the pads. We took to the gymnasium floor, and the offensive and defensive teams lined up for mock run-throughs of plays, all run at half speed. Touch football rules only, no hitting.

Pablo Vargas and I took to one side of the building and kicked repeatedly into a practice net while the A and B squads took turns running plays. Pablo and I were the only two contenders for place-kicker. He could kick long, but I easily beat him on accuracy. Although the final list of starters at each position had not been announced, it appeared I would be designated to kick field goals and extra points, and Pablo would handle kickoffs, which worked out well since he had two arms. Very handy if you needed to tackle an opponent returning a kickoff.

Coach Clay whistled everyone to a stop. He gave a hand signal to the equipment managers, who vanished into the storage area of the gym, then reappeared, dragging a giant rolled floor pad, about twelve feet square and three inches thick. They unrolled it at mid-court.

"Men, we've got a treat for you today," Clay announced.

"Bull-in-the-ring!" a Lobo shouted.

Somebody started the Lobo howl, and everyone joined in, stomping feet in rhythm, even those of us with no idea what "bull-in-the-ring" was.

"Bull ring! Bull ring!" A handful of players chanted.

Coach Lee shouted over the chant, "Helmets and shoes off!"

In a few moments, black helmets lined the perimeter of the basketball court, like so many captured heads. T-shirts flew against the wall.

Everyone's shirt but mine. I never took it off, even in the showers. I'd hang back after practice until everyone had finished showering, then shower with my shirt on, removing it only at the last minute to wash my upper body. Walking back to the lockers, where players stood wrapped in their towels and naked from the waist up, I was the inverse image of them all—naked from the waist down—towel around my shoulders, my scars and asymmetry a more important intimacy to me than my genitals.

We stood shoulder to shoulder around the perimeter of the musty, stained canvas mat, three or four deep, a wall of skin except for my white T-shirt. Half the coaches gathered on one end of the mats and half on the other. Coach Paxton, the linebacker coach, stepped into the middle of the battlefield and whistled for quiet.

"Mr. Beck, get in here," he shouted.

The Lobos howled for Beck, a senior defensive tackle and starter last year. Beck stepped out and stood next to Paxton, grinning and jumping, arms outstretched overhead as if he'd just bested Mohammed Ali.

"Gentlemen, here are the rules. Two fighters at a time. Open hand hitting ONLY." Paxton demonstrated with a slow-motion, mock hit on Beck, with his hand open and fingers spread.

"No hitting the neck or above." Paxton waved his hand in the vicinity of Beck's face.

"No hitting below the belt." He made a fast, fake jab toward Beck's crotch, stopping short. Laughter rocked the place.

"No kicking. No biting. No head-butting. No licking. And *absolutely* no kissing." Paxton puckered his lips and did a head fake toward Beck, and the Lobos screamed their delight.

"Everything else goes. Now, who wants a go at Mr. Beck here?"

The Lobos howled and five players jumped into the ring, anxious to tangle with Beck. Paxton gave a knowing glance toward Coach Clay, who pointed at Taylor. Taylor was a junior transfer from some nowheresville near Marshall, where he, like Beck, was a defensive tackle. Taylor had performed well during two-a-days, while the coaches had been riding Beck for coasting too much. Taylor was clearly a rival for Beck's starting position. The stakes were set, the howl rising.

"Howwwwwwwww-ooooooooooooo!"

Everyone cleared the mats, leaving Beck and Taylor, with Coach Paxton standing between them, one hand on Beck's chest, the other on Taylor's. The two big tackles leaned into Paxton, ready to collide when he dropped his hands and jumped away.

Clay blew his whistle, and they slammed together, arms flying, each strike leaving clear handprints across chests and backs. Taylor charged hard, pushing Beck all the way to the edge of the mat, where several Lobos caught him and threw him back into the fray. Beck grabbed one of Taylor's arms and grounded him on the mat, momentarily astraddle his waist and delivering a vicious whack-whack-whack to the chest. Rules or no rules, a stray swing here and there landed across Taylor's face. There was no whistle.

Taylor twisted and slithered his way out and back to his feet, and again buzz-sawed Beck into an embarrassing retreat across the full length of the ring until Clay whistled the match over. Paxton raised Taylor's hand in victory.

"*Howwwwwwwww-oooooooooooo!*"

Beck pointed his face at the ceiling, eyes closed, then timidly shook Taylor's hand, no doubt thinking this defeat would move Taylor past him to the top of the depth chart.

Three more battles ensued, all obvious matchups—contrived by the coaches— between players vying for the same position. Pablo was the only other kicker, so I expected him to step up and challenge me on the mats. I was almost six feet and a hundred seventy pounds, and while I had only a left arm, it was exceptionally strong, and my lower body strength was among the best on the team. Pablo was about five-ten and of slim build and was one of our weakest weightlifters. I thought I could take him.

As the coaches seemed to lose interest in the matches, I jumped into the ring ahead of several others clamoring to be the next fighter. The Lobo howl withered to a drone.

Paxton looked at me like I'd just sprouted donkey ears.

"Bastrop!? What the ...?" He turned to Coaches Clay and Lee, palms out. They both shrugged.

"Pick somebody else," came a shout from the back. "Me next Coach, pick me!" "Not Mayo!"

"You sure about this, Bastrop?" Paxton asked.

"Step out, Mayo," Ricky Vander shouted. "Leave this to the men."

"I'm ready," I told Paxton.

"OK. Who wants a piece of Bastrop?"

Paxton stared directly at Pablo with a "well, here's your chance" look. Pablo didn't move. Paxton called out again for someone to step up and fight me. The howl collapsed to cricket level. People looked up, down, everywhere but at me or Paxton.

I stood drowning in the sudden and awful silence. I caught Pablo's gaze for a second, pleading with my eyes and my hearing, sending the silent message, "don't leave me hanging here, man." I scanned the faces all around the mat, disbelieving that no one, no one, not a single player would step into the ring with me. Sunny was right after all. Such a futile idea. I didn't belong here. I belonged nowhere.

Jimmy Royce parted the wall of skin and stepped into the ring.

Holy. Fucking. Shit. Not Royce.

Jimmy Royce played linebacker so well, you wondered why other people even tried. On the field, he sensed the location of the ball the way a shark senses the electrical life force of its hapless prey, always moving to it, moving to the blood, relentless and unrepentant of the suffering inflicted on quarterbacks and ball carriers. To the coaching staff, he was a once-in-a-lifetime player, someone to build a reputation and a state championship around.

"What are you doing, Royce?" Coach Paxton asked.

"I'm gonna fight Bastrop here."

"Royce, let's get you someone more your speed." Paxton looked around the team, knowing full well there was no such thing as "someone Royce's speed." He'd been written up in football magazines and newspapers across the state, recruited by major colleges all over the country.

No hands went up and no one pleaded to fight Royce, not even Ricky Vander, who was the one person in the room with something to gain from the encounter. Ricky was the "other" linebacker, playing alongside Jimmy in every game, but was constantly overshadowed. The Vanders, especially Judge Vander, hated how Royce—the kid living in a shack with his grandmother and eight younger siblings next to the repugnant chicken processing plant—attracted all the buzz and accolades. But the coin of the realm was winning, and football was the only institution in town where pure performance could trump race or social class. Or amputation. At least for the length of time it takes to play a football game.

"OK with you, Bastrop?" Royce asked and gave me a chin tilt. The two of us had never spoken before that moment.

"Bull in the ring," I said, hoping whoever recorded my last words would think them pithy.

Royce pulled the canvas belt from the waistband of his football pants and ran one end through the D-ring that served as a buckle, making a loop around his right wrist. He asked Paxton to tie the other end of the belt to the back of his pants, through the belt loop in the small of his back.

"Pull it good and tight, Coach. Get that arm down, snug against my side."

Now each combatant had one, opposing arm.

Some Lobos chanted "Royce, Royce, Royce." The howl began to rise.

Paxton stood the middle ground between us, Clay whistled for the fight to start, and Jimmy Royce— "two-and-soon-to-be-three-time" All-State linebacker—beat the pure crap out of me for thirty seconds, which is thirty hours in bull-ring time.

I managed to slap him a time or two, I think, but I spent much of the time flying into the skin wall and being pitched back by the crowd into Jimmy's ferocious assault. He painted my torso official Lobo scarlet—even through my shirt—and one wild swing busted my nose. Clay whistled the fight to a stop and Paxton didn't bother raising Jimmy's hand. Everyone knew I'd been slaughtered. But I'd fought Royce. Something nobody else dared.

Jimmy Royce high-fived me as Paxton untied his arm.

The howl shook the room, the Lobos chanted Royce-Royce-Royce, and I doubled over—bruised, sore as hell, gasping for breath, struggling to keep my balance, rivulets of snot and blood running down my mouth and chin.

I had never been happier in my life. A happiness soon to be shattered by the killing of Wonderful Byrd.

Chapter 14
Everybody's Got Something to Hide Except Me and My Monkey

A few days later, I decided to celebrate my newfound Lobo status with a movie. The PineView Drive-In was about a half mile up the highway from Sunny's house. I'd watched a lot of movies there growing up. But I never paid for any of them.

Over the years, I'd pried one of the heavily rusted metal panels loose at the back wall, where I could squeeze through onto the grounds and find a nice dark spot to sit and watch. The walls were designed to block cars driving by or parking on a sideroad. They hadn't planned on a kid walking through the pastures at night, carrying his own lawn chair and wearing a backpack with snacks and a drink.

———

The movie that night was *Butch Cassidy and the Sundance Kid*.

About the time the Hole-In-Wall-Gang robbed their first train, I saw two cars enter the theatre and make their way toward the far back row of speakers. They parked between me and the snack bar.

One car was a large black Lincoln, and the other was Ricky

Vander's Trans Am. There wasn't much light, but I could see and hear enough to know both cars were full of Lobos. The Lincoln carried maybe four or five players whom I couldn't quite make out, but I got a good look at Ricky, apparently drunk. He had his two favorite henchmen with him in his Trans Am, Eric Duffy and Jack Roche. Duffy was a second-string linebacker, and Roche was the Lobos' starting free safety. The players moved liquor bottles and beer between the cars.

Soon after parking, the Lincoln driver and another player got out and opened the trunk, and helped somebody climb out. The guy in the trunk was tall and awkward. He stumbled and rolled his head, as if dazed, and his skin shone gray in the meager light. The other two helped him stand to his full height, the three of them with their backs to me, facing the movie screen.

Trunk-guy stutter-stepped as if on the deck of a pitching ship, leaned against the side of the Lincoln and shouted slurred words toward the screen.

"Horsey! Horsey!"

"Can't you keep him the fuck quiet?" the driver barked.

"Monkey juice," a voice from inside the Lincoln said, and somebody held out a tall bottle from a backseat window.

"Muunn-kaay jooooo," slurred the trunk-guy, snatching for the bottle and missing.

The driver pulled another bottle from the trunk before slamming it shut, then he and his buddy tried to corral the trunk-guy. Headlights from a car leaving the movie washed over them, and in that brief glare I saw their faces: Beck behind the wheel of the Lincoln, Ronnie Kerrell—the Lobos' wide receiver—at his side. And the one they'd hauled from the trunk was Wonderful Byrd.

"Her pretty pretty!" Wonderful screamed out, pointing at Katherine Ross riding a bicycle with Paul Newman.

"Shhhhhhhh, you stupid-ass monkey!"

"Get him the fuck over here already!" Ricky yelled out.

"Muunkay muunkay joooo," Wonderful said, and reached for the bottle Roche held away from him at arm's length.

"Not yet, monkey man."

Beck and Roche delivered Wonderful to the Trans Am, where he stayed for some time, hidden in its dark interior with Ricky, Duffy and Kerrell. Then Duffy transferred Wonderful—now shirtless—back to the Lincoln, this time into the backseat.

The Lincoln Lobos shuffled positions from time to time, a front seat passenger switching places with someone in the back, then another shuffle and another. When all the shuffling was done, Kerrell called for Wonderful to return to Ricky's car, and Roche struggled out of the Lincoln—his own belt and pants now undone—and walked the stumbling and dazed Wonderful back to the Trans Am.

Just before the last bank was robbed in Bolivia, Ricky moved into the back seat with Wonderful. All was quiet for a while, except for periodic muffled laughter, some from the Lincoln and some from the Trans Am. And when Ricky and Duffy emerged with Wonderful, they carried him to the rear of the Lincoln with his feet dragging the asphalt.

Butch and Sundance made a run for it, but died in a freeze-frame hail of gunfire and I watched Ricky and Duffy wrestle Wonderful—now wearing only his underwear—into the black maw of the Lincoln's trunk.

Chapter 15
Lovely Rita

Although I made the varsity football team, I was still an Akela, and as such had to fulfill one of my major duties to the school, to tutor any athletes, especially football players, who might run afoul of the academic rules of eligibility. And there was a new policy that year expanding the tutoring service beyond football players to any cheerleaders, pep squad members, and Shewolves who needed help. Each Akela was assigned four or five people to tutor. Two of my four were Jimmy Royce, and Rita Burke.

Rita was my toughest case. She was smart, but damned lazy. And her beauty constantly drove me to distraction. She would show up for a tutoring session and I'd drift away for a moment, drift to that night by Ricky's pool when I tried to mentally put Rita's face on the *Oui* girls. Or that time at the end of two-a-day practices when she leaned in so close to unsnap my chin strap that her breath filled my face and brushed my lips.

Rita's grades in English were killing her GPA, primarily because she was in Mrs. Fawke's class. Fawke was the best English teacher in the school (and possibly the state), but she required a lot of reading and writing from her students. Rita's laziness was a bad match with

Fawke's workload requirements. She seldom read the assignments and simply failed to turn in many of the short papers required weekly.

When we met one-on-one for tutoring, I'd usually begin the sessions by talking about her latest assignment on Crane or Steinbeck, then quickly find myself unable to think about anything but how her hair would feel against my face, or how her skin would smell if I could only press my nose into the nape of her neck.

Rita sensed this, of course, and as the weeks passed, she stopped sitting across the library table from me and moved to my side of the table, at first leaving an empty chair between us. Then one day, she sat in the chair right next to me, scooting her chair closer than necessary.

"Why don't we start with your draft of this week's paper on 'The Lottery'?"

She opened her notebook and handed me a page with three or four sentences, her forearm rubbing against mine in the exchange.

"Rita, you know it's supposed to be two *full* pages?"

"That's all I came up with."

I quickly read her weak, disjointed sentences.

"This is a good start," I lied. "Your last sentence would make a better first sentence. You know this is due tomorrow, right? Are you writing more tonight?"

She leaned into me, the point of her shoulder barely nudging mine. The blood in my arm and neck surged with warmth, like someone had thrown a switch somewhere.

"I'm going to an event with my parents tonight. We'll be out late, *and* I have a bunch of algebra to do."

"Fawke's going to kill you if you turn in another paper like this."

"Billy, have you ever read this lottery thing?"

"Sure."

"Ever written a paper on it?" She leaned into me again, this time more deliberately, and let her shoulder linger on my upper arm. Her long raven hair very briefly glanced my neck. Lava flowed through me like it hadn't since the night of Black Jack at the Vander Ranch. I flashed on the *Oui* centerfold girl, just for a moment, and that girl paled next to Rita.

"Oral ... I mean, we did oral reports. I don't think I wrote anything." Even my hair blushed.

"I really need a good grade on this one. Can't you help me out? You're so good at this stuff."

"We're not supposed to do the work for you."

"I wouldn't ask, but I don't want to fall more behind in algebra. Do you know how long it takes to work out all those problems?"

I knew I could write a killer paper on "The Lottery" faster than it took Rita to dress for school in the mornings. She moved back away from me an inch or two, waiting for my answer, dark eyes cutting into me, lips shining. I didn't want her moving back across the table from me, or worse, run the risk she'd ask for a different Akela tutor.

"OK. But I'll have to make it a C+, or maybe a B-. Otherwise, Fawke will get suspicious."

"You're great, Billy! I'll need it before school starts so I can rewrite it in my own handwriting. Meet me at the Coke machine at 7:45?"

She didn't wait for my reply, and as she left, she rested her hand on the side of my neck, and I impulsively turned my cheek into her wrist. I watched her all the way out of the library before I realized we hadn't covered any of the material I'd planned for the tutoring session.

Over the next several weeks, Rita and I came to an understanding. Rita would let me think I had some chance with her, and in return, I would help her cheat like hell. I wrote all her weekly short papers in English (25% of the final grade), along with her English term paper on *Wuthering Heights* (50% of the final grade).

We were in World History together during fourth period, and she somehow managed to talk our teacher into letting her move to a new desk directly across the aisle from me. In addition to writing her

World History term paper on England's colonial rule over India, I signaled the answers to her on every major exam.

Most of the exams were multiple choice, so we worked out a system where she would signal which question number she needed an answer for, and I'd signal the answers back with how many fingers I held to my face while "contemplating" my test (one finger = A, two fingers = B, etc.). Lucky for Rita, there were never more than five choices.

———

While I shamelessly danced on Rita's string, I worked Jimmy Royce hard on his reading and comprehension. Royce was wicked smart, but suffered from underdeveloped reading skills, which, of course, contributed to his struggling with almost all academic subjects. I was determined to improve his reading and writing skills not only because he deserved it, but because I wanted him to get as much enjoyment from books as I did. I wanted him to love fiction as much as he loved crushing quarterbacks.

And I wanted to help him because I sensed he was one of the few of us with a real chance to leapfrog out of our collective smallness. It was the least I could do to repay him for the beatdown he'd given me in the bull ring. I really liked the idea of having a friend who scared the hell out of just about everyone.

Although he resisted at first, he knew there was no choice but to bring his English grades up or risk missing games. While Jimmy was a lock for a full-ride football scholarship somewhere, assuming he didn't get injured, he knew he was competing against equally talented players from across the U.S. for a limited number of positions at top-tier football schools. Missing games pulled his stats down —he needed as many unassisted tackles and interceptions as possible to be appealing to elite college football programs. As I suspected, he mostly needed a little reading practice and motivation, and his literature skills steadily improved as the season progressed.

We met to discuss a paper he was writing on *Lord of the Flies*.

"How'd you get so good at this stuff, Bastrop?"

"Wasted youth, I think."

"No, I think you was just born with it. Your mama and daddy go to college?"

"My mom did, for a while."

"What'd she study?"

"English."

"She plan to be a teacher?"

"She wanted to be a poet."

"I knew it. Bastrop, you was born with it! Your mama a poet and all. Why she quit?"

"Have you finished the *Lord of the Flies* paper yet?" I asked, hoping to change the subject.

"Just a bunch of rich white kids. Camping. Crazy-ass bunch of white kids, too."

"You didn't like the story?"

"It don't make no sense to me. All a bunch of stupid shit. Pig's heads on sticks, kid named Piggy. What's up with all that pig stuff anyway?"

"That's what I've been talking about, you need to look beneath the surface of the story. The truth of the story sometimes lies in what is implied indirectly, in the symbols the writer uses. Piggy, for example, represents learning and intellect."

"Piggy's like you, huh, Bastrop."

"God, I hope not—I hope I don't have much in common with Piggy. Things didn't end that well for him."

"How about that pig head. Is that a secret message too? Hell, if the man wants to tell me something, why don't he just tell me straight up?"

"The sow's head on the stake represents evil. Golding is doing what storytellers and writers have done for centuries. He's using certain characters and objects as a shorthand way of talking about the true nature of people and the whole world, really. This book's about how everyone contains both good and evil within themselves. To one degree or another. You just don't know how much until something strips away the thin layer of civilization, strips away all the rules. That's when the truth comes out. It's all about finding the truth."

"Uh-huh. And what are you reading?" Royce nodded at the edge of a book poking out of the top of my backpack.

"*Deliverance*, by James Dickey."

"That ain't on *my* reading list."

"It's not on anybody's reading list. It's illegal, so to speak, in this school."

"Don't worry, I ain't telling nobody. Hell, I'm embarrassed for you, reading books you don't have to read. Mercy Lord, Bastrop, you were just born with a big ole hungry brain. Must've gotten that from your mama. Lucky for Korvus, God also gave you a big ole deadeye foot. What's that *Deliverance* book about?"

"A bunch of rich crazy-ass white people. Camping."

"Got any pigs in it?"

"More or less. There's some pig squealing that's disturbing."

"Tell me something, Deadeye. There any books *not* about white people? You know, no camping and chasing pigs and craziness like that? Any black man or woman written a book the State of Texas would deem worthy of reading?"

"I don't know how the State of Texas rates it, but the single greatest novel ever written was by a black man."

"Don't blow no sunshine up my skirt, Bastrop."

"No, for real. Man named Ralph Ellison. Only wrote one novel, but it was so good, he didn't really need to write another one."

"What's it called?"

"*Invisible Man.*"

"Bastrop, now you're just messing with me."

"I shit you not. I'll bring my copy to you tomorrow. But you got to keep it hidden. It's illegal here too."

"I cain't read no punk-ass science fiction shit. Rockets and monsters and invisible damn people. Hell."

"It's not even close to science fiction. You'll see, you'll love it."

"Bastrop, you all right, man. Bring me that book. I'm going to keep you from being the only freak in this school who reads a book he don't have to. What are you tutoring them other kids with?"

"Just helping them shore up any weak spots, on any subject they need."

"How about that Chinese chick?"

"Vietnamese."

"Yeah, right, her. What's up with her? She's been checking me out, you know."

"Kim-Ly just needs a little help using English in a more American style. She's doing great overall."

"I think she wants to nuzzle me up, Bastrop. 'Course, all the ladies do. How you doing with Rita?"

"What do you mean?"

"You know what I'm talking about. I see you licking your chops any time she comes down the hall. You going to trip over that tongue one of these days if you not careful."

"She's got a boyfriend. In college."

"Hell, all them Shewolves got boyfriends. Sure, she got a boyfriend, alright. Till a better one come along. Listen to me. You famous now, man. You're Mr. Never Miss. You Billy-the-Kid-Fuck-ing-**Deadeye** Bastrop. You the Deadeye! Hell with her boyfriend. She just waiting for a better one to come along. You gotta be the better one!"

It was true, I'd missed zero extra points and only one field goal all season. I still got an occasional MAYO sign on my locker door, but after some games, a DEADEYE sign would show up. And a sports-writer for the local newspaper had started referring to me as Deadeye Bastrop in his articles.

"I don't know how to talk to her, except about schoolwork. I'm tongue-tied out of class. I can't talk to any girls. I'm afraid, you know, that I'm repulsive to them."

"You got your mind all fucked up, Deadeye. You want her, right?

You got to parlay this football thing you got going. You got to put on some Deadeye swagger. Be bold and beautiful, man! Listen to the Jimmy now—no matter what they say—women don't like meekness. They might make chit chat with meekness, and they might go to the movie with meekness, and they might let meekness buy them a hamburger. But they ain't never gonna fuck meekness.

"You know that Booster Bash coming up next week? You gonna take Miss Captain Shewolf Hot-Ass Rita Burke to that party. Tomorrow, I want you to walk right up to Captain Rita and say something like this: '*Baby, your parents misnamed you. Your name shoulda been Two Skies, 'cause one sky ain't big enough to hold all that beauty.*'"

"OK, now who's shitting who? I want to date her, Royce, not kill her. She'd laugh herself to death if I said that."

"Women like to laugh, Deadeye. Listen to the Jimmy now."

"That kind of crap only works for you because you're *you*. They're not even listening to you when you lay that crap on them, they're just standing there awestruck to be talking to you at all."

"OK, Bastrop, don't take my advice. I'm only trying to quid-pro-quo you here, you know, you help me and I help you. Go ahead and admire Lovely Rita from afar. Just do us all a favor, and try to keep that long-ass tongue in your mouth so people don't have to step over the damn thing."

Chapter 16
You've Got to Hide Your Love Away

The Booster Bash was scheduled for the next Friday night, and a week after that, the Korvus High Lobos would play for the 1971 Class AA Texas State Football Championship for the first time ever, against the Radley Razorbacks at Memorial Stadium in Austin. The town was berserk.

The Bash venue was the National Guard Armory. Two daises were built on either side of the cavernous armory, and the starting offense (and their dates) would sit on one dais and the starting defense (and their dates) on the other, and the ample space between the two platforms would be cleared of howitzers and helicopters and instead be used for buffets, mingling, and dancing.

I was to sit on the south dais with the starting offensive team. The table where respect was served.

I decided to take Jimmy's advice (all but the "two skies" part of it) and go bold and ask Rita to the Bash. I knew the odds were very long. Most likely, she already had a date (of course, she would), but at least I would have made the first step toward learning how to talk to her, or any other girl, away from a classroom setting.

I approached Rita during lunch break as she sat on a bench with two other Shewolves captains. They sat amid a gaggle of other girls who stood in groupings and chattered all around them.

The Shewolves were impeccably groomed and sat quietly for the most part, looking drowsy and bored. I moved toward their bench cautiously, parting first one cluster of girls, then another, the clusters quickly reforming, as water fills in behind a passing boat. The cicada thrum of conversation rose and fell as I moved through.

"Hi," I said meekly. Rita's Shewolf companions looked at me wide-eyed. Shocked. One pursed her lips.

"Hi, Billy," Rita said. "Did you finish my paper on *Withering Heights* already?"

"*Wuthering Heights*," I corrected her, and immediately cringed at slipping into tutor mode. Or maybe it's bold—as Jimmy had advised—to correct her? Shewolves One and Two giggled.

"So, is it done?"

"No, I'm still working on it."

"It's due end of the day on Friday, you know that, right? I really need that one to pull my first term grade up."

"It's no problem," I said, "I'll have it for you first thing Friday morning. Speaking of Friday ..."

"You're a peach, Billy. Now I just wish your handwriting was more like mine, then I wouldn't have to rush so much to recopy everything. Any chance I could get it Thursday? Give me some breathing room?"

"Speaking of *Friday*," I said, "Jimmy Royce and I were talking ... and he said maybe I should see if you ..." I thought dropping Royce's name would give me a little more cache.

Rita and the Shewolves brightened a bit as I invoked Royce's name.

" ... if you don't already have plans ... maybe you would be willing to go to the Booster Bash with me ... but you know, just if you don't have any other ... ." Dear God, that was not just meek, it was meek squared. I'm never getting laid.

Rita and Shewolves One and Two eyeballed each other. Twice.

Shewolf One smiled broadly and fiddled with the stack of books in her lap, and covered her snicker with the back of her fist. Shewolf Two stared and stretched her eyes open to the point of almost launching her contacts at me. Boredom gone. Conversations paused as the surrounding coven began to realize what was happening.

Rita leaned fully back on the bench, her breasts pushing hard against the white cloth of her blouse, small gaps forming around some of the buttons, letting a brief peek of red bra blaze through. She was bemused and shocked, but pleasantly so. She sat very straight and lifted her chin slightly, running both hands through her gleaming black hair and pulling it back and letting it fall. Her football earrings danced and caught the light.

"Why not?" she said. "Now, are you sure I can't get that paper on *Thursday?*"

"Really, you'll go? That's great. Oh, oh, we'll have seats on one of the main platforms. Right out front."

"And the withering, uh, wuthering paper on Thursday, right?"

"Sure, I can do that." It was near the end of the first term, I could understand Rita was anxious about that paper, it was fifty percent of her grade, and it would be the last one I needed to do for her. I had papers due, exams to prep for, tutoring, and football practice, but I knew I could get her paper finished a day early. I didn't want the very first date of my life thinking I was a slacker.

Three minutes later, the whole school knew Rita was going to the Bash with me. Jimmy Royce high-fived me so hard he nearly knocked me over a stairway railing.

"See what happens when you listen to *the Jimmy!*" He shouted and grinned and strutted to his class like a proud papa.

Coach Lee gave me a thumbs-up as I walked past his Civics classroom. Teammates I passed in the hallway all that afternoon either smiled or scowled. Some smiled and shook their heads slowly in the kind of amazed acknowledgment reserved for those who have lived through some insane act purely by the grace of heaven, like fire eaters or high wire walkers, or the nuts who occasionally survive a plunge over Niagara Falls.

Others scowled and shook their heads in envy and pained disbelief, taking the news as final proof the universe was flying off its axis and we were at last entering the end of days, when either the sun would explode, or monkeys would fly from asses.

———

I slept little that week. I was awake at all hours, either writing one of several end-of-term papers, or thinking about Rita, or studying for finals, or writing Rita's *Wuthering Heights* paper (pure torture), or trying to picture Rita naked, or worrying about the Radley Razorbacks—our state championship opponents—and their High School All-American quarterback, or studying more for finals, or trying to picture Rita reading *Wuthering Heights* naked.

Finally, I gave up on everything except just thinking about Rita—scripting how the date would go, when I would pick her up, what I would say to her parents, what subjects to talk about during the whole five minutes it would take to drive from her house to the Bash, what route we would take to the armory, the pros and cons of taking her to the Dairy Queen vs. the Tastee Freeze after the Bash as well as the relative merits of the two FM radio stations I could get on the Lizard's radio (after much analysis I ruled out AM radio altogether).

I washed, scrubbed, waxed and shined the Lizard inside and out, wishing that wax would remove the dents and rust that had accumulated over the years. I put red cellophane tape over one of the broken taillights. I worried about the threadbare spots in the upholstery. I experimented with draping different swatches of cloth or hand towels over them, trying to make their placement look somehow random or accidental. Still, that strategy was pointless, so I just hoped it would be sufficiently dark that night. I talked a fellow Akela into buying my *Rubber Soul* album for two dollars and used the money to replace the broken headlight.

Sunny observed all of this for a couple of days, then finally spoke up.

"This girl you're taking, she don't happen to be the GD Queen of England, do she?"

"Nope," I spoke without looking up and continued scrubbing the Lizard floor mats with Pine Sol. "But she is the Shewolves captain."

Sunny pressed her face against one of the Lizard's windows, making a greasy spot where I'd just Windexed.

"You ain't got my good hand towels in there, do you? Those are just for company. And under no circumstances are my embroidered dish towels to leave this house. You hear?"

"When was the last time we had company?"

She didn't answer.

"Here's forty dollars." She threw the bills onto the driver's seat. "Why don't you see if you can get a decent jacket or something. And don't forget to take some flowers with you. Girls like flowers. And, make sure you bring her home before midnight. Most white people don't let their girls stay out past midnight."

"Yes'm."

"Y'all ain't gonna daince are you?"

Shit shit shit. I forgot people would be dancing. I had boogied a few times late at night, alone in my room, to Aretha or the Stones, but I hadn't danced with anyone since third grade. Well, not with a girl (I wasn't counting the Mrs. Santa Claus disaster). I added it to my "to-do" list for the week: check library for dancing book, carve out time to practice dancing.

"Ah was at a daince once."

I dropped my sponge and stood.

"This I got to hear. When on earth did you ever go to a dance?"

The closest thing to a dance I'd ever seen Sunny do was when she swayed around with a rattlesnake held overhead at Howard Granger's Church of All Truth, where she'd started going—to my dismay—a couple of Sundays a month since I started high school. Although I loathed the place, I'd go with her sometimes and sit in the very back row, being there just in case she, or anyone else, needed a ride to the hospital.

"Just the once. Ah mean, outside church. Course church daincin is different 'cause it's sacred, showing your love of Jesus. All other daincin is devil daincin."

"How old were you?" I was sure she was bullshitting me.

"Fifteen, Ah believe. Papa was trying to marry me off, but Ah didn't give him much help in the matter. It was a big barn daince. Barn ain't there no more, burned up a long time ago. A bunch of us girls stood around, waiting. There was a lot more girls than men. We stood and watched people as they two-stepped and sashayed around, and after a long while, this tall, skinny, ugly fella with big round spectacles asked me if Ah would hit the floor with him."

"So, you danced with the tall, ugly guy?"

"Oh, hell, we dosey-doed around a few times. Then he tole me Ah dainced pretty good. But Ah think he was just hoping to hug me up. Ah tole him he dainced pretty good too, and he said, 'Thank you for saying that—Ah ain't never dainced with a white woman before.'"

"*He* wasn't white?!" Now I knew for sure she was messing with me.

Sunny glared at me, and her neck flashed red.

"Well, hell yes! Now you know better'n that! Of course, he was a white man." She fell silent and expressionless for a long moment, looking into the middle distance, thinking deeply.

"Um-humm, Ah'm pretty sure he was white."

———

The Friday of the Booster Bash, I ached with exhaustion. Over the week, my initial thrill and shock that Rita would go with me kept morphing from euphoria to terror and back to euphoria tinged with lust, and back to dread, then to lustful terror, and finally into something akin to a dreadfully happy state with an undertone of lust.

On the drive to pick her up, a bolt of panic struck me. I had no idea what I was doing—when she got into the Lizard, from that point on, I'd be a baby with a loaded gun.

I wore my best clothes and a new blazer (thank you, Sunny) from Shorty's Discount Warehouse and (according to Sunny) the only tie my grandfather Turner Bastrop ever owned, a red silk number with horizontal gold bars. The corsage was small, made of several thumb-sized yellow rose buds. They were sold out of red since scarlet was one of the Lobos team colors (scarlet and black), and in big demand for the Bash. The corsage was in a clear plastic square box, small enough to fit in the side pocket of my new blazer.

The Burkes lived in a neighborhood called Elmwood Park, the most exclusive neighborhood in town. There was only one way in and out of the place, so cars seldom drove into the area unless they were visiting or otherwise on official business.

Most Elmwood Park homes sat on large, heavily wooded lots, thick with hardwood trees and large magnolias and live oaks. Many of the lots connected to a common area known simply as "the woods," which was basically a private park for the residents, with horse trails, and deeper in the woods, a small lake in the middle of a grassy meadow. It was widely rumored that the two most expensive houses in Elmwood Park belonged to the Burkes and the Vanders.

I arrived at the Burke address at seven sharp and thought it would be polite to park on the street parallel to the house, since there were several cars already in the circular driveway. I sat in the Lizard for a few minutes and gathered my nerves, and surprised myself by actually relaxing.

This was a great time for me. I was a straight-A student and a record-setting football player in a town that worshipped football, taking one of the most gorgeous girls imaginable to an event where my teammates and I would be feted and celebrated as heroes as we stood on the cusp of delivering to our elders their most precious, most long-sought treasure: A Texas State Football Championship.

But most importantly, I was about to take a major step into the mainstream, to begin the process of molting out of my freakishness and into ... just another guy. That's all I ever wanted. To be nothing special.

Through the front door, I heard the sounds of a party: subdued music, the hum of multiple conversations. I rang the doorbell and Vanessa Burke answered, glass of wine in hand.

"Yes, may I help you?" she asked, smiling.

"Hi. I'm Billy Bastrop."

Vanessa pulled the wine glass closer into her body and tilted her head very slightly and again said, "Yes?"

"I'm here for Rita. For the Booster Bash."

Dr. Burke came around the side of the door and stood next to his wife. Vanessa's smile dissolved, and she turned to her husband.

"Oh dear," she said, looking first at Chester Burke and furrowing her brow, then looking at me, her eyes darting from my face to my empty blazer sleeve.

"Well, I'm afraid Rita's not here," Vanessa said.

Her words punctured me like a spray of bullets, and I felt my spirit gush from those new wounds and puddle on their marble porch.

"She's out with David," Dr. Burke explained, matter-of-factly, like that would clear everything up.

"David's up from SMU. He's in town for the weekend," Vanessa said. "And oh, I know now, you're Rita's tutor, right?"

"Vanessa," Dr. Burke said, "this is Billy Bastrop, the kicker."

"Oh, yes. Yes, of course. The sidewinder. Billy, you do such a good job."

"What brings you over, Billy?" Dr. Burke asked. "Shouldn't you be over at the Booster Bash about now? We're all headed there shortly."

Inside, people milled about with small plates of food, some with glasses of wine, some with bottles of beer, chatting, laughing. From somewhere inside the house, I heard the voice of an elderly woman, raspy and muted.

"Chestuh! Chestuh! Somebody has parked a junked car in front of the house."

A boy about ten years old ran over to the door with a party napkin. It had a gold football printed on it.

"Billy, would you sign this for me?"

I stood frozen. Couldn't speak or move. I'd lost all will and energy, my tenuous grip on civility and consciousness slipping, slipping.

Dr. Burke reached inside his blazer and handed me a pen, and repeated his question. "What brings you by, son?"

I signed the boy's napkin, asking him to hold it with both hands against the Burkes' doorjamb so it wouldn't move as I put my name on it, and all I could think to say to Dr. Burke was, "Just something about final exams. Sorry, I disturbed your party."

I crossed the lawn to the Lizard. Several young children chased each other beneath drapes of Spanish moss, the trees strung with hundreds of soft, amber Christmas lights.

A blonde girl about six years old stood on the curb and watched me.

"What happened to your arm?" she asked as I passed her.

"Here," I said, and lifted the little corsage from my pocket.

"I won't be needing this."

Chapter 17
Helter Skelter

I passed the armory, bright and vibrant with dancing Lobos and their dates and families, bathed in the warmth of well-wishers on a cold winter night. Two searchlights— visible across the entire county—shot their beacons into the clear December air, the night otherwise moonless and black. I couldn't go in and sit there next to Rita's empty seat—a billboard of my gullibility and stupidity—sit there and validate how thoroughly I'd been duped.

I kept driving and pushed the Lizard hard, barreling recklessly down the narrow, paved road that edged the lake, the beacons at the armory still poking into the blackness, out on the horizon. I whipped left onto the gravel of Potter Road, barely braking for the turn, and fishtailed in the old car, gravel crunching under tires and ricocheting wildly off the Lizard's belly, kicking up a fog of pale dust. Potter Road was a seldom-used gravel road that skirted the edge of Town Lake, the town's public water reservoir. It split off the primary road that circled the lake and wound through a cypress bottom and finally emerged from the woods and dead-ended into a small meadow atop a low bluff right above the lake. It's where people went to be alone.

I passed through the damp, ghostly bottomland, headlights raking across the impenetrable fortress of bare trees on either side, and emerged into the meadow at the end of Potter Road. There was one car there—a black Porsche—parked with its nose almost kissing the chain-link fence that stopped people from accidentally plunging off the bluff and into the lake.

Two people stood beside the car. Probably drinking or doping, I figured. Just shadow figures in the darkness. I drove past at a steady speed so they'd know I wasn't stopping and would not disturb them. It was a guy and a girl. But the shadowy girl caught my eye, something about her. The tilt of her head. The way she flipped her hair. It was Rita. Yes, Rita, for sure. Rita and the famous David.

The two of them leaned on the Porsche, impervious to the chill, and David—David the college boy, David just up from SMU for the weekend—had Rita bent over the hood of his Porsche. He pumped her from behind. Rita lifted on her forearms and bounced with David's rhythm. She arched her back and pushed her rump into him. David pumped faster, and Rita slung her hair to one side and pointed her chin at the night sky. She gave out long contrails of breath, her breath crystallizing in the cold air and collecting into a thin fog around them.

"Fuuuuuck," I said. Yeah, she had been misnamed. Should have been *Delilah* Burke. Deceitful, manipulative little cozener. Could I have been more blind, more oblivious? On some level, I guess I knew it all along. But my situation was self-inflicted. Sure, I wanted in her pants, but she wanted in my head. And in the end, I'm the one who ended up with the short end of the dick.

———

The Lizard seemed to take over driving for me, and I leaned back and turned on the radio, unexpectedly picking up a station from Chicago, some thousand miles away, a pleasant surprise that happened from time to time when the atmospheric conditions were just right. The

Lizard turned onto the interstate and ran wide open toward Dallas for twenty or thirty minutes, then took a random turn and followed a narrow blacktop road into a place dark as hell and parked. Nothingness. I sat there in the deep black comforting of nothingness and drank in the Chicago music: Dylan, Jefferson Airplane, Kinks, Cocker, Beatles. The world went away for a while.

I awoke on an asphalt road bisecting two cotton fields, a blaze of headlights in the rearview mirror. A clarion truck horn blared at me.

"You broken down?" A man's voice came from the oversized pickup behind me. I cranked the Lizard and waved out the window, and pulled over as far as I could on the narrow road to let him pass. Then I took off my blazer and tie and threw them into the backseat and sped toward town.

———

It was nearly midnight when I rolled the Lizard slowly by the courthouse.

Ricky Vander, Eric Duffy, and Jack Roche were on the square, throwing a half-size rubber football back and forth in long, high arcs. I cruised right by them.

As I passed, Roche yelled, "Hey Mayo!" I turned my head his direction and heard a dull thump on the side of the car. The toy football. I parked the car, got out, and picked up the ball.

"Keep driving, Mayo," Ricky said. "Unless you're here to give us all blow jobs."

He'd picked the wrong night to fuck with me. I tossed the ball at his face.

"Whoa. Look who's sprouting balls now," Ricky said. "Aww, they grow up so fast."

"Where you been all night?" Duffy asked. "You skipped the Bash. Out looking for Rita? Not in your trunk, is she?" The three of them snickered and slapped at each other like first graders. Drunk.

"They're out by the lake. Potter Road," Roche said. "That's where I'd take her."

Ricky stepped over nose-to-nose with me, exhaling rum fumes and staring me in the eyes, daring me to look away. He jabbed the point of the ball into my chest. Pressed it. "All this time you're driving that junker around town, Rita's got David's big ole college cock in her mouth." He grinned at me with the most perfect teeth Judge Vander's money could buy.

I tried to hold the stare, but my concentration broke. Ricky won the stare-off as I squirmed at the vision of Rita and David he had just put in my head. Rita, where she belonged. He seemed very pleased with the anguish tattooed across my face.

Ricky took a step back and flipped me the ball. "You want to hit me with this ball? Do it like a man. Lobo up."

He took off running, hand high overhead for me to throw him a pass. Was this an invitation into the inner circle of the Crown Prince of Knope County? A chance to join the Three Pricketeers? I admit this small offering felt good after Rita snuffed me out like a stale cigarette. Good and wrong and empowering and disgusting all at once. I took the bait. With shame, but I took it.

I threw a perfect spiral strike, and Ricky snatched it one-handed on a dead run right on the center stripe of Watson Street. We had downtown Korvus to ourselves. Nothing much stirred that time of night.

"Touchdown strike by Mrs. Claus," Ricky hollered down the empty streets. He ran back toward the square and threw the ball wildly at Duffy, who missed the catch and let it bounce into the evergreen shrubbery ringing the courthouse. Duffy retrieved the ball and a fifth of Bacardi from beneath the bushes. He took a long slug from it. Then Ricky took a drink and handed it to me.

"I hope that's yours," I said.

"Fuck yeah. Hide in plain sight is our motto."

"Drink up, Mayo," Roche said. "We won't tell your Mama."

"Aunt," I said, and took a drink and gave it back to Roche.

"That's a pussy sip," said Ricky. "Take a real drink."

I gulped the rum, and Roche snatched the bottle, guzzled it and bulged his eyes in mock reaction, then smacked his lips loudly and screamed, "Monkey juice!"

A police car slowly cruised by, checking us out. Roche shoved the bottle inside his jacket. Ricky and Duffy waved, and the cop waved back and then sped away down Magnolia. The police weren't likely to hassle a group of Lobos on the cusp of winning a state championship. Not for anything short of murder.

I should have left Ricky and his wingmen to their drunken game and called it a night. But my humiliation by Rita burned in me like hellfire, a fire I kept throwing Bacardi on. The rum, and the sudden unexpected camaraderie—even backhanded camaraderie from cretins—kept me on the square that night.

It was rare for these three to speak to me at all. Their tone had lightened. They seemed to be easing up, including me in their midnight romp. The daily posting of signs on my locker had almost stopped. Maybe Ricky was over Falcon?

Roche handed me the bottle and I guzzled from it. Cringed and coughed.

"Down and out, Bastrop," said Ricky. "Let's see what you got."

I ran down one side of the courthouse square, holding my arm up in anticipation of Ricky's pass.

I ran maybe ten yards when Ricky threw a bullet right at my head. The ball came so hard and fast I had no chance of catching it, but I did manage to get my hand on it and deflect it to the ground, where it bounced wildly across the parking lot and rolled across the street—straight across from the front doors of the courthouse—into the narrow alley between Calder Jewelry and Lewis Hardware.

I started up the alley to get the ball and stopped short, mystified as the ball came flying back out on its own. Wonderful Byrd had thrown it. He walked out of the alley and stood before us in the streetlight.

"Ricky's ball. Ricky play ball," Wonderful said, pointing to where

Ricky, Duffy, and Roche gathered. They leaned against the front grill of the Lizard, waiting for me to throw the ball back. Roche drained what was left of the rum and Duffy opened a new bottle.

"Ricky, my friend," Wonderful said, reaching for the ball on the sidewalk, and nearly tumbling over headfirst.

I grabbed the ball and stuck it in my armpit, then caught Wonderful before he fell into me. I stood him upright. He could barely stand and stank of beer and piss.

"Go home," I said to Wonderful, "you need to go home right now."

I jogged away, back toward the others. Wonderful stood motionless for a moment, then followed me.

"Here comes your friend," Roche said.

Wonderful stagger-stepped slowly toward us, a pink-eyed specter paled in a whitewash of streetlight.

"What do you want, freakass?" Ricky asked and drank from the fresh Bacardi bottle.

Wonderful pointed at the rum and grinned first at Duffy and Ricky, then pointed and said, "Moonkay joooosse. That!"

"Not tonight, tamale boy. Monkey juice just for us tonight," Duffy said, and the Lobos laughed.

Wonderful shuffled closer, coming toward me. On his last step, he lurched forward, his nose almost glancing my face, his breath sick-sweet with puke and alcohol. Then he reached down and gently and deliberately tapped my crotch with the back of his hand.

"It hard yet?" Wonderful asked.

"What?" I jerked backward, bumping the Lizard. The street danced a rum dance around me, and it took a long beat for me to decide if I'd heard what I'd heard, or were my liquor ears fucking with me.

"Y'know. Hard? Wonnerful do it?" He stuck a finger in his mouth. Moved it around. "For moonkaay joooo?"

Ricky lunged forward and whacked Wonderful in the chest with the Bacardi bottle. "Stupid fucking nigger!"

"What the fuck, Bastrop?" Duffy said. "You going to stand for that?"

"Asshole tried to rape you, man," Roche said.

Wonderful fell back but stayed on his feet, then slid along the full length of the Lizard and headed toward the courthouse entrance before disappearing down the steps to the public restrooms.

Ricky ran after Wonderful. Duffy and Roche followed Ricky, and I followed them.

We entered a nasty place, the floor grimy and slick from a leaking urinal, a single fluttering fluorescent bulb throwing patterns of shadow and gray. Wonderful sat slumped to the floor near one of three urinals, his back propped in a corner.

"You gotta kick his ass, Bastrop," Ricky said. "You can't let him get away with that."

"Kick his fucking freak ass," Duffy said.

"He's just drunk," I said.

"The fuck?" Roche said, "You just gonna let him grab your dick?"

"Maybe tamale's just confused. Maybe he thought y'all was in private." Duffy grinned and winked at me.

"Yeah, that's it. You know, Mayo, we heard you like to grab some dick when you get a chance. Oui? Or is it wee-wee?" Duffy and Roche shook with laughter.

Ricky didn't laugh, but sucked down the remaining rum and shattered the bottle against a commode.

"You gonna kick his ass or what?" Ricky glared at me.

"Bull-in-the-ring!" Roche shouted. "Gotta git your licks in."

"Fucking A, bull ring, bull ring," Duffy mock chanted.

"He doesn't know what he's doing," I said. "He's just drunk."

"He's a fucking queer," Ricky said. "Or maybe you just love him like you love Royce? I guess we all knew you loved the darkies. But you a queer lover too?"

Ricky grabbed Wonderful by his collar and pulled him from the corner and head butted him to the floor.

Wonderful sprawled across the damp floor on his back and cried out, blood flowing from his nose. He tried to rise, but Roche drove a kick into his ribs, knocking the wind out of him. Wonderful collapsed again, lying still and gasping for breath.

"Duff, git your lick in," Ricky said. Duffy kicked Wonderful in the side, and he rolled over face down and moaned and cried.

"Call my daddy. Call my daddy, come get me." Wonderful said in sputters and heaves, his voice muffled as he spoke into the filthy floor.

"Get your lick in Bastrop. Bull ring."

Fuck. If I don't do something, they're going to ride my ass all the way to Austin. Maybe I should just give him a little pop. I lined up and took a sidestep the way I'd taught myself from Jan Kubicek's book. Wonderful tried to gain his feet, but fell back to his hands and knees, his whole body shifting right, left, back and forth.

I lined up as if facing a ball and tee, leaned forward, took a quick approach step, then kicked—aiming at his ribs—planning to hit hard enough with the flat top of my foot to satisfy the Lobos, but not full force. But he shifted toward me as I swung. My foot caught Wonderful in the jaw and flung his head with a nauseating thwack into the hard leading edge of a urinal.

Wonderful fell face down on the floor. This time limp and motionless.

Silent.

Ricky grabbed a handful of Wonderful's hair and lifted his head, peering into his slack face. "Fuck! I think he's dead!"

I bent and puked in the corner and fell against the dank tile wall. Despite a belly of rum, sobriety surged into me, the word *dead* knocking me sentient. I stared at Wonderful—couldn't stop staring—so gray in that dim, strange light. So cold.

Ricky dropped Wonderful's head and shot toward the stairs and yelled back at the rest of us. "Run like fuck!"

Ricky, Duffy, and Roche rushed upstairs and out into the night, scattering. I slipped in my vomit and sprawled on the floor. Not five feet from Wonderful. I struggled to my feet, wiped my hands on my clothes, and headed up the stairs, following the Lobos into the dark and leaving Wonderful Byrd dead.

Dead on that piss-stink floor.

<h1 style="text-align:center">Chapter 18
Within You Without You</h1>

The morning after the Booster Bash, Sunny sat at the kitchen table drinking coffee and eating biscuits with red-eye gravy. I filled a Flintstones jelly glass with murky tap water and sat across from her.

"Y'all enjoy the party?"

I couldn't speak, just stared at my useless arm propped in a dining chair across the table from me. My teeth vibrated, and I listened to the bones in my skull shift around and my bowel screaming at my stomach. Was Wonderful really dead, or did I dream that?

"Mr. Garth stopped by this morning looking for one a his dogs. Said the courthouse burnt last night, and somebody was in there. Fella turned to a crisp. The whole place burnt to nothin' but a shell. Now ain't that something?"

I shifted my stare to Sunny, hearing the words, but not grasping the meaning. Not at first.

"They saying it coulda been electric. Or maybe a hobo sleeping in the bathroom caused it. Garth says Judge Vander's fixin' to head up a group to investigate."

I knew instantly that Ricky had told his father about last night and that Arch Vander was already on the move to cover Ricky's tracks.

"You feeling alright? You're looking poorly. Why don't you get back in bed."

"Yeah," I said. "I do feel godawful."

———

The Boosters chartered a Greyhound to take the team to the state championship game, a six-hour drive to Austin, giving us a nice break from the usual bone-rattling and uncomfortable yellow-box school buses. I slept most of the way, surrendered to exhaustion, having slept very little over the six nights since Wonderful died.

We gathered in our assigned locker room at Memorial Stadium two hours pre-game, as was our custom. Brand new uniforms hung in the lockers. White jerseys with scarlet and black lettering, and bright, silky scarlet pants.

But all eyes were on the new helmets. The suffocating black headgear had been replaced with shiny new helmets, deep ruby in color. Even the "snarling wolf" team logo on the helmets had been refreshed and redesigned. It was now more graphically vibrant with demonic red eyes and a more aggressive snarl, mouth agape, canines bared like daggers.

I rotated my new helmet all around for a close look. We were supposed to be red wolves (*canis rufus*), the wolf species indigenous to East Texas and other parts of the South. Instead, our new logo was based on the Eastern timber wolf or gray wolf (*canis lupus lycaon*). I didn't have the heart to tell anyone we had the wrong wolf. We dressed and took the field briefly for some warm-up exercises before heading back into the locker room.

We sat quietly. Almost no one spoke, but if they did, it was in a hush. Some prayed, some puked. We could hear the opposing bands playing, and the crowd responding to cheerleaders, first Korvus, then Radley, then Korvus, then Radley again.

Coach Paxton told us a story about his senior year of high school in New Mexico, and how he played on the team that won the State Championship, the best moment of his life. Then Coach Clay took the floor and spoke of courage and honor.

Coach Weller gave the signal for us to gather around, and we circled the gathered coaches and the Lobos knelt on one knee, helmets in hand, and Coach Weller prayed to God to protect us as we rode into battle, and if it was within His grace and if we were worthy, to reward us with victory. We stood in unison and strapped on our wrong-wolf helmets and lined up two by two to take the field. As we moved toward the door, we could hear the Radley fans begin their cry of "sooey-pig" to call in their Razorbacks.

"Woooooooooooooooooooooooooooo Pig! Sooey!"

Korvus answered, howling to call in the Lobos.

"Howwwwwwwww-oooooooooooo!"

Ten thousand people screamed, for or against, and we sprinted in.

Pablo kicked off, and the Razorbacks took the ball on their twenty and moved methodically down the field, scoring on a TD pass after ten or twelve plays. It was 7-0, Radley.

The Lobo offense struggled, as it had all season, and we had to punt several times. But the defense held strong, as Jimmy Royce and Ricky Vander rained hell on Radley's High School All-American quarterback, Ezra Kane. Royce knocked down several passes and sacked Kane for major losses all night. Ricky intercepted two passes and ran one back for a touchdown. By halftime, the game was tied, 7-7.

Late in the third quarter, things turned sour for us as our quarterback, Jeb Lancer, was hit hard while trying to pass and fumbled the ball. It rolled almost to the Lobo goal line before Jeb recovered his own fumble. But Jeb's bad luck continued on the next play, and he was sacked in the end zone for a safety. Razorbacks 9, Lobos 7.

The clock hated us. The Lobos found themselves down to the last seconds of the game and trailing by two points. But we had possession of the ball on the fifty. Jeb completed a long pass to Vasquez, who was knocked out of bounds on the Radley five. Twenty-three seconds left. The chant went up from Korvus: *Deadeye, Deadeye, Deadeye.* They were calling my name.

Coach Clay ran one more play, a reverse up the middle. We lost a yard. Twelve seconds left. Time out. Then Clay gave me the signal, and I took the field and lined up for a short kick that would win or lose everything.

The whistle blew, the clock rolled, and Jeb—who would hold the ball—looked at me for the sign. I nodded, and Jeb signaled the center. A perfect snap to Jeb. Ball on the tee.

I stood barely six feet from Jeb, but he was invisible to me. I didn't hear the crowd or see the maniacal Razorback rush pouring over, around, and through the Lobo blockers, desperately trying to hold them out. I neither saw nor heard Jeb's screaming pleas: *Kick! Kick! Kick!*

All that existed for me at that place and time was Wonderful's head perched on the tee, his nose and mouth leaking blood onto the turf of Memorial Stadium.

Newspaper accounts later described me as standing there as if frozen solid, as still as a concrete lawn ornament. No one in the history of Texas football had ever seen such a thing.

Jeb snatched the ball from the tee and made a frantic run for the goal, was caught, pitched the ball wildly to another Lobo, who pitched it to somebody else, all in a sad, clumsy comedy of an ending to the Lobo season as the clock hit zero.

———

When I ran off the field, Coach Clay viciously tackled me to the ground. He straddled my midsection and throttled me. People poured out of the stands and onto the field from both sides of the stadium, and players and coaches and referees and an assortment of law enforcement personnel—Korvus police, Radley police, Austin police, Texas Highway Patrolmen, Texas Rangers—all ran headlong into an erupting riot.

Jimmy Royce grabbed Clay and pried his hands from my neck, and a bevy of Lobos then attacked Royce—swinging their helmets as weapons—and we all collapsed into a massive dog pile.

Civilians and police dove into the pile, some to break it up, others to egg it on. Royce broke Clay's wrist and clavicle, but in the melee, Jimmy's left knee was destroyed, ligaments and cartilage torn apart. Kneecap shattered. He never played football again. Never made his escape from behind the pine curtain.

————

As the riot subsided, I was escorted by two Texas Rangers to the Korvus band bus (a standard, yellow-box school bus). Coach Lee said it would be best if I rode back home separately from the rest of the team.

No one in the band physically attacked me, but there were plenty of boos and "Mayos" as I boarded the bus. I sat in the very front, alone on one of the bench seats, right behind the driver, Mr. Maxwell, who was also a janitor at the high school.

Maxwell was a tattooed ex-marine who had fought in the Pacific during WWII. He was tall and wiry, bald on top with his side hair cut so close to the skin it was almost invisible. He flared his nose and squinted at me through thick, black rimmed glasses as I boarded the bus, still wearing my full football gear. He didn't say a word, just shook his head slowly and clicked his tongue against his upper lip.

I took my seat directly behind Maxwell and put my helmet next to me on the seat. Maxwell glared at me in the wide interior rearview mirror mounted above the windshield.

It was approaching midnight as the band bus left Austin for the long drive home, and within an hour, most of the band was asleep. I floated in and out of sleep. It seemed every time sleep would overcome me, the bus would roll or lurch and I would awaken, check the mirror, and see Maxwell staring me down.

We drove across a silent, dark world, nothing to see but our own headlights lighting nothing. I leaned my head against the cold, freezing window and watched my breath frost the glass in a bus full of sleeping band members, and the drone of the motor in the black stillness overtook me.

Someone approached from behind, moving to sit by me. I grabbed my wrong-wolf helmet, moved it to the floor to make space. Wonderful took the seat next to me. He scooted across the seat and draped an arm around my shoulders and leaned awkwardly into me and tilted his head against mine, pressing wild, wiry hair to my temple and cheek. A hug. It was not forgiveness but commiseration, because he alone knew what my life would be like as I replaced him as the pariah of Korvus, Texas.

———

We pulled into a squalid interstate rest stop around 4 a.m. The lights in the men's room were out, and nothing but anemic moonlight seeped in through high, narrow slits, giving the urinals a ghoulish presence, as if they stood displaced from the world. Just floating there in space, waiting. I looked at the urinals but saw Wonderful. Heard his cries.

I knew then I'd spend the rest of my life reliving that night and trying to answer the most inscrutable of all questions: Why?

Rejection? Isolation? Frustration? Rita? Rum? Everything and nothing?

Most men, as they reach the far side of midlife, can look back on maybe a moment or two in their youth when they had the opportunity to take that final step from boy to man. It may have been a time when they had to choose to stand alone against a crowd. They might have faced a situation that required them to sacrifice their own best interest to provide aid or comfort to someone in need.

Or their chance may have come when they decided to own up to some serious error in judgment or behavior, and voluntarily face consequences and punishment. They had the opportunity, in that moment, to choose manhood over childhood, to choose the hard right over the easy wrong.

My moment came that night in the basement men's room of the Knope County courthouse, when Wonderful rose to his hands and knees, moaning and trembling, swaying his head slowly side to side, his nose bloody, a thin line of pink spittle dripping from the corner of his mouth. A man would have told that gathering of mindless brutes to fuck off. A man would have picked Wonderful up off the goddamn floor, washed his face, and driven him home.

But there were no men there that night.

Chapter 19
I'm So Tired

I was lost and terrified for weeks after Wonderful's death, wracked with guilt and grief and the fear that Judge Vander would find a way to make me the lone culprit, and keep Ricky, Duffy, and Roche protected from blame. It wasn't paranoia, it was logic.

The Vanders wouldn't allow any taint to arise and damage Ricky's college football chances. If burning the courthouse didn't do the trick of getting everybody off the hook—or any of the other three Lobos blabbed to anybody—then they would need a villain, a lone gunman. And who better than me, the heteroclite, the new Oswald?

Most nights after Sunny went to bed, insomnia drove me outside with a flashlight to wander aimlessly across the pastures. One night on Mr. Garth's land, I banged my head on a bucket hanging from a tree limb, hidden from sight. There was a full bottle of Jim Beam and a half bottle of vodka inside. Somebody's stash. How unlucky for them.

———

I woke up cold and half-drunk under the stash tree just as the sun threw a pink blaze across the horizon. I stumbled and weaved my way home. Sunny was frying eggs and bacon and was taking a pan of biscuits from the oven when I bolted through the back door too fast, caught a hoop rug with my foot, and flopped belly-first on the kitchen floor, sobbing and blubbering.

She spun around, sending biscuits skidding and bouncing across the floor toward me.

"You scared the GD piss outta me! Get off that floor. Where you been before the break a dawn?"

"I'm so sorry, Sunny. I'm sorry."

"Oh, hell. It's just biscuits. Ah can make more. Are you crying?"

"Not the biscuits. Wonderful. I'm sorry about Wonderful."

I tried to push up but fell back down face-first, then rolled on my side, and threw up yellow sour liquid.

"Lord in heaven. You're sick as a dog. Pneumonia Ah bet. Ah thought you had more sense than to be out this time a year without a coat."

She grabbed my arm to pull me up, then immediately fell back toward the stove.

"Swanee! You smell like you been dipped in whiskey. Better tell me you ain't been drinking!"

"Wonderful. Sorry."

"What the GD hell you talking about? That white nigrah boy wandering around town all night? They saying he gone missing."

I sat up and looked Sunny in the eyes.

"He's dead."

She helped me into a chair, and I haltingly told her the unaltered truth. The more I spoke, the less I sobbed and the more sober and coherent I became. I told her everything. When I finished, we sad-eyed each other for several seconds until Sunny stood and lit a Camel.

"Lord God."

"I didn't mean to hurt him. I didn't. I swear. I haven't told anybody else. But I'm scared and don't know what to do. It's driving me crazy."

"Ah won't tell nobody but Jesus. And He's gonna be pissed. Ah'll tell you one thing right now though, you gonna have to finally get yourself baptized. Jesus'll forgive you killing somebody on accident, but only if you join the church and get cleansed in His water. Now gwon to bed and sleep off that whiskey," she said, looking around the kitchen.

"Ah gotta clean this mess up."

———

A week later, Sunny and I were sitting with Brother Howard Granger in his small, bare office. She had nagged and cajoled me into meeting with the sleazy malcontent to decide the fate of my soul. And how could I argue with her? My actions were a clear confirmation of her belief that I was lost and godless and, without intervention by the good reverend, damned to an eternity of dangling from the end of Satan's fork, roasting in an endless sea of hellfire.

The meeting began with Brother Granger and Sunny praying. Then Granger looked at me and said, "How come you ain't never been baptized, old as you are? Don't you love Jesus? Your mama here thinks it's time you got yourself saved."

"She's my *aunt*," I said.

"He loves Jesus, Brother Granger. He loves Jesus more than anything," Sunny said.

"Well, let's hear him profess it."

I looked at Sunny, her lips quivering, tears in her eyes. She looked back and forth at me and the preacher, waiting for me to accept my invitation to salvation, checking Granger's face for any signs of anger, for any signs that he would turn me away as unsalvageable.

I tried to speak, tried to say the words she wanted me to say—

indeed, the words she deserved to hear—but then stopped myself. I despised this man, and it took all my strength to sit before him and watch Sunny submit to him. She had always seemed so strong to me, despite her incessant negativity and paranoid, insane ways. A lone woman, making her own way in the world, raising someone else's child, proving that indeed one's character is measured by how you treat someone from whom you have nothing to gain.

And Sunny surely had nothing to gain when she took me in. But her strength was always there, if sometimes obscured. As far as I knew, she feared only three things: the thought of eternal damnation, any body of water larger or deeper than our bathtub (she was maniacally afraid of drowning), and Brother Howard Granger, because to her, he stood in the path to Jesus, and Jesus was her only path to hope.

Brother Granger, the self-appointed shepherd of souls, was himself soulless. I sat in the back of his church on many of the times Sunny went, and watched him take money from the poor, the sick, the ignorant, and the scared. Watched, horrified, as he convinced her to take up serpents again.

His congregation was mostly people of meager means, but they gave to The Lord what they could. Granger collected, and the leaks in the church's tin roof continued to leak. Cracks grew wider and longer in the broken pews. New hymnals never arrived. The missionaries got little for the starving children of Asia, India, and Africa.

Time and again, the desperate would line up in front of him, and he promised to remove their diseases or fix their twisted spines or atrophied legs. And they rejoiced at first when he laid on the hands, but they also kept on dying or limping. It's said that the whoring of flesh is mankind's oldest profession, our oldest story. Men like Granger made me think that pimping for immortality—humanity's primal and enduring desire—was truly our oldest profession.

And now his pimping had gone electronic. He had his own radio show for a half hour every morning, right after the "Farm and Market Price Update" on local AM station KRVS 1350.

"Do you not profess it?" Granger asked as Sunny squeezed my shoulder, trying to urge some response from me. "Don't you want to accept Jesus as your Lord and Savior?"

I looked away from him without answering. Sunny dropped her head and sobbed quietly. I scanned around the small, crummy office. There was a picture of Jesus delivering the Sermon on the Mount hanging above a bookcase that was completely barren except for three Bibles and a couple of legal pads. An anemic electric heater puffed hot air at us with a loud metallic hum and rattle.

A few feet from the heater on the back wall stood two large terrariums, one holding three or four diamondbacks, the other holding a group of intertwined copperheads. I recognized the smaller of the copperheads as the snake Sunny had held overhead in church two Sundays ago.

Beneath the terrariums were the two serpent boxes Granger and the others used to transport the snakes to church services. The serpent boxes were by far the nicest possessions of the church, expertly constructed from high-quality oak, with perfect dovetailed corners and brass hinges and fittings, and each decorated on top with a finely carved cherrywood cross.

"Look here. I know you've had some trouble in your life. Good Lord took your little sister. Took your true mama. Sent your daddy away. And He took your arm. Why do you think that is? That He takes so much from you, yet leaves you here on this earth? Leaves you behind?"

I fought it, but I welled up at these words, and immediately hated myself for it. I wiped tears and looked at his sharp, cleaved face. He fixed a piercing stare on me through heavy-lidded eyes, and drew his lips narrow and tight and reptilian.

"The Good Lord told us that *'he gave his only begotten Son, that whosoever believeth in him should not perish, but have everlasting life.'* Look, your aunt here is going to heaven. She is one of the best women I have ever known. She is a true believer, and she truly loves Jesus. Don't you want to be able to walk through them pearly gates one day and see her again, after she's dead and gone? I didn't know any of your other people, but if they was believers, don't you want to see them again, see that little sister and your true mama? They'd be waiting for you."

There was a long silence before he said angrily, "C'mon boy, you've got to believe in *something!*"

I was really neither a believer nor a disbeliever. The core of my heart on this subject was empty. Granger's and Sunny's brand of religion seemed too much from the realm of Paul Bunyan and Pecos Bill, with the walking on water, the magically replicating fishes and loaves, the blind seeing and the dead walking.

As for the great theme of love that ran through Christianity, I found that very appealing. I loved the idea of a single, brilliant point of light and goodness in an otherwise cold and uncaring—if not actively hostile—universe. I loved the idea of an unbreakable thread of love connecting all of humanity in a great circle across eons of time, connecting all who ever sought redemption for their infractions. Connecting people who truly want to be better people.

While there were things I could admire about Sunny's faith, I still abhorred the absolutism of the fundamentalist Christian litmus test that demanded prostration to the self-righteous, self-appointed gatekeepers to that great, infinite circle of promised love. Gatekeepers like Brother Howard Granger.

It was tempting to entertain the fantasy of one day going *poof* and appearing in a perfect land and running headlong across green pastures into the waiting arms of Lucy and Julia. And while that fantasy was so irresistible, so very seductive, it seemed too cartoonish, too childish. I was clearly no longer a child. Killing Wonderful had drained the last few drops of childhood from me, and it seemed to me that only a child could believe in Santa or the Sandman or that there could ever be a storybook reunion of my dead family.

I stared at Sunny as she sat in a submissive heap before the holy man. I thought about her and what I owed her. I thought about Wonderful and how he would probably be helping his mother and dad make tamales at that very moment, the three of them laughing and hugging, if I had not cracked his skull in a wrongheaded, drunken attempt to gain the approval of assholes.

I owed Sunny and I owed Wonderful, and I didn't know where to find the currency to repay them, or what kind of currency it should be.

Sunny reached over and put her hand on mine. Finally, I forced a bucket full of disgust back down my throat and locked eyes with Brother Granger.

"I do truly love Jesus and accept him as Lord and Savior. Brother Granger, would you please baptize me so I can be with my Aunt Sunny and Christ in heaven?"

This I did for Sunny. It was the only thing I had to give her in exchange for the love, care, and protection she had selflessly provided me. I knew Sunny's mind well; I knew how concrete she was in her thinking. Sunny believed in the literal, immediate effect of the process and ritual of salvation just as much as she believed that she would go to a heaven in the actual sky above our heads, just beyond the clouds. She believed that saying the words, "I believe in Jesus and accept Him as my Lord and Savior," and being dunked in a tank of water by a holy man would literally save me from burning in hell for killing Wonderful Byrd. In her mind, I would be saved and forgiven forever at the very moment my head went underwater. Problem solved.

"Praise Jesus!" Granger said, and Sunny bear-hugged me, and the two of them launched into a prayer of thankfulness. I bowed my head, but I didn't really hear the prayer because Granger's earlier words still rang in my head: *"You've got to believe in something."*

But all I could believe in at that moment was this: I believed that Wonderful was dead and there was nothing I could do for the rest of my life to change that, or ever amend for it. I believed that in the moment immediately before Howard Granger dunks me in a tank of water, I would be the killer of a helpless, simple-minded boy, and in the moment immediately *after* Howard Granger dunks me in a tank of water, I would still be the killer of a helpless, simple-minded boy. Only wetter.

Even if Granger's baptism absolved me for Wonderful's death, what about the other two men I'd kill in the next fifteen years?

I was going to need a lot more sacramental water.

Chapter 20
You Can't Do That

My baptism was scheduled for the following Sunday at Granger's Church of All Truth, located in an empty warehouse—a windowless and largely airless metal building—on one corner of the Pentameter Corp refinery's property. Granger had somehow managed to get permission to use the space free of charge.

Four people were to be baptized. Three young kids (twin brothers and a girl from another family), all about ten years old, and me. The four of us sat together in the front pew just to the left of the crude, unpainted plywood pulpit that Granger used. The main portion of the service went on for two hours that day, with the Spirit descending multiple times into the congregation, moving them into long episodes of singing, often with different sections of the room simultaneously singing entirely different hymns, or even extemporaneous hymns previously unknown to Christendom. And there was much dancing, or at least rapid flailing of arms and legs, clapping and keeping time to *a cappella* songs (there were no musical instruments allowed in Granger's church, only the human voice).

Granger announced to the congregation that there would be no taking up serpents or laying on of hands during this particular service. Then he launched into a sermon on the message and meaning of John the Baptist, and the story of the baptism of Jesus by John. A few minutes before the sermon ended, he gave a signal to one of the ladies of the church, who came forward and led the four of us out the front door and across a mud and gravel road in front of the church building to one of the refinery's concrete block office buildings, which had bathrooms where we could change clothes (there were no bathrooms in the warehouse).

She gave each of us a thin, white cotton baptismal robe and a brown Piggly Wiggly bag, then told us to go into the bathrooms and take off all our clothes except under shorts or panties, and put our clothes in the grocery bags.

"Y'all did remember to bring extra underwear to change back into later, right?" she asked.

She led us back across the path and into the small foyer of the church, where we stood and listened to the congregation singing joyously, and waited for Brother Granger to call us in. There was a large, galvanized metal stock tank in one corner of the front of the church, just behind and to the left of the pulpit. The tank was about ten feet long and five feet wide and came up almost waist high to a grown man. It was usually covered with a ragged brown tarp, but today the tarp was gone and the tank had been filled with water. Two deacons of the church stood next to the tank beside a set of wooden steps to help us in and out.

The congregation was small, probably about thirty people, but they made a big noise, their voices and joy amplified and reverberated by the tin roof and smooth sheet metal walls and bare concrete floor. We walked into the main room of the church, and everyone leapt to their feet. Brother Granger raised both hands overhead, and the singing wound down and was replaced by raucous shouts of "Praise Jesus," "You are saved!" "Come to the Lord," "You are loved!"

Granger shouted above the din, "Let's pray. Let's pray." All heads bowed and Granger prayed to Jesus to please accept his newest followers into the flock. He ended the prayer by quoting from the Book of Mark:

"He that believeth and is baptized shall be saved; but he that believeth not shall be damned. And these signs shall follow them that believe; In my name shall they cast out devils; they shall speak with new tongues; they shall take up serpents; and if they drink any deadly thing, it shall not hurt them; they shall lay hands on the sick, and they shall recover."

Granger climbed into the tank fully clothed, cowboy boots and all. He gave a signal, and the twins were lifted over into the water, the water about chest deep to them. The congregation quieted except for an occasional, softly spoken "Yes Jesus" or "Praise God." People moved out of their seats and formed two lines on either side of the aisle, leading up to near the edge of the tank.

Granger told the twins to profess their faith to the flock who stood there to greet them with open arms, once they were reborn from the water. The boys spoke softly, one at a time, announcing their acceptance of Jesus to the congregation. Granger got down on his knees in the water between the two little boys, and he said loudly, "I baptize thee in the name of Jesus," and with his hands behind their necks, he pulled them backward and under the water, and just as quickly pushed them back up.

The church roared with approval and shouted praises, and the boys were lifted out into the arms of their parents, and they proceeded down the aisle to accept hugs and laughter from their new peers in Christ.

Granger then baptized the girl, and she squealed with delight upon emerging from the water and practically swam across the tank into her mother's arms. The crowd clapped and shouted praises, and she walked down the aisle, trying not to slip on the water left there by the boys.

One of the deacons nodded at me. I moved toward the tank, and the deacon took my arm to help me climb in. I waded over to where Granger stood in the middle of the tank, and Sunny moved to the head of the reception line. All eyes were on me, and a joyous clap began in the back, and then spread into a rhythmic, unified clapping, and shouts went out of "Come to Jesus" and "Jesus loves you."

"Do you accept Jesus Christ as your Lord and Savior?" Granger asked. "If so, profess it to your friends and neighbors."

I looked across the congregation and every person, every single man, woman and child stood beaming at me, clapping their hands, some being moved by the Spirit to prance and spin across the aisle in my honor. I was deeply shocked and touched by this very sincere outpouring of greeting and acceptance from this tight group of humble, caring people.

They were truck drivers and mechanics, waitresses and short-order cooks, roughnecks and brick layers, housekeepers and grocery clerks. The men were sunburned and sweat-bleached, wearing work clothes that had been freshly washed for Sunday service. Many had hands so cracked and stained from oily work that they could never be fully cleaned, their fingernails blackened and scarred from hard, dirty labor.

Several were missing a finger or two, long ago traded to the sawmill or the chainsaw for the right to earn a paycheck. Most of the women wore no makeup and very simple jewelry, if any at all, and they wore long, muted, flowing dresses. Many of the women, regard-less of age, wore their hair long and straight, but bundled it up high on their heads. Everyone laughed and smiled freely and invitingly at me and clapped loudly and in unison for my impending salvation.

Why do they care if Granger dunks me or not? How can they be this overjoyed about what happens to *me*?

I looked all up and down the line of good people there, looked many of them full in the eyes, and could see only honest motive in them. All this joy, shared by people connected in a great circle by a common set of beliefs, literally standing there with open arms to embrace me as one of them, to embrace me as a reborn believer like them.

I could lie to Granger, but I couldn't lie to these decent people.

And then it occurred to me that if I didn't believe in the Forgiver, who was left to forgive me for trying to lie my way into heaven?

I moved away from Granger and waded back to the edge of the tank and climbed out of the baptismal waters. The church fell silent, as if long abandoned, as if it had never been occupied at all. And Sunny—poor Sunny—burst into tears; her knees buckled, and two deacons by the tank caught her and eased her into a seat. I walked to the front door of the warehouse church, my wet gown trailing across the floor, and stepped out into the March chill of a late Sunday afternoon.

Granger followed me out and shouted at my back, "You're taken by Satan today! There will be no mercy on your soul!"

———

I walked past the Green Lizard, leaving it there for Sunny to drive home. If she was too upset to drive, I was sure someone in the congregation would make sure she and the car made it home.

I gathered the sopping overlong robe up into my hand to keep it from dragging the ground, and walked as fast as I could manage in bare feet, and wondered how I must look to passersby—like an especially homely bride, either late for the ceremony and determined to make it to the altar on time, or hurriedly escaping a shotgun wedding.

I walked randomly at first, but the cold eventually forced me to turn toward home, maybe six or seven miles away. My legs grew numb, but I knew I could make it.

Soon, a Texas Highway Patrol car pulled up alongside me.

"That's a mighty pretty dress," said the officer, tipping his cowboy hat to me.

"I'm sorry, officer, was I speeding?"

"Hey, what's your story? Car broken down somewhere?"

"I'm walking home."

"Hell, you're wet. Ain't you cold?"

"Somewhat."

"How far you going? You're liable to freeze if it's far."

"About four or five more miles, I guess."

"Git in."

I got in the patrol car and told him I lived on 271 South, just down from the PineView Drive-In.

"Hey, ain't you that place kicker? The one who froze up and lost us the state championship?"

"Yeah. That was me."

"Can you tell me just one thing? Just what the goddamn hell were you thinking? Just kick the goddamn ball. Just kick the thing!"

"Long story. Thanks for the ride, though."

"Okay, you got to tell me. Why in the name of heaven are you walking down the highway in a wet dress?"

"It's a baptismal robe."

"Oh, right. Sunday. You just get baptized?"

"Almost."

"How do you get *almost* baptized?"

"Just had second thoughts."

"So how far up on you did the water git?"

"About waist high."

"So, you're telling me you was half-ass baptized?"

"That sounds about right."

"And you just up and walked out?"

"Walked right out the door."

"Well, hell. I reckon you can rest comfortable knowing that, at the least of it, your privates and your rear end will make it to heaven."

We pulled into Sunny's driveway, and I thanked him again for the ride. I was midway to the house when he shouted out to me. "I see a whole shitload of stuff in this job. But I ain't never seen an ole boy abandon his own salvation before."

Chapter 21
The Inner Light

Sunny barely spoke to me for a month. But late one afternoon, as I came home from my shift at Piggly Wiggly, she was waiting for me in the kitchen, drinking coffee.

"Ah want you to drive me over to Conifer for the camp meeting this weekend," she said.

"When? I'm supposed to work Saturday and Sunday."

"Tell 'em you can't work this Sunday. You ain't supposed to be working on Sunday anyway. That's the Lord's day. You should know that."

"I need the money."

"Ah don't know what the shit for. Ah get enough Texaco checks to feed us and keep us in gasoline. What you saving for? Going somewhere?"

I knew then she'd found my Canadian tourism brochures. I kept them well hidden at first, but got less and less careful with them, in some ways hoping she would see them and that would be a natural opening to ease into a conversation about my plans.

In the aftermath of Wonderful's death, I made two decisions. I decided it was time to begin my education, so I dropped out of

Korvus High School to devote all my spare time to reading. And I decided to emigrate to Canada.

Canada. Beautiful mountains. Crisp air. Clean, clear, cold waters. I'd never been there, or even met anyone who had ever been there, but based on several books and PBS documentaries, I loved the place. Canada. Pristine wilderness and sophisticated cities. Waterfalls and polar bears.

I researched it thoroughly. No passport needed. English-speaking for the most part. Much closer than South America or Europe. There were several established enclaves of American expatriates and draft dodgers in Canada. Where could I buy a big coat and a furry hat? What kind of food do they eat up there?

Canada. Friendly, polite, intelligent, non-racist people. Mounties and hikers and kayakers. That was the place. That was where I could have a future. Rand McNally showed the most direct route there from Korvus: drive to Texarkana, then Little Rock. Through Memphis and Nashville. Then Louisville and Cincinnati. Finally, cross the border at Detroit.

I bagged groceries at Piggly Wiggly and worked part-time at the Knope County Library to build a bankroll to buy a car. It was going to take a while to make it happen, but I was determined. Canada. The very antithesis of East Texas.

The last thing I wanted to do was drive Sunny to a Jesus fest. How could I show my face to Granger's congregation after aborting my own baptism? Those people didn't want to see me there. Some might be openly hostile about it. But I knew how deeply my behavior had hurt and embarrassed Sunny. She had been quite cold toward me since the "almost" baptism, but now was asking for a small favor. It seemed like the least I could do to help mend things between us, and maybe help soften the blow when I told her my plans for Canada.

"OK, I'll drive you to Conifer, Sunday. What time?"

"There's a sunset service, so let's get there 'fore dark."

Several Holiness churches gathered for this event, which adhered to no formal schedule but managed to occur about every five years, or whenever the Spirit moved the various preachers to call for it. Congregations from all over East Texas, and some from as far away as Arkansas and Louisiana would gather at isolated meeting grounds somewhere in the piney woods, usually a different location each time, meeting for a week at a time.

Sunny was giddy. "Tonight you'll see the true love of Jesus," she said as we drove into the pastoral countryside past the little town of Conifer, just a few miles south of Korvus. "You'll see it with your own eyes, and you'll hear it and feel it. You're gonna see how the Spirit can save you. Can just flow right through you and keep you harmless. You'll be blessed tonight. At long last! Billy Wayne Bastrop, you will find your path. You're gonna be washed in the Truth."

We thought we were near a key turn, so I drove slowly, with Sunny reading aloud some confusing directions she had written on a torn piece of grocery bag. She slapped her notes on the car seat and shouted, "Ah hear music! Ah hear the Lord's music!"

I heard it too, and we turned off the paved road onto a red dirt path, immediately crossing over two cattle guards that shook the Green Lizard side to side with a rhythmic thump-da-thump thump. Unlike Brother Granger's Church of All Truth, many of the other attending churches allowed musical instruments—in fact, relied heavily on them as an enhancement to worship.

We first drove a quarter mile through a thicket of trees and emerged into a stretch of open pastureland, the lay of the land immense and blank except for an occasional clump of trees here, a pond there. Another path veered off to the right, leading toward an expansive pecan orchard where long, straight rows of two-hundred-year-old trees stretched into the distance. To the left, a dirt road climbed gently toward the high point of the landscape—a broad plateau.

Trucks and cars and tattered old school buses, now repainted and relabeled by the churches that used them, were parked all across the pasture below the plateau. It appeared as though the first two dozen vehicles had been parked with a disciplined and orderly plan, but halfway through, either the desire for order or the ability to maintain it had fallen away. The remaining vehicles were crammed in chaotically, like survivors of one of those massive, interstate pileups you see on the news, where people abandon their cars the instant they stop rolling.

We walked up a cow path leading to the top of the hill, and Sunny struggled with the climb. Once on top, the relative flatness at the summit of the hillock stretched out before us, maybe fifty yards wide and at least a hundred yards long. To the west lay the shore of Tall Pines Lake, guarded by a shallow marsh full of cypress knees and the short, jagged remnants of tree trunks, long ago killed by rising water when the Coushata River was dammed to create the lake.

As we crested the hill, a stiff wind of music hit us. Two crude, knee-high, wooden platforms had been freshly built for this occasion, side by side, near one edge of the plateau. They were so new, sawdust ringed them like fresh pine snow. One platform was for musicians, who had just launched into a rocking version of "Look What The Lord Has Done." The other platform was for the many preachers who would speak. It was equipped with an antique steamer trunk, which stood on one end to serve as a lectern, and an old lion-footed dining table to serve as an altar, with a long white banner printed with "Jesus Saves" draped over it. There were two pickup trucks parked at the base of the hill, each holding a hulking diesel generator, and three men were just finishing the task of stringing electrical cords out from the generators and up the hillside for lights.

The service had not yet started, but the music was already frantic. There were guitars and mandolins. Fiddles and upright basses. A dulcimer or two. And tambourines, boxes full of tambourines. By the time Sunny and I made it to the top, about sixty worshipers milled about, and a line of at least fifty more were making their way up the cow path behind us. Dozens of people stopped at the music platform first to grab a tambourine, before making their way out into the open-air sanctuary that was covered by a large brush arbor.

People gathered under the arbor and sang, everyone seeming to know all the words by heart. There were no benches or pews because everyone would be on their feet during services anyway, stomping, dancing, and clapping, and seats of any kind would be as useless as urinals in a nunnery.

Sunny waded into the thick of the congregation, and I walked to the far back edge of the arbor, trying to disappear off stage, so as not to offend any members of her home congregation who might be in attendance, as I was sure none of them had taken my abandoned baptism very well. I planned to hang out alone in the back shadows for a while, then sneak back to the car and listen to the radio while I waited for the services to end, or for Sunny to get tired enough to want to go home, because these kinds of services had been known to run for hours, sometimes until dawn. That's why the women brought boxes of food and coolers full of iced tea and lemonade and laid out a covered feast on creaky picnic tables that stood just behind my hiding location, past the butt end of the arbor.

The sun had almost fallen into the lake when I saw two teenage boys, feet caked in mud, dragging a burlap sack—*Tejas Grove Pecans* stenciled on one side—up from the murky margins of the water. The boys made their way across the fields to where a dozen men stood with serpent boxes arrayed at their feet.

"Y'all need any more snakes?" one of the boys hollered out.

"Oh, you cain't have too many," a man yelled back. "Bring 'em on!"

The boys deposited the tow sack next to one of the serpent boxes and wisely stood back. Howard Granger stepped forward, dressed in blue pinstripe pants and a black suit coat, a yellowed white dress shirt, and black cowboy boots.

He bent over the sack, and several wild strands of hair broke loose from their pomade and flopped out like antennae. He prayed briefly over the sack. Then he held it open with one hand and quickly lifted out a four-foot cottonmouth water moccasin with his free hand. The snake was thick and muscular and appeared jet black in the twilight. It writhed in his hand and wound its upper body around his forearm, the snake itself almost as thick as Granger's wrist, flashing its pearly white-mouth warning. It lunged outward toward the other men, and they fell back as one groaned, "Whoa!" and "Look out mama."

"He's a good one!" Granger grinned at the boys, who backed up another few feet.

"Don't fear the snake unless you don't love the Lord our God," Granger admonished the boys. They moved further back.

Granger flipped open the lid to one of the serpent boxes and held the cottonmouth over it, and almost as if commanded, the snake turned its head down into the box and disappeared. Granger and another man reached into the sack and took out four more thick water moccasins and distributed them across several serpent boxes, then began a procession to bring the boxes up the hill and place them on the altar.

Someone flipped a switch, lighting strand after strand of bare light bulbs, loosely woven along the sides and down the center of the brush arbor. The music shifted to Hank Williams' "I Saw The Light" and an anorexic teenage mandolin player stepped up to one of the microphones, her vibrant red hair—a bushel of curls—bouncing wildly as she played, her body ducking up and down as if dodging an invisible attacker.

She sang high and sweet and nasally, the occasional cracking of her voice oddly enhancing and endearing her performance. Everyone there (save me) sang out heartily along with her.

———

The lake swallowed any last remnants of sunlight, and on an otherwise calm night with a sky as clean and clear as grocery-store ice, a rogue gust of wind swept across the lake and shot across a thousand yards of marshes and open pasture, pushing up and over the hilltop where we stood listening to the dodgy redheaded singer.

The gust hit with sudden, breathtaking force, engulfing us in a hazy cloud of dirt and twigs and dead grass, and shifted the whole assembly of the brush arbor hard to one side, like a ship listing after striking rocks, its poles letting out a long, wounded-dog moan. A few patches of willow branches and brush were torn from the arbor and thrown violently down the hill into several parked cars. The lights went dead, leaving us blind and stinging from the dust and debris.

What had been raucous music and joyous singing and clapping dissolved instantly into stony silence. And again, without warning, the lights stuttered back on, but only for a moment or two before one strand of bulbs broke loose from overhead and slung itself against one of the gnarled cedar trunks. Several bulbs shattered as if shot, and a shower of sparks and glass peppered a section of the congregation. The lights flashed off again, only for a second, and crackled back on to stay, and the hilltop gathering beneath the brush arbor was once again fully illuminated.

The stunned silence was pierced by an Arkansas woman they called Aunt Lizzy. She screamed as if stabbed with a ragged knife, then began to jerk and twist around in circles on her two walking canes. She was standing somewhere near the middle of the congregation, and people moved around quickly to give her room.

Aunt Lizzy appeared to be well beyond eighty. She was a Pentecost prophetess Sunny had told me about, who traveled a circuit of churches and camp meetings with her grandsons. Many snake-handling churches had a prophetess or two, typically older women who didn't handle snakes themselves, but would be moved by the Holy Ghost in other ways, such as going almost cataleptic and speaking in tongues, and when not speaking an unknown tongue, to speak out prophesies in actual English.

Her two canes were carved to resemble serpents, with each serpent's head forming a handle, and the end of each snake's tail forming the cane tips. One cane was of a lighter, caramel colored wood, and the other a very dark walnut or cherry.

Lizzy was the first to receive the Holy Ghost that night, and she turned herself around and around on her canes in a circle, and began chanting "ho-eee-iii-plee-plee-plee-hotch! ho-eee-iii-plee-plee-plee-hotch!" She skidded forward, lunged, then spun in circles, shrieking like a panther on the attack.

She moved in an erratic pattern, but each of her maneuvers gained ground toward the preachers and musicians at the front. Each circular move was preceded by her high-pitched screech, then followed by a new phrase in the unknown tongue, and each time she completed a circle across the ground, a dozen people on either side of her began wild, disjointed movements and dances, some speaking in tongues, others shouting in English, "Praise Jesus" or "Amen Lizzy" or "Show us the way Lizzy."

Aunt Lizzy moved ever forward, infecting the crowd as she went. A bald preacher in a denim jacket leapt to the pulpit and held his Bible overhead with both hands and screamed, "The Holy Ghost has moved on us, brothers and sisters! Brought down to us by a mighty wind. It's hit us hard tonight! Praise Jesus, brothers and sisters! They's folks all over the world trying to find the Holy Spirit, but we got it right here with us tonight!"

"Praise God!" someone shouted.

"They're lookin' high and low for it!"

"Amen!"

"But we got it here! Right here!"

"We ain't lookin for it now!"

"The Holy Ghost rode into us on a Holy Wind!"

"Just blew right in!"

The fiddlers played a short riff to welcome Aunt Lizzy as she made it to the music platform. She made no attempt to step up onto the platform but instead turned and faced the crowd.

Some stood silent and reverent, some fell to their knees, praying softly or loudly, others sang and clapped, some bouncing around the hilltop back and forth under the arbor, spinning and jumping and calling out the Lord's name.

Aunt Lizzy hollered out one last raspy phrase in the unknown tongue, and then slashed both canes through the air, like the two swords of a withered, arthritic samurai. She began to prophesy. In English this time.

"Jesus will speak to us. Without words, without us even knowing it. He will speak without speaking. Look for the signs that follow after Him. Look and you shall believe. He will speak to you any way He can. He will use dreams and haints and angels. And He will use demons. Because even the demons believe in God."

I was so mesmerized by Aunt Lizzy's performance; I didn't see Sunny as she approached me from the side. Her voice snapped me back into the moment.

"Cain't you see it?" She waved her hand toward the congregation. "Cain't you feel it washing over ever'thing and ever'body here? The Good Lord gives us power over them snakes. Power over all demons try to take up in your heart. Ah'm gonna show you. Once and for all. Gonna prove the power of faith. Then you'll know yourself what you gotta do to live in the Light."

Chapter 22
She Said She Said

Brother Granger called for the attention of the congregation. The music stopped and all eyes focused on the pulpit. He stepped up and preached for about five minutes before inviting Sunny to come forward and give her testimony.

I couldn't believe what I was seeing. Sunny moved to the front, repressing all her secretive, reclusive impulses. It was stunning but also clarifying. This is why she maneuvered me into driving her here. She's showing me she'll go to any lengths to save me, to bring me to her faith. She's even willing—at great pain—to fight every instinct ingrained in her and speak in public, and before God.

"My mama and daddy came to East Texas from up somewhere in the coal country of Kentucky, up near the border with West Virginia," she began. "His name was Turner Bastrop and her name was Pearl Willis, 'fore she married him. They tole me their people come down from the great mountains that run like a spine far up north and into the east. They left on their journey with a wagon and a mule, and not much to put in the wagon but a few sacks a corn meal and half a deer carcass."

"*Amen. They was poor people,*" someone sang out.

"It took 'em months and they liked to starve, but my daddy was wily and able, and they scrounged food along the way and they finally made it to Knope County."

Amen. They had a long hard trip to Texas.

"My mama got sick after they'd been here a few years. She laid in the bed for months, and never could breathe natural. Then the consumption ate her up, and Jesus brought her home to be with Him."

Help her, Jesus.

"Ah was twelve and my little brother Cecil was nine when she passed."

Jesus, be good to Pearl. Jesus watches over the little children.

"We sharecropped cotton for a while, on the old McKain farm, a bunch of y'all will know where that is. Our daddy really didn't have no use for younguns. To him, Ah was a grown woman who ought to be able to do what any grown woman could do. Cook our meals, warsh all our clothes."

It's alright, Sister Sunshine.

"After Mama passed, Daddy started working in the oil fields, and he made good money for many years, and the Texaco company paid him in stocks as part of his wages. He saved all them stocks and told me to never, ever sell 'em, because when he was dead and gone, the Texaco company would send me dividend money ever few months, and while Ah wouldn't be rich, Ah wouldn't starve neither. This was the Good Lord's blessing to me, and Ah have always given a goodly share of this money back to the Lord."

Sunny glanced over at Brother Granger, whose head was bowed, as if in prayer.

Sunny paused for a long while before turning to look at the four preachers. Then she turned back to face the crowd.

"A year or two after mama passed, my daddy began to lie with me as if Ah was his wife."

Did I hear her clearly? What? No. Please God no. I fought for a breath.

The amen chorus fell silent.

"He tole me Ah was his play purty."

No. No. No. No. I slumped to the ground, back against one of the poles supporting the arbor, and howled and wiped tears with my T-shirt.

The amen chorus had no amens.

"Ah didn't know no better for a long time. Then Ah got an urge to start reading the Word."

Amen.

"Ah got my mama's Bible and started reading it front to back."

Sister Sunshine got on the right path.

"Then one night when we were in his bed—a night blacker'n tar —when my daddy rolled over on me, the room filled with a light brighter than the noontime. It was the Holy Spirit come to me, and He said, 'You are not here in this place. You are with Me.'"

Splinters of glass roiled in my throat, and I clawed at the dirt. Sunny—Sunny—oh, my dear God, Sunny.

Praise Jesus!

"And Ah been with Him ever since."

Tell it, Sunshine!

"And it was terrible for Cecil too. Cecil was slow to learn things, and ever'body knows a little boy can't work good as a grown man. A little boy leaves gates open. A little boy can't put tack on a mule proper."

Jesus help little Cecil.

"My daddy beat Cecil bad. Beat him all the time." Sunny let the tears flow.

Give her strength, Jesus. Tell it, tell it, Sister Sunshine.

"Ah hate to say it, but Ah got to tell the truth here before the Holy Ghost." Her tears stopped, and her voice became very steady and deliberate.

"My daddy beat the love of Jesus out of that boy. He beat Jesus out of him and made a hole big enough for the demons to get inside."

"Rot in hell, Turner," I whisper-shouted to no one and pulled my shirttail over my face. Wiped tears.

No, Lord!

"Cecil went bad, and Ah tried to bring him to Jesus, Ah did. Ah knew he would be protected if he could find his way into the bosom of Christ."

Praise His Name!

"I tried to cast the demons out myself. But Ah didn't know how, Ah ain't never had no Bible teaching, never been taken to church."

Jesus help little Sunshine.

"Ah found Jesus, but all Cecil found was the bottle. Y'all pray for Cecil."

Jesus help Cecil find the right path.

"Cecil got demons in him. Pray to Jesus to run them out. Run them out with the Holy Ghost."

Run them demons out!

"Cecil hurt his own children. Hurt 'em bad. Y'all pray for my brother's soul."

I struggled to my feet. Yeah, Cecil. Where the fuck are you, asshole? Where?

We're praying, Sister Sunshine.

Sunny cast her eyes into the night sky and said, "Jesus, please keep little Lucy by your side. Be with her as you were with me."

She addressed the congregation for the last time.

"And y'all please pray for Cecil's boy, Billy Wayne. He's still trying to find his way. Help him find the right path."

Jesus help Billy Wayne.

Several people looked my way, and a few walked over and gave me a back pat or softly spoke encouraging words. People who didn't know me kneeled beside me and prayed for my soul, then helped me back to my feet. My hands were filthy, and my nails filled with black dirt and I wobbled on my feet, looking across the way at Sunny, drenched in her pain.

Brother Granger anointed Sunny's head with oil and took her hands in his. As the two of them prayed, two other preachers walked to the altar. They prayed over the serpent boxes and started flinging the lids open.

Granger said to the congregation, "Don't take up a serpent if you ain't been anointed by the Holy Spirit. But if you have, you shall have no reason to fear. These are the signs that follow them that believe, that they shall take up serpents."

He handed Sunny a four-foot timber rattler, and she held it overhead and walked gingerly back toward the crowd, looking up constantly toward the snake, or perhaps looking directly up into heaven. The snake twisted its head from side to side as if inspecting the handiwork of the brush arbor and slashed at the air with its tongue. Sunny grinned ecstatically and looked up into the night sky and screamed, "Praise Jesus."

The musicians came to life, and the congregation started to clap and stomp their feet, and the whole crowd parted down the middle to form an aisle the full length of the arbor. Fiddles and mandolins wailed as a very tall man skipped down the aisle toward my position, clapping and shouting. He spun and headed back toward the front, soon to be replaced by one or another person, sometimes pairs of worshipers, running or dancing the length of the aisle, praising Jesus, or shouting or moaning out random noises, the sound a fusion of joy and terror and madness. I took three or four steps back toward the picnic tables where it was darkest.

Granger and another man each took up a large rattlesnake. A preacher from Louisiana held aloft a pair of copperheads. For the next half hour, twenty or more people carried serpents, passing them overhead, one to another.

As Sunny circled the music platform with her rattler, the Louisiana man passed her another. I'd never seen her handle two at once. She draped one around her neck and held the other overhead with both hands, swaying from side to side, face to heaven, mouthing unheard words, tears down her cheeks. The skyward snake's head hung low, and it licked out toward Sunny's face, waving its tongue, tasting the night.

Sunny and her two snakes headed back toward the altar, back toward the row of serpent boxes. I moved impulsively forward from my semi-secluded spot, not really knowing why I came forward or what I would do if things went wrong, but sensing that things were on the edge of spinning out of control.

I had no power to do anything, of course, but moved anyway, the way a parent throws an arm across a child in anticipation of a car crash. Your arm won't do any good, but you throw it up anyway. I moved down the outside perimeter of the brush arbor, mostly in the dark, trying to stay out of the way of any random worshipers who might try to hand me an unwanted viper.

The music reached a frenzied pace, with what started as a hymn devolving into a fractured, hallucinogenic version of its former self. Several rattlesnakes and copperheads escaped from their boxes, crawling across the dirt floor of the arbor and rushing into the blackness beyond.

At least a dozen serpents were still in circulation, and shouts of "Jesus saves," and "see the signs of Jesus," rang out. A pastor from Conifer named Brother Lancy—sweating profusely and screaming in tongues—turned a serpent box upside down and dumped a writhing pile of snakes onto the altar. Sunny took a third viper from the altar pile before the creature could slide off onto the floor, an obsidian cottonmouth the teenagers had brought up from the lake right before sunset. Some in the crowd gasped and murmured when she took the third one. They'd never seen that done before. No one else that night carried even two.

She swayed at the hips and shuffled down the central aisle, her head cocked to one side, her face rapturous and her eyes fixed on the night sky, fixed on a point far out among the stars, a rattler wrapped one full turn around her throat, its head sliding down along her left breast. She held the other rattler at about its mid-body, letting it droop from her right hand. The third snake, the cottonmouth, wound itself as a caduceus around Sunny's left wrist and forearm, its tongue licking the air around her face.

One by one, people returned snakes to the boxes, and the crowd seemed to come out of a mass trance. The music wound down to something sounding more like music played by humans and not crazed demons, and Brother Lancy reverted to speaking English and called on everyone to join him in a prayer.

Sunny was the last worshipper to return her snakes to a box. She eased in the first rattler. Then the second. I stood near her now, the serpent box between us on the ground.

She gently unwound the cottonmouth from her forearm but stumbled as she bent to place it in the box and dropped it hard to the ground, the hefty viper hitting with an audible *whump*. It curled with its back against the box and flashed a snowy mouth, and Sunny impulsively reached to retrieve it, as if reaching for dropped car keys.

The first bite was into Sunny's upper forearm. It was a solid hit, its fangs sinking so deep and injecting such a full dose of venom that she skidded immediately to her knees, her upper body an easy kill-zone target for a second strike. The snake lunged forward again, and this time caught Sunny on the left side of her neck, just below her jaw line, fangs again piercing firm and deep.

As the moccasin coiled for a third strike, I impulsively reached across the box and snatched it just below the head—a lucky catch to be sure—then stepped over the box and stomped down on the snake's midsection. I stood on the viper and jerked the head upward with all my strength. Terror and rage gripped me, and I don't know how many times I did it, but I jerked it up with all my strength, again and again, until it burst at a point about midway between its middle and its head. I left the bottom part on the platform in a heap of blood and snake innards and threw the front part of the snake as far as I could, letting it sail into the darkness surrounding us.

Chapter 23
I Want to Tell You

By the time I got Sunny to the hospital, she was unconscious and convulsing, having been heavily envenomated in the brachial artery of the forearm and the carotid artery of the neck.

I sat in the ER waiting room for two hours, mostly staring into the glass face of a vending machine, counting the packages of peanuts, Oreos, and Snickers. Counting them over and over, and then counting the ceiling tiles, then the floor tiles. A middle-aged couple sat in tears near the swinging doors that led into the patient care area, whispering to each other and waiting for news of their son, who had lost control of his pickup and hit a tree.

A mother came in carrying her toddler, who she feared had eaten rat poison. A beautiful young woman wearing a DQ uniform waited for news of her boyfriend, who had been nearly crushed to death on a nearby drilling rig. We all sat there together, a random collection of bonded strangers, waiting for the dice to roll, waiting for a doctor to tell us what the next chapter of our lives would be.

Just after midnight, a tall, frail doctor came out to talk to me. He was about sixty, walked with a noticeable stoop, and kept his face tilted downward as he spoke so he could see clearly over the tops of his reading glasses, which he never removed.

"Mr. Bastrop?" he said, looking around the room.

"Here," I said, raising my hand.

He walked over and I stood. He didn't offer his hand.

"I'd like to speak with you about your mother."

"She's my aunt. Is she going to make it?" I asked.

"She's still alive but hasn't regained consciousness. We've been monitoring her closely since we administered the antivenin. Because her bites were so deep and into major arteries, she received an unusually large amount of the snake's venom, and much of it got into her blood very quickly. The antivenin will help, but it's probably too late to avoid rather serious organ damage."

"How long till you know the damage?"

"It's hard to say. For now, we're watching all her vital signs, looking for erratic heartbeat, respiratory shutdown, kidney failure. We're running some blood and urine tests that will help us manage her care."

"Do you think she'll wake soon?"

"I'm afraid she's showing signs of going comatose. The good news is her brain activity looks strong for now. We're going to watch her very closely, and we'll let you know of any changes right away."

He nodded to me and turned away to talk to the couple about their son.

———

By three a.m., the waiting room had cleared of everyone but me. I stared at the vending machine and calculated how many nickels it would take to empty the remaining inventory. I tried to read an article about bass fishing, and then one about lawn care, and then one about how to crochet a baby blanket, but I could never get past the second paragraph of any of them.

A young nurse wearing pale blue scrubs came through the

swinging doors and said, "Mr. Bastrop, you can come back and see your mother now. She's awake."

I jumped up. The nurse held the door for me, and as I passed I said, "Thank you. She's my aunt."

The left side of Sunny's face was bloated but seemed to have receded since we first arrived at the hospital. Her arm was badly swollen and splotched with hand-sized patches of deep purple, variegated with brown and greenish stripes. Skin pushed up and partly over her left eye, leaving only a small, blackened slit where her eye socket should have been.

"Billy, honey. Honey." She reached out with her good hand and I held it. She had never called me honey in her life. She had never called anybody honey.

"How do you feel?" I asked.

"Ah feel like the shit the dog won't eat." Her words were slurred, but her voice was stronger than I expected.

"Do you remember what happened?"

"Hell yes. That GD cottonmouth got me."

"Too many snakes this time, Sunny."

"Not too many," she answered. "Just the right number. One for me. One for Cecil. One for you. No, all for you really. To let Jesus know the demons ain't consumed you yet. You're worth it. You're worth all the snakes. Jesus gave me power over any demon a snake can hold."

"But you were bitten," I said.

"Just 'cause Ah dropped that last one. The Holy Ghost must've left my body 'fore Ah tried to pick it back up. The Spirit probably thought Ah was done handling."

Sunny took two or three labored breaths, said, "Billy, it burns my ass you bringing me here. You shouldn'a done that. It's an insult to Jesus. Ah was under His protection. He said we can take up serpents and fear them not."

"You would've died."

"What kinda sense does it make to take up serpents in Jesus' name and then go running to the GD doctors if you get bit? That's just plain crazy." She looked at me with as much disappointment as she could manage from her contorted face.

"I was trying to keep you *alive*."

Sunny smiled at me and stroked my forearm. She struggled for a moment with her breathing, then said, "Billy, listen to me. Go home and get my Jesus box. Get it right now. You know the one Ah'm talking bout, the shoebox with all them little paper Jesuses in it? Get it and bring it to me. Ah need that box. Ah need it bad."

"Sunny, can't it wait? I need to stay here with you. I should be here in case the doctors need me for something."

"They ain't gonna need you for nothing. Please, Billy, get me the box."

An older nurse came in and took Sunny's temperature and blood pressure. "How's your pain?" she asked.

"Painful," Sunny said. "Hurts like a sumbitch."

"I'll check with the doctor and see if we can give you something stronger."

"Ah need something from my house," Sunny said to the nurse, and pointed at me with her good hand. "Tell him it'll be alright for him to run git it for me."

"Close by?"

"'Bout ten minutes."

"Run on and get your mama what she needs. She should be fine till you get back."

"Aunt," I said as I stood up to leave.

———

I knew she kept her shoebox full of precious Jesus pictures in her bedroom somewhere, so I began my search. Nothing near the bed except her Louisville Slugger leaning against the headboard. Nothing under the bed but some folded quilts and blankets. Nothing on the nightstand but her massive main Bible, several auxiliary Bibles, four cartons of unfiltered Camels and three Bic lighters.

The bottom drawer of the dresser looked promising at first, as it was filled with papers: the title to the Green Lizard, deed to the house and five acres of land, a fat raggedy folder stuffed full of Texaco stock certificates and her checkbook (balance of $246.34). Underneath the stock certificates was an envelope labeled "Will" in Sunny's distinctive and unmistakable handwriting.

"Ha!" I spotted a shoebox shoved far back into the drawer. But it was filled with cash instead of paper Jesuses. Shit, I thought, she really shouldn't be keeping stock certificates and a box full of cash in the house.

I rummaged through her closet, tossing aside old gossip magazines and newspapers and at least a dozen Bibles. Wedged into a wall of miscellany on the top shelf of the closet were several shoeboxes of various sizes and colors. One caught my eye right away because Sunny had drawn a cross on one end of it.

"Yes!" It was stuffed with Sunny's Jesus pictures.

I closed the lid and rushed back to the hospital.

The old nurse signaled me through the swinging doors to the critical care area.

"Doctor said she's slipped off into a coma now. Her breathing's gone shallow, so he put her on a ventilator. And her heart's racing and erratic."

She dragged a cold metal chair up near the bed and motioned for me to sit.

"You should probably just stay in here with her now. I'll be back to check on y'all."

She pulled the curtain around us and stepped through the slit to attend the patient in the next bed.

I watched the monitors: blood pressure, pulse, blood oxygen saturation. The ventilator beat a long, slow rhythm: *phush-whooo. phush-whooo. phush-whooo.* Other than the rise and fall of her chest, and her unswollen eye shifting from time to time beneath its closed lid, not a single muscle moved over the span of her body for the next hour. I watched the oxygen count drop, and the pulse alternate between long periods of very high numbers, and equally long periods of very low numbers.

Sometime during the second hour, I felt an electric panic jolt out of my gut and rush into my throat, flushing my face and head with sudden heat, as I realized she was not going to make it, that I was going to sit on a hard metal chair behind a translucent curtain in a corner of Knope County Memorial Hospital and watch her go.

I couldn't look. I couldn't be there and I couldn't *not* be there. I felt trapped in this curtained hole, this dying hole where the old nurse had left us, Sunny's remarkable testimony at the snake-infested camp meeting filling my head.

I told myself to stop whining. I told myself my anguish was tiny compared to Sunny's father raping her as a twelve-year-old. She couldn't be there and she couldn't leave. I thought of little Sunshine and how her abuse eventually snapped her mind. All she could do was go rushing into a bright light full of Jesus and stay hidden there for the rest of her life.

And although I suppressed it and kept it a secret even to myself, I did love her. I'd denied it for so long, having the bone-headed notion that love—especially familial love—had to be all or nothing, that to love Sunny meant I had to accept all her dark and noxious corners.

I stood and hugged her. Hugged all the good parts of her.

———

By her bedside, I couldn't count packages of peanuts or Snickers, so I decided to count Sunny's Jesuses. Surprisingly, I felt much better at first, as I dug through the box and pulled them out, one by one. The

Jesuses were little markers of my childhood with Sunny, each one giving me a rush of memory.

Many of the clippings were from purloined material, her snatching a Jesus calendar off the wall of a gas station while the attendant was distracted, or us smuggling a Jesus fan out of church on an especially hot Sunday. She detested the Jehovah's Witnesses who came to our door, but while she hid herself behind the couch, she would send me out, six years old, to talk to them on the front porch so she could still get their free literature, which was chock full of prime Jesus-clipping material.

One night, soon after arriving to live with her, I heard Sunny in her bedroom reading Bible passages aloud and praying, often tearfully. Her main Bible was a monster she'd bought from a door-to-door salesman. It was thick as a five-pound sugar sack, but heavier, with oversized gilt-edged pages, and stuffed full of extras like fancy maps and genealogical charts and full-page color artworks by Da Vinci, Raphael, Michelangelo, and others.

My personal favorite was the painting of David slaying Goliath, where the future king of Israel stands with his foot on the giant's chest, sword swooping down to behead the stoned, helpless mutant. All words spoken by Jesus were printed in red ink. This way, anyone impatient with The Word could quickly scan the pages to find the most important parts of human meaning and destiny, unencumbered by context or subtlety. That was Sunshine's main Bible, the one she cherished, but she had at least a dozen more, lesser Bibles.

That night—not long after I'd first moved in with her—she sat up in bed with a pair of scissors and one of her smaller auxiliary Bibles in her lap, four or five other Good Books strewn to either side.

"C'mon in, long as you don't start jabbering at me," she'd said, not looking up. "Ah'm trying to pay close attention here."

"Can I look at the giant's picture? In the fat Good Book?"

"Ah don't want to get that one down for you right now. Just look at some of these others here till Ah'm done." She pointed around the bed with her scissors at the lesser Bibles, then bit her lower lip in concentration, twisting and turning the scissors and slicing across a page of scripture.

I flipped through pages in the nearest reserve Bible, a children's Bible next to her foot, hoping to find another version of David chopping off Goliath's head, or equally interesting violence. A single person had been cut from most of the pictures, leaving behind a gathering of shepherds here, a flock of cherubim there, a party of gesturing dinner guests—minus one—on yet another page, and an empty cross on a hill next to two more crosses that still bore their dead.

When Sunny finished clipping Him from another scene, leaving behind a horde of people with no one to serve them fishes and loaves, she stuffed it into a shoebox that already brimmed with paper Jesuses. Then celebrated by opening a new sleeve of Oreos.

"Can I do it?" I asked.

"What?"

"Cut outs. Cut the paper dolls."

"This?" She held up the freshly clipped loaves-and-fishes Jesus, bright colors on the front, words of the gospel across the back.

"No, no, no. You don't never cut a Bible. That's a terrible sin."

I sat by her hospital bed and listened to the incessant whoosh of the ventilator and counted. But the shoebox I sorted through contained more than portraits of Christ. Deeper in, I found the newspaper clippings that made clear what Sunny meant at the camp revival when she said, "Cecil hurt his own children. Hurt 'em bad":

Angelina Man Indicted in Death of Daughter

A 42-year-old Angelina man who was on the run for six weeks and suspected of beating his 2 year-old daughter to death, was indicted Thursday on one count of murder. Cecil Bastrop faces up to 15 years in prison if convicted on his charges. Additional assault charges are pending regarding severe injuries sustained by Bastrop's 4-year-old son. Authorities charge Bastrop assaulted his son with a machete, and the boy lost his right arm in the attack. Both alleged incidents occurred at the family's home on Simms Road, 2 miles east of Angelina, Texas.

Angelina Man Convicted for Death of Girl, Assault on Boy

Cecil Bastrop, a 43-year-old Angelina man was convicted of manslaughter and assault today in the blunt force trauma death of his 2-year-old daughter, and a machete attack on his 4-year-old son. After two weeks of trial, it took the jury only 90 minutes to return the two verdicts. Bastrop faces 10-20 years imprisonment at the state correctional institution in Huntsville, Texas. Bastrop worked as a mechanic at Ollie's Truck Stop on Highway 59 near Angelina, and also worked as a seasonal sugarcane cutter. When asked to comment on the outcome, Angelina County Sheriff Oren Tyler said, "This case hit me especially hard. It's been gut-wrenching for everyone involved. I'm happy to see the jury return a conviction."

I spilled the box of Jesuses on the floor, and they scattered like ashes. I grabbed the trash can to vomit, but only managed some dry heaves and then pushed out through the slit in the curtain and found my way to the Green Lizard. I couldn't think of anywhere else to go, so I just locked the doors and sat in Sunny's old ugger and let all sense of time and place dissolve.

There were no tears. The sun shone brightly in a perfect sky as I sat and stared out across the hospital parking lot. The flags atop the flagpole were lifted by a steady breeze, and their chain clanged against the aluminum pole. A lawn mower hummed in the distance.

At least now I knew where Cecil had been hiding my whole life. Back in his hometown. Hell.

.   .   .

A man knocked on the Lizard's windshield, breaking my stupor. He wore a gray speckled suit with a red tie and horn-rimmed glasses.

"Your name Bastrop?"

"Yes, sir." I couldn't look him in the eye. I knew why he was looking for me. I knew what he was going to say.

"Are you Mizz Bastrop's next of kin?"

"Yes, sir."

"I'm sorry to have to tell you, but Mizz Bastrop has passed."

I nodded at him.

"We need you to come back inside the hospital so we can do some paperwork to send her over to a funeral home."

I followed the man back into the front entrance of the hospital, where Sunshine Pearl Bastrop lay dead. Killed by the snakes of God. How many people learn the price of their soul? Mine was three serpents.

As we walked down the central hallway toward his office, we passed the old nurse carrying a sandwich wrapped in wax paper and a tall bottle of Coke.

"Sorry about your aunt," she said.

"Mother," I corrected her.

"She was my mother."

Chapter 24
You Never Give Me Your Money

A week after Sunny's funeral, I drove two hundred miles south of Korvus to Angelina, looking for Sheriff Oren Tyler—the man quoted in the newspaper article about my father's trial. A woman at the courthouse told me Tyler had not been sheriff for over ten years. Now he owned a gun shop at Main and Third, about five blocks away.

I walked into Oren's Gun & Pawn and saw two men in their late twenties, wearing jeans, T-shirts, and cowboy hats. They leaned over a counter, peering through the glass top at an array of handguns. They glanced at me briefly, then stared back down at the guns. A man came out of the back room, pistol on his hip, carrying a pump-action shotgun with price tags on the trigger guard.

He was about fifty-five with a silvered goatee and bushy eyebrows and a full head of hair slicked straight back, mostly dark on top but almost completely gray across his sideburns and both temples. He was average height, but solid, trim, and muscular, especially his upper body and forearms. "XXX" was tattooed in dark blue ink across his left forearm, right below the point where he had rolled back the sleeves of a khaki work shirt.

"Be with you shortly," he said to me as he showed the shotgun to the cowboys.

"I'm looking for Sheriff Tyler," I said.

"I'm Tyler, but not sheriff anymore," he said. One of the cowboys jerked the shotgun to his shoulder and shot an imaginary quail or duck flying overhead.

I busied myself looking at a large poster titled "Game Birds of Texas." The cowboys bought the shotgun and a muscular revolver and holster, and four boxes of ammunition for each weapon, and left.

"How can I help you today?" Tyler said. "You've got to be twenty-one to buy a handgun."

We faced each other over the pistol case. "I'm looking for information, Mr. Tyler," I said. "You don't know me, but several years ago, you arrested my father. Cecil Bastrop."

"Bastrop? God, yes, I remember him. I'll never forget that whole sad mess. Cases like that stand out around here. You his boy?" He motioned at my empty sleeve.

"Yessir."

"My condolences for all you've lost, son." He walked out from behind the display case and shook my hand in the awkward right-hand-to-left-hand maneuver I had become so familiar with.

"I'm Billy," I said. "My sister's name was Lucy."

"Where you live, Billy?" Tyler asked.

"Korvus. About two hundred miles north."

"Knope County? I know it well. Got a brother who runs a deer lease not far from there. You got family up there?"

"I've been living with my aunt. She took me in after ... well, after everything. She died about a week ago."

"Yeah, I remember her from the night it all happened, and from the trial. Big woman, right? Sorry to hear. She was a real force of nature. Sunlight was it?"

"Sunshine."

"What for you now?"

"Not sure."

"How old are you?"

"Seventeen."

"See, until you're eighteen, the county will be after you. They'll place you somewhere."

"You mean like in a foster home?" Damn. I hadn't thought of that.

"Most likely. But they move slow as Christmas, so if you fly under the radar, you might make it to your birthday before they get their shit together. Good thing for you, I ain't a sheriff no more, I'd be obligated to make a call up to Knope County and rat you out." He jabbed me playfully in the chest and smiled.

I cleared the foster-home panic from my eyes and smiled back at him.

"Sheriff Tyler, would you be willing to tell me what all happened?" I pulled the two newspaper clippings from my jeans.

"I found these in my aunt's things, and I was never told any of this. She always told me it was a car wreck that took my arm and killed Lucy. I'd like to hear the whole truth of it."

"I'll talk to you. You sure as hell deserve that much. But you should know, everybody says they want to know the truth. That's what you're supposed to say. What kind of asshole walks around saying, 'No, no, don't tell me the truth. I don't want to know that.' But once you catch the truth, there ain't no cure for it. It's been known to eat away a man's good sense. It's the oddest damn thing, people unable to resist the one thing they would be happiest without."

"I need to know," I said.

"People as old as me, we give the truth a wide berth. We know that truth's just a sad, lonely bastard. He's that mean motherfucker who'll get you drunk and steal your money and get you arrested. You often see him sitting over in the corner of the bar alone, nursing a drink. 'Cause nobody really wants anything to do with him. They say they do. But they don't really."

Tyler put on a gray Stetson with a sweat stain around the brim, took off his gun belt and locked it in a filing cabinet. He walked over to the front door and flipped the sign from "Open" to "Closed."

"You hungry?" he asked. "Let's walk over to La Leonera. Ever had cabrito?"

———

La Leonera was across the street from Oren's Gun & Pawn. It was a small, storefront spot that over the last hundred years had probably had a long litany of shop lives: tobacco to dress to drug to hardware to insurance to video to enchilada combo plates. A husband-wife team with one hired waitress scrambled around taking orders and refilling iced teas and shouting in Spanish to a frantic, grouchy cook in a too small kitchen.

"Antonio. Victoria," Tyler tipped his hat to the owners as we settled into chairs at a small table with a red ceramic tile top. "They do a helluva nice job here."

Antonio rushed over to warmly greet Señor Tyler, and the two of them spoke rapidly in Spanish. Belly laughing at whatever Tyler was saying, Antonio flashed a mouthful of dentures at me.

"We're having the cabrito," Tyler said to him.

Antonio smoothed his mustache and shouted at the waitress to bring "two number fours."

Tyler and I ate our *cabrito al pastor* and started talking. He told me he hadn't known my parents well but had a passing acquaintance with them. Angelina was a small town and, as sheriff, he either knew firsthand about a lot of people, or would hear things about them. My mother, Julia, was a lot younger than Cecil, smart and attractive and ambitious. He remembered seeing her name in the newspaper a time or two, local girl wins literary award, gets something published somewhere, that sort of thing. During the trial, he heard she was nearly finished with an associate's degree at Crockett Junior College, and she aspired to go on with her education and teach English Lit someday.

The sheriff's department had a contract with Ollie's Truck Stop, where Cecil worked as a mechanic, to tow and impound vehicles as needed, and to do maintenance and repair work on county vehicles, including all the sheriff's department's patrol cars. Tyler would run into Cecil from time to time when his patrol car needed work, and Tyler or one of his deputies had thrown him in jail several times for DUI.

They'd also arrested him for fighting with other drunks at various low-dive honkytonks in the south of the county. They suspected Cecil had nearly beaten a man to death one night in an argument over which of the two of them was most likely to go to hell. The other man—when he regained consciousness—refused to press charges, admitting he was wrong. Cecil was for sure the most likely of them to make it to hell.

"And we had to make calls out to your house on Simms Road," he said. "He beat your mama a time or two."

"Do you know what their problems were?"

"Problems? Their problems were: he was a crazy-paranoid-jealous drunk, and they lived in Deep East Texas. Those are two of the biggest damn problems anybody can have."

"You didn't arrest him?"

"She'd never press charges. You got to understand, that's a hard thing for a woman in that situation to do. Your kids might get taken for a while. Then the ole boy always gets out. She probably figured the beating would be worse next time if she was the cause of him going to jail."

"Trapped," I said.

"She could no more break out of her situation than a character can break out of a George Jones song. Trapped just that bad. Happens all the goddamn time," Tyler said. "There was a rumor or two that she and a professor at the college might have been a little too close. My guess is Cecil found her out and snapped. Took it out on you kids."

"Must be a hard job. For you, I mean." I said, "Knowing what's really going on with people beneath the surface. Knowing about the crazies, knowing what will probably happen. Not being able to do anything to stop the inevitable. Just having to wait and wait until they cross that line, knowing it's just a matter of time. Like you know how the George Jones song is going to end, but all you can do is listen to the radio and wait. Didn't you ever just want to shoot the radio and save everybody a lot of misery?"

Tyler piled his tableware on his empty plate and pushed it aside and leaned back in his chair. His forehead tightened and his unruly eyebrows bristled. He pointed his dark eyes at me and said, "Every day. Every damn day when I was with the law. And every day since. But the theory is, that's what makes us different from monkeys. We got procedures. We got due process. Don't they teach that in high school civics anymore?"

Two men stopped at our table to shake hands with Tyler and make small talk. While they talked, I retrieved the two newspaper clippings from my pocket and quickly read them again. The two men left, and the lunch rush was over, leaving Tyler and me as the only two remaining customers.

"Why did you say this case, my family's case, hit you 'especially hard'?"

"Did I say that?" I showed him the clipping. He looked out the window and across the street toward his pawn shop.

"Oh, hell. Some reporter probably just made that up."

He shifted in his chair when he spoke, and his tone seemed phony to me for the first time. I felt like we had really connected from the beginning, and were genuinely talking man-to-man, in fact, my first ever man-to-man talk, but something was off; there was a sudden evasion.

"You were the sheriff here for over twenty years. You must have seen a lot of bad stuff happen. What was it about our case that got to you?"

"I got called to the hospital that night your sister died, and you were cut. Dispatcher said some lunatic woman had hijacked a Greyhound bus and brought two badly hurt kids into the ER. And on top of everything else, it looked like somebody had tried to drown them."

"Sunny hijacked a bus?"

"You don't know that part neither? She was taking the bus to Angelina to pick up her car that Cecil'd been working on for her. And out the window, she sees the damn car—way out in the boonies, halfway down the embankment, about to slip into Black Bayou. She screamed bloody hell for the driver to stop. Witnesses on the bus said somebody—it was too dark to tell who—was pushing the car into the water. Turned out it was Cecil. Turned out you and your little sister were in the backseat, the little girl limp and lifeless, and you bleeding to death."

A shiver hit me. Hackles rose under my shirt. Tyler looked as sad as a pallbearer and patted my forearm.

"Were you there?" I asked, words catching in my throat. I clenched my eyes against the tears.

"No. There's nowhere near where anybody coulda called us. Everything I know is from talking to the passengers afterwards. They said the car slid off into the bayou before the bus driver and your aunt could get out of the bus with a flashlight, and it was sinking fast. It was Sunshine who spotted you and your sister. And she was frantic. Running up and down the bank hollering for help, begging the bus driver or anybody to jump in and get you kids before the car went under.

"Nobody'd go in. Claimed they couldn't swim. Or were afraid of snakes. Got to admit, there's a shitload of snakes in Black Bayou and God knows what else. Didn't stop your aunt plunging in."

"Sunny couldn't swim. Was terrified of water," I said. "But snakes? No problem."

"Maybe she couldn't swim, but she got both of you out of that car and back to land. The damn bus driver was down on his knees with a heart attack by then. Sunshine threw the two of you up on the bus and drove it to Angelina Memorial herself. That's when the call came into the sheriff's office.

"You ask me why your case got to me so bad? Any time kids are involved, it just kills your soul. I can't explain it. There was just something about that little boy, about you, as I watched there in the ER while the doctors worked to stop the bleeding. I knew they'd have to take the arm. I'd seen a lot of boys in the war with their arms and legs mangled, and after a while, you could tell with just one look if a limb would stay or go. You were cut that bad. The girl was already gone, wet and broken and covered with a sheet, and you were cut. Just the horror of it.

"And I felt that cut myself. A cut I knew would never heal. I can't explain it. That's just how I felt. I wanted to blow the asshole's brains out. Motherfucker claimed he didn't mean to cut you like that. Claimed he was trying to swat you down. Stop you from running from him 'cause you'd gone hysterical over your sister being hurt. Swat you down, my ass! With a machete? Jesus."

His words pried things loose in my head. Snippets. A flash of me snatching away Lucy's doll. Lucy crying. Daddy screaming at us. More crying. Daddy knocking her into the door frame.

Tyler paused a moment and sipped his coffee.

"Your case got under my skin in a bad way back then, and that scared me because I'd never let it happen before. It just crawled up in my ass and lived there, eating away at my insides. I couldn't go to bed at night without imagining how it happened over and over, some drunken bastard beating and cutting his kids, *and I mean little kids.* And then the stupid motherfucker huffing and puffing and trying to hide what he'd done by pushing the car with the kids inside it into that god-awful cesspool swamp."

He put a little more sugar in his coffee.

Tyler continued, "It didn't make any sense. Why would I let it get to me after all those years, after all I'd seen and done? I was with the 82nd Airborne during WWII. A fucking Ranger. We were badass. I mean, trained fucking killers. Determined and remorseless. I'm not one of those assholes who brag about all the blood and guts and depravity of what happens in war. Most guys like that are liars, and never saw half of what they claim. But let me just tell you, truthfully, since you are a young man seeking truth, no matter how heinous you think war is, it is far, far worse than anything a sane man can imagine."

He gazed around the dead calm of the restaurant and put some money on the table as Antonio brought a fresh cup of coffee.

"So even though I had witnessed—and been a party to—brutality on a massive scale during the war, and then as a lawman seen mankind at its worst for years, I'm suddenly going to be pushed over the edge by what I see at the Angelina hospital the night you and your sister were brought in? It just didn't make any sense. So many good people had died and been mutilated all over the world during the war. For what? What had been accomplished? We still lived in a world where some worthless scumbastard like Cecil Bastrop could take a machete to a kid. Then it hit me—the truth everybody says they seek but don't really want to know—hit me. It didn't make any sense because *it don't make sense*. The world just doesn't make any goddamn sense. There's your truth."

He stared into his second cup of coffee for a long moment.

"I took up drinking again. My wife left for real that time. No matter what I did, I couldn't shake loose from that one night. I guess I had been teetering on the edge for a long time without any clue of what was hiding down in here." He pointed at his gut.

"I even went as far as talking to a shrink a couple of times in Houston. After that, I knew my days working in law enforcement were over. I got out because I wanted to start shooting the radio like you said. Wanted to stop the song. Hell, I thought I *had* stopped it until you came walking into my shop today. Yeah, I knew who you were the minute you came through the door, like some old haint showing up to rattle his bones at me. Looks like fate's connected us ole Billy boy." Tyler gave me a big grin. "That's why I'm telling you all this and nobody else. It's owed to you."

We left the restaurant and walked to the Lizard.

"Is he still in the Huntsville pen?" I asked.

Tyler's eyes widened, and he tilted his head slightly to one side.

"You don't know?"

"No, I don't know anything."

"He was released about six years ago. Served seven years of his sentence."

"Seven! That's it?"

"That's it."

"Anybody know where he is?"

"I heard his probation officer lost track of him about a year after his release. Just seemed to vanish after that. My guess is he either got himself killed or is maybe in prison in another state somewhere."

"I want to find him," I said.

"No, you don't. No good will come from that."

"I've got to stop the song."

"Look, I know you've got a lot to sort through here all of a sudden. You came looking for some truth, and now you've caught it, and like I said, there's no cure for that.

"You're going to carry it with you all day, every day. That's going to be hard. You would've had a much longer, happier life not knowing the details. Right now, if I was you, I'd concentrate on getting back home to Korvus and figuring out how to dodge the Knope County children's services people for the next few months. Go on home and mourn your aunt's passing and work through everything in your head."

"Will you keep your eyes and ears open for him?" I asked. "Let me know if he ever shows up?"

Tyler shook his head in resignation and smiled sadly at me.

"Sure. I think a man in your situation has the right to that kind of information." It was the first time anyone had ever called me a man.

Tyler took a pawn shop business card from his wallet and wrote a number on the back.

"Shop number on the front, home number on the back. If after all is said and done, after you've worked things out in your head and your heart, and if you find this whole thing has crawled too far up your ass and is eating at you night and day, then call me. Will you do that?"

"Yes, sir," I said.

"I mean it now. Call me. Don't go after him alone. You're going to need help."

At the time, I thought Cecil would be the second man I'd kill.

I was wrong.

———

The next morning, I sat at Sunny's kitchen table with her shoebox full of Jesuses. I reburied the two newspaper clippings among them, because that was clearly what she'd been doing. I could see her praying over the clippings before pushing them deep down among the stolen saviors, her own unique method of exorcism.

I took a sip of coffee and dug through another box and pulled out a tattered copy of an obscure literary journal with one of my mother's poems in it. I had just started reading it when Howard Granger knocked on the front door.

I opened the door but kept the screen latched.

"Billy, we got some business to discuss," Granger said.

"What kind of business?"

"Sunshine's will," he said, "she wanted the church to get half of everything."

"Like hell," I said.

Granger took a folded piece of paper from his back pocket and waved it at me.

"Look yourself."

I slipped the latch, took the paper, and let the screen fall shut. It was a Xeroxed page in Sunny's unmistakable handwriting:

April 10, 1965
  <u>Sunshine</u> <u>Pearl</u> <u>Bastrop</u>
  Will and Testamint
  On my deth give have of ever thing to Billy Wayne Bastrop. Give

the other have to The Church of All Truth Brother Howard Granger Preacher or who the preacher is if Brother Granger is dead or gone.
Sunshine Pearl Bastrop

Sunny had signed it, and a witness had signed, Eunice Gates. Eunice was a church member and Granger's sister-in-law.

"I don't know anything about this," I said.

"There it is, plain as day," he said.

"I bet it's not legal."

"Bet it is, praise Jesus."

"I'm not giving you half of anything."

"Just what I'd expect from a heathen with no love of the Good Lord."

"Get the hell off our property," I said, and pushed the paper back out the door, letting it fall to the concrete porch.

"I'll just come back with the law."

He scooped up the paper and took one step off the porch, then looked back as I was closing the door.

"Boy, how old are you?"

I closed the door and locked it. He shouted at me through the door.

"I know you ain't even eighteen yet. I'm coming back with the law and with them county children's care people. You ain't old enough to conduct business with me on this will. And you ain't old enough to live out here on your own."

I pulled back the curtain and shot him the finger.

"Half's better than nothing, boy," he said. "You think about that."

I didn't know how much time I had, so I moved as fast as I could. I ran into Sunny's bedroom and took the top drawer of her dresser out, the one with all the money and titles and deeds, and ran it back into the kitchen and dumped the contents into a wicker laundry basket. I fished out the envelope with "Will" written across the front and tore it open.

Fuck it all, what he said was true. It matched Granger's Xerox copy.

I ran to my bedroom and randomly piled clothes on top of the papers in the basket. I threw it all in the trunk of the Green Lizard and went back for more. Two trips, three trips. I hauled my stereo and speakers and all the Beatles and Stones and Hendrix I could grab.

On my last pass, I filled my Army backpack with as many books as I could stuff in, most of them from the Knope County Library. Finally, I made sure to get the Canadian Tourism Commission brochures and the Rand McNally atlas.

I didn't want to leave any clue as to where I had gone.

———

About an hour down the road, somewhere near Texarkana, I turned the radio to AM1350, KRVS in Korvus. There was Granger, screaming and raving about heathens and communists and the love of Jesus. As I reached the edge of the little AM station's range, a few miles west of Texarkana, Granger began to fade and crackle. I pointed the Lizard toward Little Rock, punched it, and let her run full out—whopper-jaw be damned.

Let the big Lizard eat up the road until I'd escaped the sound of his voice.

Chapter 25
Mean Mr. Mustard

Canada is a long, long way from East Texas.

I conked out for the night just short of reaching Nashville, and checked into a rancid motel in Bucksnort, Tennessee. Well past noon the next day, I woke up starving and went to the Exxon next door, hoping for some kind of food. Pint of milk. Ho-Hos. Peanuts. I reached into my pocket to pay and came up empty.

"Be right back," I said to the clerk, who never looked away from a tiny television wedged between jugs of pickled eggs.

Back in the room, I opened Sunny's shoebox of cash. I grabbed a twenty, and it occurred to me I had no idea how much money was in there. Four, five hundred bucks maybe? I counted it four times before I convinced myself. $25,520. That was about three times the median annual household income in 1972, based on the last term paper I wrote in my American History class. Three years' worth of money for a whole family. Sunny was the queen of frugality and it had rubbed off on me; this much money would last me a long time.

And then there were the Texaco stock certificates, which I also hadn't counted and wouldn't know what to do with anyway. I didn't know if it was possible for me to legally convert those into cash or not, or even how to do it if I could.

How much does a cabin cost in Canada? Or at least a trailer. No. No trailer. Trailers probably aren't even allowed in Canada. Parking a trailer in the gorgeous landscape of Nova Scotia or British Columbia would be like pinning a turd on a tuxedo.

They likely have only cabins, and not shithole, rickety Abraham Lincoln cabins, but cabins made of long, straight, redwood trunks with smooth, evenly applied mud or goop or whatever they call the stuff they put between the logs, and neatly stacked river-rock fire-places and chimneys.

Maybe I could start a business. A bookstore. A bookstore that serves coffee. I was beginning to feel a little better, less like a fugitive, and more like an international entrepreneur. The money and stock could never leave my side. I dumped some books from my olive drab backpack to make room for Sunny's little fortune.

After retrieving my breakfast and gassing up the Lizard, I was off again for Canada.

———

Late day, I crossed the Ohio River east of downtown Cincinnati with great clouds of gray smoke pouring from the Lizard, out either side of the hood. I took the next exit—Kellogg Avenue—and rolled into French's Highway 52 Fuel & Motor Center.

As I bent over the engine, waving away steam with no clue how to fix it, a rattletrap flatbed piled with junk slammed into the Lizard's rear. The crash crumpled a shark fin, bent a fender against a tire, and shattered a taillight, shoving the car into my waist and nearly drop-ping the hood on my head.

The driver flung his door open, jumped down and gingerly ran his fingertips over the wounds to my car. He was short and fat, but fat only in the belly, his belly pushing out from below his rib cage and flapping over his belt. He had an abbreviated, boyish face, almost devoid of a chin. A glimpse of scalp shined through here and there beneath a veneer of glistening black hair. I took him to be about forty.

His truck was overloaded with all manner of metal junk: rusted-out refrigerators and washing machines, car doors, axles, sections of steel pipes of all sizes and lengths, large panels of rotted tin, car engine blocks and car parts, and at least a dozen defunct air conditioners. The junk hung precariously over the back of his vehicle and bulged over the sides, all of it piled well above the flimsy wooden side rails. There were two or three haphazardly placed chains criss-crossing the mountain of crap to hold it in place. The lettering on the truck door read "French's Salvage – Kellogg Avenue – Cincinnati, OH."

"You're OK, right? You weren't in the car, right?" said the driver.

I walked to the back of the car to inspect the damage.

"I'm OK. But you crunched up my car pretty badly. That wheel won't turn now." I pointed out where the right back fender caved in against the tire, cutting into the rubber.

"No problem. No problem at all. I'll take care of this. Don't worry about that. Look, I'll make this right. Let's just not get any police or insurance people involved, OK? Insurance guys are pricks. It'll take forever. My rates will go up. OK? I own a towing business and I own a body shop. I can get this all fixed up for you. You know, if you're looking to buy a car, I have a little used car dealership just up the road here."

"I don't need a car. I just want this one fixed."

"No problem. I'm letting you know 'cause this car might be on its last legs, is all. Let me go back inside the truck stop—I'm the owner here—and make some phone calls, and we can get this in the shop for a few days and fix it up good as new for you. Where do you live? I can have somebody deliver her to you when she's done."

"I don't live around here. I'm traveling," I said.

"Oh. Oh. I see now. Texas plates. You headed back home to Texas? Yee-haw! I never been there."

"North," I said.

"Traveling alone, are you?"

I paused a long beat before responding. Nodded yes.

"No parents, nobody else?" He scanned around the parking lot while raking a comb through his thin hair, straight back.

I didn't answer.

"OK, OK. I own a small motel not far from here, about five miles away. You can stay there a day or two, on the house, of course, and I'll get everything fixed right up. It's not the Ritz, but you'll be fine there. Let me give you one of my cards, and I'll write a note to the manager to set you up gratis. Then I'll call somebody to come pick you up and take you over there."

He climbed into the truck cab, found a business card, and handed it out the door to me. It read: Stu French, French Enterprises, and it listed a phone number and a street address on Eastern Avenue in Cincinnati. Then he began scribbling a note on the back of a receipt he pulled from a crumpled pile of papers on his dashboard.

I leaned against the truck, waiting for the note. There was a low, slow creak. Then a sharp *pow!* like a gunshot—but not a gunshot, a chain snapping—sending an avalanche of rusted crap crushing down on me from atop French's truck. All manner of things heavy and metallic smashed into my head and shoulders, knocking me first to my knees, then flat out on my face. I lay there dazed, hornets buzzing in my brain, and my vision blurred, the landslide of junk pinning me face down in sudden darkness, dead washing machines and engine blocks and long sections of heavy iron pipe pressing me into the concrete. I fought for a breath. Every piece of me hurt like salt in a cut.

There were voices. A little light. A little more. From the corner of one eye, I saw two pairs of greasy boots and one pair of nice loafers shuffling around the oil-sheen pavement. Stu French and a couple of his mechanics were digging me out.

"Don't move, OK. I can take care of this. I'll get you fixed up. No problem," French said.

Fuck how? Does he own a hospital too?

———

"Your arm is broken in two places," the ER doctor at Cincinnati General Hospital said as he held X-rays overhead and eyed them closely.

"And your left knee is badly sprained."

"Don't worry," Stu French said. "I'm paying for everything. Doc, heal him up real good for me. Don't worry about no insurance. I'm covering all the expenses. Cash, OK? Minimum of paperwork, OK?"

"We'll set the bone and put a cast on it right away," the doctor said.

"How long will it take my arm to heal? How long before I can drive?"

"The cast should come off in about six weeks. But I don't recommend a return to normal activity for eight to ten weeks."

"And my leg?"

"The good news is, the X-rays don't show anything broken in your leg or knee. I'd say stay off it for at least a week, and then gently try it out by walking around your house. Come back here or go see your family doctor in a week when the swelling has reduced, and someone can do a full assessment of the mobility of your knee.

"For now, go home and prop it up and put some ice packs on it. We'll pack it in ice here before we release you today. I'm assuming you're going home to family who can care for you? You're going to need a lot of attention for a while, since you're going to be without the use of your only arm. You're going to need help eating and bathing. And even going to the bathroom."

"Crap." Canada was rapidly fading in the distance.

"Not to worry, Doc. We'll see to it," French said. "We'll take him to see a doctor I know to check his leg. He's a good doc—a golf buddy of mine. And we'll figure something out for his feeding, etcetera. No problem. I can work all this out. How about some painkillers? Give him plenty of painkillers. I'm buying."

The hospital people set my arm and applied the cast. They were kind enough to shape the cast to let all my fingers and thumb dangle free.

"Normally, it wouldn't be done this way," the casting woman explained. "But since you only have one arm, you need as much dexterity as possible."

The doctor wrote prescriptions for painkillers and anti-inflammation drugs as well as antibiotics because of the cuts and lacerations on my head, face, neck, and chest. They put me in a wheelchair and a gruff, bearded orderly started pushing me toward the hallway.

"Wait. Don't forget my backpack over there." The pack holding all my cash had been on the ER floor in the corner the whole time. The orderly dropped it in my lap.

"Just like I had in 'Nam. Heavy. What you got in here, bricks?"

"Books," I lied.

"Better than bullets, I guess."

French and one of his employees named Odell rolled me out to a white panel van with "French Dry Cleaners" written on the side, and rolled the wheelchair right up into the back of the van, then blocked the wheels so I wouldn't bounce around and ram my leg—which was packed in ice and immobilized and sticking straight out—into the back doors of the van in case of a sudden stop. They soon delivered me to a place on Eastern Avenue in Cincinnati, an area of town everyone called the East End. And some people called it Little Appalachia.

———

"This is not a motel," I said as Odell rolled me out of the van. It was a large brick building that had once been blood red, but the paint had long ago faded and peeled, revealing the original brick color as dull terracotta.

The front faced Eastern Avenue, and the rear of the building looked out across the short span of a dirt and grass levee onto the broad expanse of the Ohio River, the water over five hundred yards wide, with Dayton, Kentucky, a straight shot across the river.

The place was three stories tall with soaring arched windows in the front, each window covered with splintered and weathered plywood. A rectangular tower rose from the middle of the building in the front, rising to a point about forty feet above the central pitched roofline, where it abruptly stopped, leaving an awkward, chopped-off appearance.

"Used to be St. Vitus Church," Odell said as he pulled me backwards in the wheelchair up a considerable flight of concrete steps to the front door.

"See up there," he pointed at the truncated tower, "that's where the steeple used to be, used to rise another hundred feet or so."

He hauled me up the front steps one step at a time, about as carefully as he'd haul a wheelbarrow full of cinder blocks, jolts of pain stabbing through my arm and shoulder and down the back of my leg as I rocked backwards up every single goddamn step.

"How do you like it?" Stu French asked. "I bought it for next to nothing from the diocese about five years ago. Gonna turn it into apartments. They made me tear the steeple off the tower, though, so it'd look less like an active church."

"Where's the motel?" I asked. No response.

French opened one half of the heavy, medieval-style, split-arched doorway, and they rolled me inside the ex-church and into a two-bedroom apartment on the same floor as the entryway, which, because of the climb up the front steps, was almost a full story above street level.

"This is the only unit we've finished so far," he said. "But we'll eventually get there."

From what had once been the church foyer, a door opened into the living room of the apartment. Off the living room, a hallway ran from the front of the building (the street side) to the back of the building (the river side).

There were two small bedrooms on either end of the hallway, one facing out over Eastern Avenue, the other with a view over the river toward Kentucky. Between the two bedrooms was a tiny kitchen and a bathroom.

"We just put this tub in last week." Stu grinned proudly and pointed at it. It was an old ceramic-coated steel tub on clawed feet, yellowed and scratched and beat all to shit.

"It don't look like much now, but it works fine."

The place looked like a troupe of chimpanzees had built it. None of the interior doors were on hinges but lay stacked against the living room wall. There was crudely hung drywall in a couple of rooms, but the rest were bare studs. The floors were mostly exposed plywood—in many spots buckled and warped—and splotched and strewn with enough scattered paint and drywall mud to suggest Jackson Pollock had been at work on a new masterpiece. I thought I recognized the kitchen stove and refrigerator as some of the rejects that fell off Stu's truck and stranded me in Cincinnati.

The only furniture was a twin bed in the street-side bedroom. It had a slotted, metal rod headboard and footboard, and looked like a discarded prop from a WWI army hospital movie. I suspected it had been delivered and set up right before we arrived, having come, no doubt, from French's Used Furniture. Because surely, somewhere in the East End of Cincinnati, such an establishment had to exist.

Chapter 26
Don't Pass Me By

They left me in bed with my leg propped on my Army pack. Hours and hours passed.

Near dark, I heard a girl's voice echo through the empty spaces of the ex-church.

"Hello?" she said.

"Hi," I answered.

"They told me to bring you some food."

"Come on in."

"Where are you?" she asked.

"This way. Down the hall to the left. Toward the street."

The girl didn't immediately step into the room but grabbed the door frame with one hand and leaned in slowly and cautiously. She was maybe ten or eleven. Tall for her age, and very thin. She wore a gray, hooded sweatshirt and jeans frazzled at the hems. She had skittish blue eyes and corn-silk hair, about shoulder length, in desperate need of washing and brushing. The girl stood in the doorway and pulled a package of cold wieners from the pouch of her sweatshirt and held it up for me to see.

"You can come on in," I said. "What's your name?"

"Mae."

"I'm Billy. Nice to meet you, Mae. I thought maybe everybody left town."

She walked into the room cattishly, looking around at all the nothing there.

"It's not much, but the rent's really cheap," I said.

Mae didn't smile, but slowly walked over to within arm's reach of me and tore open the pack of hot dogs. She took one out and put the rest of the pack at the foot of the bed, on the sheets now wet from my melted ice pack.

Mae tore the dog into three pieces and reached to place a piece in my mouth, holding it very lightly with her thumb and forefinger, as if feeding a wild, wounded animal.

"What, no mustard?" I said. Still no smile. She solemnly fed me the next piece, and the next.

"I really like your shoes," I said. They had originally been nondescript white—and now very dirty—sneakers, but someone, I assumed Mae, had decorated them with multicolored swirls and crisscrossing angular lines and geometric shapes, all obviously hand-drawn, and looking a little like something Jimi Hendrix might have doodled on a napkin between recording sessions.

"Did you do that with some kind of markers?" I asked. She gazed at her shoes, and stuck one foot forward and back on its heel for a second, but said nothing in response.

"Did Mr. French send you?" I asked Mae as she sectioned apart another hot dog for me. She nodded.

"Is he your dad?"

Mae hesitated. Bit her lip. Then she nodded.

"Where do you live?"

She pointed out the window at a house directly across the street. Since I couldn't move around much in the bed, my view up and down Eastern Avenue was limited, but I could see the house Mae was pointing to very clearly.

It was an old Victorian. Very narrow across the front, but running long and deep into the lot, and backing up to a steep hill that sloped up two or three hundred feet to Columbia Parkway, a major thoroughfare running from downtown Cincinnati out to the eastern suburbs. The house sat on the far left of a row of six similar houses, each separated from the next by alleyways barely ten feet wide. Immediately to the left of the French house was an old single-story building housing several storefronts.

Mae fed me three more hot dogs until I said, "Enough." She stuffed what remained of the package in the pouch of her sweatshirt and headed for the door without a word.

"Thanks for the hot dogs," I said. "Can I get something to drink?"

She turned around in the doorway and nodded yes.

"Like some water or Coke or something in a big glass I can put here on the windowsill. That I can reach by leaning over? And a straw. A really long one. Don't forget the straw, OK?"

She nodded.

"And tell your daddy or Odell I need to talk to one of them, OK?"

She was gone. From the window, I watched her trot down the long flight of steps and across the street to the old Victorian.

———

As soon as Mae left, I pissed my pants.

Darkness came with no lights on anywhere in the apartment, so I either fell asleep or fell into some kind of fugue state induced by exhaustion and stress. Either way, I was gone from the world, or at least I hoped so, because Wonderful Byrd showed up several times during the night. He brought a cheeseburger and put it just beyond my reach. I heard a horse clip-clopping down the street outside the window. It was Falcon with Wonderful on board, waving as he passed. Near dawn, he stood at the foot of my bed and sang an *a cappella* version of "Everybody's Got Something to Hide Except Me and My Monkey" from the *White Album.*

It was almost noon the next day when Odell finally showed up with a pitcher of water and some straws.

"What the fuck happened to you guys? I'm dying here," I said.

"Been busy," Odell shrugged.

"Did you ever think I might need to piss?"

"Oh. Yeah. No, I didn't think about that."

"Take this brace and bandage and crap off my knee. I'm going to walk. Fuck what the doctor said."

Odell took all the stuff off my knee and put my backpack on the floor next to the headboard.

"Now the pants. Take my pants off."

Odell stood up straight and looked at me and crumpled his face.

"What?" I said. "I sure as hell can't do it."

"You pissed your pants?"

"Thanks, Sherlock. I had no idea."

Odell pulled my jeans off and dropped them on the floor.

"Underwear too," I said.

"You're kidding."

"Hell no, I'm not kidding. Get them off me."

Odell pulled my pissy underwear off and threw them on top of my pissy jeans and wiped his hands on the sides of his pants.

"Now cover me with the sheet."

Once covered, I said, "Did you guys get my medications?"

"Right here," he said. Odell pulled three bottles from his shirt pocket and rattled them.

"Hold them up so I can read them," I said. "OK, give me two of the white ones, and one each of the other two."

Would the narcotics make my Wonderful sightings better or worse? I didn't care.

Odell gave me the pills and held the water pitcher up to my mouth. Then I told him to set it on the windowsill and put a straw in it. After Odell left, I experimented with standing up and walking. My knee shot harsh jolts of pain into my calf and up my thigh and privates with every step, but I was determined not to be left at the mercy of these imbeciles.

Was this a kidnapping? Was I a hostage for some inexplicable reason? I decided to wait before formulating a strategy to escape. It's hard to play a game without knowing what the game is. And like Stu, I didn't want officials involved like police or social services. I was afraid Judge Vander or Howard Granger, or both, had warrants or BOLO alerts or whatever out on me.

I limped half-naked down the hallway, taking one step with my good leg and half-dragging my injured leg along with me, stopping frequently and resting against the bare wall studs until I made it to the bathroom.

My arm was bent ninety degrees at the elbow in the cast, and turned so it crossed my stomach at the bottom of my ribcage. But the fingers were free. So, if I bent over at the waist, I could reach my privates and direct the flow of urine into the toilet. I didn't need a fancy maneuver when naked, but experimented with the technique for later, when I could get some dry pants back on. I also worked out a plan for cleaning myself after defecating, but I would need Odell to get me a section of water hose for that. I sure as hell didn't want that cretin wiping my butt.

I wasn't entirely sure he could manage his own.

———

"Why you want this piece of hose?" Odell asked when he finally showed up with it.

"So you don't have to wipe my ass," I said.

"I sure the fuck ain't wiping your ass."

"Then ram some of it good and tight up the bathtub faucet," I said. "And put plenty of duct tape to hold it on."

Odell left, and I tried it out. It worked.

After using the toilet, I stepped into the tub and leaned over to turn the water on with my free fingers. I gripped the hose with my loose fingers and leaned forward, pointed the hose where it needed to go, and cleaned my nether regions. I'd just invented the first hillbilly bidet.

It wasn't perfect, but it enabled both Odell and me to live much happier lives.

———

Several days later, my walking had improved considerably.

My injured knee hurt like a bitch if I put too much weight on it, or if I moved too quickly in a lateral motion, but the swelling was down, and I was resting against the wall studs much less frequently as I made my rounds.

Since I was living pants-less—Porky Pig style—I kept a sharp watch on the street for Mae and her daily delivery of frankfurters. When I saw her coming, I'd get in bed and drag the sheet and blanket up above my waist.

My new mobility allowed me to scout the surroundings, since I could now get to all the windows. Although I'd lost track of time, I knew it was not yet June, since school buses were still running every morning and afternoon. One bus stopped a half block down from St. Empty, the name I gave my new prison, the former but now defunct St. Vitus.

Mae never got on a school bus in the mornings, and she never got off in the afternoons. Maybe Stu or Mae's mother drives her back and forth every day? But I never saw a woman come or go from the house, and I almost never saw Stu drive anywhere. I'd see him come out of his house around ten each morning and walk across the empty lot between his house and the row of businesses next door. He always walked around to the back of the building, then disappeared inside.

From the signage, I could make out four names on the storefronts: Polly's Café, French's Dry Cleaners, Aunt Ruby's Clothes & Consignment, and Rory's Tally-Ho Club. But Stu wasn't going through the back door of French's Dry Cleaners, he was going into Rory's Tally-Ho Club every morning and almost never coming out.

Mae showed up once a day with the hot dogs, wearing the same clothes every time. After the first couple of days, I told her to bring a plate and a long, sharp stick or a long serving fork, like the kind people use on Thanksgiving for the turkey. She brought a long fork. The revised feeding procedure was for Mae to tear up several dogs on the plate, and then I could use the fork to spear a piece and then tilt it up high enough to reach my mouth. Mae sat on the floor and watched in fascination as I did this.

"These are delicious," I said. "Do you make them yourself? Old family recipe, perhaps?" Mae smiled a little for the first time.

"Where do you go to school," I asked.

"Mac ... uh ... Mac ... McKramer," she said.

"Is that far?"

She shrugged.

"Do you ride the bus?"

She shook her head No.

"Does your daddy take you?"

She shook her head No.

"Your mom then? Your mom takes you to school?"

She shook her head No.

"So you go to school, but nobody takes you?"

She shrugged again.

"Please God don't tell me Odell is responsible for taking you to school."

She fiddled with her shoelaces and ran her fingers across the toes of her dirty psychedelic sneakers, and after a long pause, said, "My daddy takes me."

"Does your mom live with you and your dad?"

"No. She didn't want me. So I came to live here."

I decided I was quizzing Mae too much. She was naturally sad and introverted, and my questions were clearly making her uncomfortable. And I felt like a real asshole for making her say that aloud, that her mother didn't want her.

While she might have been uncomfortable answering my questions, Mae didn't seem to be in any hurry to leave. In fact, she was staying longer and longer each time. She spoke little, and then only in response to a direct question. But she liked to walk around the apartment with wonderment, and she loved to go to the back bedroom and look out over the river at all the houses and buildings across the way in Kentucky, or at boats or barges moving up and down the waters. While it was good for both of us to have some company, I had to be careful and not let her stay too long, especially since I was buck naked under my covers.

"You better go home now," I said.

She nodded. Got up to leave.

"I have a special request for dinner tomorrow, OK?"

She turned and looked at me quizzically.

"Do you think you could find me some hot dogs somewhere?"

She laughed. An audible laugh. First one.

"And tell your daddy I need my car."

————

Mae wasn't the only one wearing the same clothes for a week.

I still wore the same shirt from when I drove out of Texas, buttoned only around my neck like a small, filthy cape.

My pants and underwear lay in the same heap where Odell had tossed them that first day. All my other clothes and other worldly possessions—except the backpack with Sunny's money that I had managed to always keep in sight—were still in the Green Lizard, and I had no idea where French had taken it.

I watched up and down the street every day, hoping to see Stu French or Odell or some other French employee drive it up Eastern Avenue and park it in front of St. Empty.

I watched, but it never came.

The next morning, I stood in the front doorway of the church with the door partially open and only my head sticking out so as not to expose my nakedness to the world. I waited for Stu to leave his house to walk over to the back door of the Tally-Ho Club. I didn't know if I could be heard or not from that distance, but I planned to scream like a tornado siren. At last, I spotted him.

"Mr. French! Mr. French!" I shredded my throat screaming at him. He kept walking.

"Mr. French. Stu French. Stuuuuu Freeeench!" I kept shouting it. He finally glanced my way and paused. My heart jumped. He crossed the street and climbed up the steps of St. Empty to me.

"Well, hey there. How are you mending?"

"Where's my car? I need all my stuff from the car." Stu pushed the door open, and I stepped further back inside the church, where I couldn't be seen from the street.

"Jesus, are you walking around naked in here?"

I turned my back to him and leaned into one of the walls to shield myself, and spoke to him over my shoulder.

"That's what I'm trying to tell you people. I don't have any clothes. You left me so long that first day I wet my pants. They've dried out now, but there's no way I can put them on by myself."

"OK. OK. No problem. I'll get somebody over here," he said.

"Didn't Mae tell you I needed my car?"

"What? Who?"

"Mae. Your little girl."

"Where did you see her?"

"You know, when she comes over with the hot dogs. I need something else to eat besides hot dogs, by the way."

"Odell, that moron! I told him to take care of you. *Just him.* Christ, what a shithead. OK, OK, I'm going to kick Odell's ass and get this all fixed up. No problem."

"And my car. I need my stuff. I'm losing my mind in here with nothing at all. No clean clothes, no books, no one to talk to except Mae."

"Yeah. Yeah. About the car. As it turns out, the shop's a lot busier than I knew. Major backup. But we'll get to it soon, I'm guessing only a few more days. You can't drive anyway, so no harm, am I right? In the meantime, I'll send Odell or Booker over to handle the clothes situation."

"And my books. I've got to have something to do here besides stare into space."

I'd already re-read the paperbacks I had in my backpack and read the entire journal containing my mother Julia's last published poem for at least the twentieth time.

"Not to worry. I've got it," Stu said, and patted my back as he left.

———

No one came for two days after that.

Not Mae, not Stu and definitely not Odell. No food, no water (although I had the butt hose in the bathtub that I could drink from if I got desperate enough). The school buses had stopped running, and it was getting hotter and hotter in the apartment. Even if my arm had been free, the window frames were so thickly painted over that I doubted they would open. I grew up thinking it was cool "up north." I was wrong and learned that Cincinnati rivaled East Texas on the humidity scale, each night in bed in that airless apartment was like being trapped under a feverish, sweating hog.

Sleep was near impossible except in short fits, and I would have welcomed even fitful sleep if Wonderful had stayed away. Sometimes it was just footsteps in another room. Or his disembodied cries. On the worse nights, his scream would jolt me upright from a brief bout of sweaty sleep, "Call my mama! Call my mama! Call her, come get me."

For much of each day, I camped out near the front door of St. Empty with the door standing partially open. That let me catch a breeze now and then and scan the street for any signs of my captors.

I paced around and around the perimeter of the apartment as both mental and physical therapy, slowly rejuvenating my knee, which was still shaky but getting better and stronger every day.

The windows in the kitchen and bathroom faced a small, neglected park directly east of St. Empty. There was a softball diamond with a ragged, chicken-wire backstop and a few scattered picnic tables. On one of my circuits around the apartment, I saw people gathering for a game.

All the players were adults, mostly men but also a few women. I leaned against the kitchen sink and watched as one team took the field, and the first batter stepped up to the plate. It was Odell. Odell struck out, and then Stu stepped up to bat and hit a triple on the first pitch.

I guessed they were all employees of French Enterprises. It was all very informal, no umpires or uniforms, but plenty of beer and snacks. A company softball game on a lazy Saturday afternoon. I started screaming Odell's and French's names, pointlessly, of course, since they couldn't hear me through the window and would have ignored me anyway.

When they were done, all the equipment—bats, balls, and several gloves—went into two large canvas bags stenciled "S.A. French" on the side, which Stu and Odell gathered up and walked back across the street and down the block to French's house. I rushed around to St. Empty's front door and started screaming out again at Stu and Odell, but they never looked up, and quickly hauled all the ball equipment into the house.

Odell showed up the next morning and immediately picked up my jeans and underwear from the floor where he had left them the first day.

"Gonna wash these for you," he said. "And I brought you breakfast." He dropped a McDonald's sack on the bed. "Egg McMuffin."

"Unwrap it and put it on that plate and hand me the long fork."

Odell did as I said, then took my clothes and headed for the door.
"Where's Mae?" I asked.
"She's gone."
"Gone where?"
"Went to her mama's."
The fucker was lying.

Chapter 27
With a Little Help
from My Friends

Odell started leaving an Egg McMuffin and a Coke (with lid and straw) inside the front door of St. Empty every morning, but he never returned the jeans and underwear he took to wash. I lay in wait for him several mornings, but it did no good to shout and demand my car and my stuff back. There was always an excuse. I could cuss and rave at Odell as much as I wanted, but his last word was always, "I can only do what Mr. French says."

French came out of his house and went to the Tally-Ho every morning, and every morning he ignored my shouts. My plight was not accidental; French and his enterprises could not be that incompetent. He wanted me for something.

A storm of fears hit me. What? Why? Are they going to kill me? No, they would've done that by now.

Unless they look in my backpack.

Then they'll kill me for sure.

———

I poked in every corner of my brain for a plan. Could I bribe Odell?

Get him to buy me some pants and drive me somewhere for a thousand dollars? How about two thousand? I dropped this idea as too risky. If anyone found out about the money, I would be powerless to keep them from taking it. They could take the cash and the Lizard and drop my naked body in the Ohio River, and five months later, some fisherman would find me fifty miles downstream. No one would have any idea who I was or where I had come from. Or care.

I could see a phone booth two blocks down from the Tally-Ho. There was also a Metro bus stop there. Maybe I could get to that phone booth and call the police, and take my chances with them. But I didn't have any coins of any kind. A hell of a thing—over $25,000 in cash in my backpack and no way to make a damn phone call.

I couldn't walk naked into Polly's Café and ask to change a twenty. And while the police might temporarily rescue me from French, they were going to ask a lot of questions, which would connect me back to Texas, and probably expose my whereabouts to both Granger and Vander.

French had me trapped. What could I do after all? Walk out of St. Empty buck naked? Yes, I thought. That's exactly what I'm going to do. I'd wait until the Tally-Ho closed around three a.m. and the neighborhood went dark and quiet, and if Stu French wouldn't come to me, then I would kick on his front door and wake him in the middle of the night and raise hell until I got some answers. No way he's calling the police.

I floated in and out of restless sleep until all the lights were off at the Tally-Ho Club. Almost no one was on the streets. I gripped a pillow in my loose fingers and let it hang like a giant fig leaf over my genitals, then headed down the stairs of St. Empty to Eastern Avenue.

At street level, the headlights of a parked car popped on, and I dropped back and slipped around to one side of the old church. The car drove off, and I trotted as best I could on my weakened knee over to French's house and up onto the wraparound porch.

I kicked the front door several times with my bare foot. I kicked and kicked and shouted. Dogs barked three doors down, but no lights came on in the French house, and no one came to the door. I walked all around the house, searching for some sign of life.

There was a detached garage on the back edge of French's lot, but no cars. I stepped up on the back porch of the house and pressed my face against a glass panel in the back door and looked into Stu's darkened kitchen. I kicked the back door. No response.

Defeated, I sat on the back steps and looked up the hillside at a stretch of railroad tracks running parallel to Columbia Parkway. As I sat there in the muggy night air, sweating and deciding my next move, I heard a soft, weak murmur.

At first, I couldn't locate the source, but soon narrowed it down to French's basement. It was so faint it would have been impossible to hear had it not been in the dead silence of three-thirty in the morning, something like the muffled cooing of a dove. Was it a radio left on? Or a small puppy or kitten?

The foundation of the house was rough-cut blocks of limestone, some of them broken and crumbly, stacked to a height of about three feet, completely encircling the house. There were narrow basement windows set among the limestone blocks, two windows on the east and west sides of the foundation, and two in the back.

I bent to see in one of the windows on the back side, but it was blacked out from within, either painted with black paint or covered in dark cloth. I tried another window, and it too was blacked out. All the windows were covered from the inside.

Basements were an entirely new concept to me. Coming from East Texas, I had never seen a house with a basement, so I thought, maybe this is how it's done up here, you black out your basement windows? But looking around, none of the other houses on the street had blacked out windows.

I decided my naked midnight raid on French's house had been a failure, so I retreated to St. Empty to come up with another plan.

My new plan began the next morning.

I stood behind the front door of St. Empty and stuck my head out and hollered at people walking by. Since I was naked except for my fig-leaf pillow, I called out only to men for the first two hours.

During the third hour, I called out to anybody. Some would stop and look for a moment, then move on. A few would shout back and say, "Sorry" or "I'm late for work" and keep moving. Most people just picked up their pace to hurry past the weirdo shouting from an abandoned church.

About noon, I saw an older man coming out of Polly's Café with a large brown paper sack. He was driving a pickup with lettering that read "Keller Welding, Repair, & Steel Erectors."

"Sir! Sir! Sir!" I shouted. "Can you help me out, please? Please?"

He put his sack of food in the cab of his truck and climbed the steps of St. Empty.

"What's going on, friend?" he said.

"I know this sounds crazy, but I'm kinda trapped in here." I positioned the door between us so he could only see my face.

"What do you mean, trapped?" He flashed a nearly toothless grin at me and chuckled.

"It's really hard to explain. The guy across the street hit my car a few weeks ago and I got hurt. Basically, I'm stuck in here without any clothes or any food, and nobody's come around for days."

"You talking about the guy who lives right over there?" His eyes flared, and he stabbed a finger at French's house.

"Yeah. Mr. French."

"Well, son, if you've got tangled up with Stu French, then there's not too much you can tell me that I won't believe. That is one sleazy bastard. Why don't you let me in? Tell me what's up."

He stepped inside and looked me over, looked at me standing there naked with my only arm in a cast and clutching the ridiculous modesty pillow to my crotch.

"Lord God," he said and shook his head, and then began to survey the shitty conditions inside St. Empty. "Lord God."

I sat on the bed and told him the story of how I'd become the prisoner of St. Empty, and the bizarre conditions of my captivity.

"Son, you're like a little bug that fell into the spider's web. Sit tight for a while, I'll be right back."

He walked across the street to Aunt Ruby's Clothes & Consignment, and on his way back, grabbed the brown bag from his truck.

"Got you some clean clothes here," he said. He helped me into some new pants (still no underwear) and a clean plaid shirt, which he buttoned around me like a cape.

"Thank you. Thank you," I said, tearing up despite my best efforts. He picked up the edge of a sheet and dabbed my eyes.

"My name's Billy Wayne Bastrop."

"I'm Loy Dean Keller," he said. "But people who know me call me Lodean. Where you from?"

"Texas."

"A cowboy, huh?"

Lodean took a hamburger and a can of root beer from the brown bag. He put the hamburger on my former hot dog plate and retrieved a large Old Henry folding knife from a scratched-up leather scabbard on his belt. He cut the hamburger into several pieces and handed me the long fork Mae had left there.

"Eat up, Cowboy," he said. "I got to get back to work. And I'm taking you with me."

Chapter 28
Fixing a Hole

L odean and I drove down Eastern Avenue a couple of miles, hugging the Ohio River. We soon reached a fork where Eastern angled away from the river, and Kellogg Avenue split away and ran alongside the Ohio.

Not far out Kellogg was Lodean's home and workshop in a heavily industrialized area. All up and down the highway were rough, low-rise metal buildings, some as small as houses, others as large as football fields.

A sprawling petrochemical tank farm lined a long section of the riverbank alongside mountainous piles of coal, iron ore, rock, and salt in open-air storage pits, recently offloaded from barges floating down-river from Pennsylvania or West Virginia. Across Kellogg from the tank farm sat a multi-acre junkyard stretching at least a mile, with the entire complex surrounded by a high fence made of corrugated tin panels and declaring in red letters ten feet high, "S. A. French Salvage."

It was early summer, and while the hillsides and neighborhoods of Cincinnati were rapidly turning luscious green, this section of

Kellogg was immune to changes of seasonal color, set in a permanent palette of gray, rust, mud and rot.

Lodean gave a running narrative as we drove through the East End, pointing out various structures he had built or repaired or improved: a warehouse here, an overhead crane there, the awning on a used car dealership, the pipe-framed fence around the coal yard.

As we rode, I sized him up. He had a sixty-five-year-old face—carved by cold winters and burning summers—on a thirty-five-year-old body. He retained most of his hair and much of it was still black and lay in tight curls across his head, although he kept it covered with a grimy Cincinnati Bengals ball cap. Bushy, scraggly sideburns hung from the Bengals cap toward a boxy jaw. Lodean smiled his snaggle-tooth smile constantly and laughed easily, and you could see right away that if a fight broke out, you would rejoice to have him on your side and curse the gods to see him lining up against you.

Lodean owned about three acres between the tank farm and a large marina, right on the river. There, he had a modest, white, two-story wood frame house with a small porch on both the front and back, both with porch swings.

Some distance past the house was Lodean's workshop. We drove past the house and up to the workshop, which was yet another metal building with a calico quilt look to it because Lodean had built it from discarded and leftover sheet metal of various colors and styles scrounged from job sites. But it was solid, and the roof didn't leak, and this was where he made a living for himself and his wife, Ada.

Parked next to the workshop were a couple of well-used and muddied trucks and another larger truck with a crane mounted on it. The crane sported a sixty-foot boom towering into the sky at a steep angle, the whole contraption scarred and tattered around the edges and looking to be almost as old as Lodean himself. Old and knocked around but very able. All the vehicles' doors were hand-stenciled—no doubt by his own hand— with "Keller Welding, Repair, & Steel Erectors."

Lodean drove his truck right up to the gaping front doorway of his shop. I could see a crew of three men working inside, sparks and smoke swirling around them. They dropped their tools and welding leads when they saw us, eager for lunch. We got out with the burgers and the drinks, and everyone sat at a table in one corner of the building. Lodean put my Army pack at my feet.

"This is Teasly, Selvin, and Pinky," Lodean said to me as he put the sack of burgers and drinks on the table.

"Billy," I said. They took off their heavy leather work gloves and threw them on the table. Without his gloves, I could see that Pinky was missing the little finger from his left hand.

Lodean's men passed the bag around and Pinky was the last to get it, and he said, "Lodean, we missing a burger. Here, you want the last one?"

"You take it, Pinky. I done ate," he said and winked at me.

"Man, what happened to you?" Teasly said and pointed at my cast.

"I was stopped for gas, and a truck loaded with junk backed into my car. When I went to look, a load of scrap metal fell on me and broke my arm. Hurt my knee too."

"Ouch!"

"French's junk," Lodean said. "He told Cowboy here he would fix his car, then put him up in one of those shithole slums he owns, and then put Odell in charge of looking after him. That was three weeks ago, still no car."

"Frenchie! Goddamn that cocksucker," Selvin said, and threw a wadded-up napkin at the table.

"Odell's a retard," Pinky said. "Everybody knows that."

"I don't think he's an official retard," Teasly said. "He's just not real smart."

"All right, that's what I mean. I don't mean he's no drooling retard. I'm just saying if I somehow got my boots filled up with piss, I wouldn't look to Odell to do the pouring."

"Where'd they put you up?" Teasly asked me.

"An abandoned church on Eastern Avenue. I think it used to be called St. Vitus."

"Vitus? Patron saint of dancing. And snake bite. That place was condemned," Pinky said. "I bet Stu French bribed somebody to get his hands on it."

"Don't matter to Frenchie. Fuck that sorry bastard," Selvin said. He spit tobacco juice in a Minute Maid can. "Lodean, you and Ada worshiped up there, didn't you?"

"Yep. Used to be nice. Once upon a time."

"Ain't that where you had Robby's funeral?" Pinky asked.

"Did," Lodean said. "Right there at St. Vitus." He took a sip of Coke and stared out the open door of the workshop.

"Fuckin asshole French," Selvin said and pushed back from the table, picking up his gloves.

Lodean and his crew finished their burgers, and the boss stood up and said, "Boys, get on back to work. I gotta check on Ada." He walked off toward his house.

"His wife is deranged," Pinky said to me once Lodean was out of earshot.

"She ain't fucking deranged, Pinky," Teasly said, shaking his head in disgust. "There ain't nothing wrong with her mind. She's got a palsy is all. A shaking palsy."

"Lodean takes real good care of her," Pinky said. "That's all I'm saying. She shakes so bad, he has to feed her."

———

Keller and his men worked the rest of the afternoon, and I watched from a distance, obeying Lodean's number one rule: never, ever look directly at the flash and glow of the welding, unless I wanted to add blindness to my growing set of disabilities.

"Come with me, Cowboy," Lodean said when they were done for the day, "I got something to show you."

I followed him out the back door of the shop with my pack hanging from my loose fingers. He pointed at a small travel trailer, rounded on either end and covered in bright silvery metal. Lodean opened a padlock on the front door and motioned me to go inside.

It was quite small, probably no more than sixteen feet from end to end and appeared barely used. There was a cramped bed on one end, a small table on the other end with built-in wraparound seating, and a toy kitchen in between, complete with a miniature sink, a two-burner stove, and a suitcase-sized refrigerator.

It also had a stainless-steel toilet, lavatory, and shower stall crammed into a broom-closet-sized bathroom right next to the bed. Practically all the space at the head-and-foot level held storage cabinets with firm latches.

"How do you like it?" he asked. "It's practically brand new. Nobody's set foot in it since I parked it here."

"Nice."

"It's French's," he said. "I built him a warehouse upriver from here, and the bastard never fully paid up. Still owes me seven thousand dollars."

"So, he gave you this trailer?"

Lodean laughed and reset his cap.

"Hell no, he didn't give it to me. One day, a couple of months ago, I just hooked onto it and drove off. I'm sure he knows who got it. He can have it back any day he wants. For seven thousand dollars."

"He didn't call the police?"

"Trust me, Cowboy, Stu French ain't never calling the police. He settles his own business, one way or another."

"Jesus. Seems like he owns everything in Cincinnati?"

"No, but he owns about half of everything down here in Little Appalachia."

I shook my head and smiled at Lodean's audacity. He patted the little sink and grinned a big, broken grin.

"You're welcome to set yourself up in here, instead of sleeping in that rathole you're stuck in. You'll be a lot safer out here. And who knows, once you get that cast off your arm, I might turn you into an ironworker."

"Thank you for the offer. It's very tempting, but I'm afraid if he thinks I'm gone, I'll never get my car back. It's got all my clothes and possessions. And I really don't want to lose that car. It's important to me."

We walked back to the workshop.

"If you can work out your business with French, and you want out of that shithole, you're welcome to hang out here till you get back on your horse. Let me see to Ada, then I'll run you back to St. Vitus."

I took my pack and waited for him at the shop where I marveled at the skill and efficiency of his crew as they measured and cut several long I-beams using acetylene torches.

When Lodean returned, he said, "Ada's not doing too good, so Pinky will drive you back. Now listen, Cowboy, I'm going to come over and check on you every day about noon and then again after work. And I told Pinky to put a lock on the inside of that door for you. You can't sleep in there every night with that door unlocked. Not in this neighborhood."

———

"You're sure lucky it was Lodean who found you," Pinky said as we drove. "I've worked for a lot of people, and I'm telling you, he's the best man I ever met. He's generous as fuck, and will never, ever let you down."

"I'm beginning to see that."

"And he hates that motherfucker French."

"I can see that too."

"French got his boy Robby killed."

"How?"

"Robby and his daddy had a falling out. Robby didn't want to do construction work, so he went to work for French. That broke

Lodean's heart, 'cause he knew it would lead Robby to no good. He was afraid his boy would end up in prison working for that bastard."

"Prison? Really?"

"Yeah. French is into all kinds of monkey business. We built a warehouse for him about ten miles upriver a while back. Lodean don't want to admit it, but I got buddies who tell me French uses that building to stockpile speed and pot and shit. He's got all kinds of people down in Kentucky supplying the stuff, then he has it boated across the river directly into that warehouse. He's got drivers who haul it into downtown Cincy, or up to Columbus—big business up there with Ohio State—or over to Indy. Even as far as Chicago, I hear."

"Did Lodean know he was building a drug warehouse?"

"Hell no. French told us it was for road salt. But everybody knew he was a slippery snake. At the time, it was just another job. Anyway, Robby worked as a driver for French. He and one of French's apes named Booker were running a load to downtown Cincy, to a neighborhood called Over-The-Rhine. I guess the deal went bad or something, so when the shit started flying, Booker drove off and left Lodean's boy behind. That's how Robby got beat to death."

"When?"

"About five years ago. Have you run into Booker yet?"

"No. Just Odell."

"Odell's pretty harmless. But watch out for Booker. He's one damn mean hilljack."

"I've only met Stu and Odell so far. And Mae."

"Who's Mae?"

"Stu's little girl. About twelve. They sent her over with some food."

"French ain't got no kids. But he's rumored to have two wives who don't know about each other. One down in Louisville, and another one over at Indy."

No kids? My bowel jumped. Then who is Mae?

"French and Booker is the cause of Selvin being deaf in one ear."

"Selvin's deaf?"

"In one ear, he is. Selvin made the mistake of borrowing money from French. He was late paying up, so one of French's boys got him in a headlock while Booker held an ice pick to his ear. Selvin tells it different, but knowing him, he probably fought back, and Booker jammed the pick in."

"Jeez."

"Oh, you can't miss Booker. He's about a head taller than you or me, muscled up with carrot-top hair and glasses with thick black frames."

We parked in front of St. Empty and Pinky said, "Well, here we are in Frenchie Town. Did you know that's what they call this stretch along here? That's what they call it anyway when they ain't calling the whole East End Little Appalachia. Hell, people call us Toothless Appalachians down here. Though not to our faces."

Pinky gave me a big smile and pointed at a gap in his teeth on the left side of his face.

"It bothers some people, what they say. But shit, it don't bother me none."

At St. Empty, Pinky grabbed my backpack and a tool bag and a four-foot section of iron pipe from the bed of his truck. Once inside, he drilled holes on both sides of the double doors, and mounted metal brackets to each door about thigh-high to me. Then he closed the doors and dropped the pipe across the brackets, barricading the door from the inside like a castle keep.

"That'll keep the wolves out at night," he said, noticeably proud of his handiwork. "Step over here and see if you can get it out with your loose fingers there."

I could do it, slide the pipe sideways, and then remove it from the brackets and lean it up in a corner so I didn't have to bend over very far to grab it again.

"How about other doors?" he asked.

"I think they're mostly boarded up. Or padlocked from the inside."

"Good. Lodean says for you to bar this door every night, you hear?"

"Will do."

Having secured me, Pinky loped down the steps to his truck and drove off into the gathering dusk of Frenchie Town.

Chapter 29
Nowhere Man

Lodean came by every day for the next three weeks, bringing me food and helping me change clothes. Because of his kindness and help, I was able to survive until the first week of July when I got the cast removed—thanks to Pinky driving me to the clinic.

Fully armed, so to speak, it was time to rescue the Green Lizard.

———

French stood on the sidewalk in front of Tally-Ho at dusk, talking to a tall red-headed man wearing glasses. Booker, I assumed. They went inside and I crossed the street and followed them in.

I took a chance and left my backpack inside St. Empty rather than risk taking it into the Tally-Ho with me, cramming it into the space between the wall and the refrigerator. I figured I could see anybody going in or out of St. Empty through the front windows of the bar.

Inside Tally-Ho, a long bar lined one wall where a bartender stood counting money and writing notes in a book. Three men sat drinking at the bar, and two men played pool at one of the tables near the front door. A row of booths lined the wall opposite the bar, all empty except for one against the back wall, and that was where Stu French sat with Booker.

"Well, well, well," French said, "looks like Texas is all healed up."

"Mr. French," I said, "where's my car?" Booker put his glasses on and stood, facing me. Pinky was right, he was a full head taller.

"No problem with the car," French said, eyeing my arm. "Nothing to worry about, it's very safe. Got it in storage for you. You couldn't drive it anyway, so we've been taking good care of it."

"Where is it? Exactly?"

"It's safe."

"When can I get it?"

"Not so fast, we need to discuss how you want to pay."

"Pay? You said you'd cover everything. You ran into me, remember?"

"Oh, no no. I didn't run into nobody. Booker, did I run into somebody?"

"No, you didn't hit nobody, Stu."

"Your load of metal fell on me. Your crap broke my arm."

"You owe us for rent and food," Booker said.

"Don't forget medical," French said and sipped coffee from a china cup, trimmed in silver and gold around the brim and handle.

"I don't owe you shit."

Booker took a step toward me.

"And, you owe us for storing your car," Booker said.

"So, you're not giving my car back? Is that it?"

"Not till we get paid."

"Time to call the police," I said, and started out. The two pool players moved to block the door.

"Sit down over here, Texas," French said. No choice really. I sat in the booth across from him.

"I had a friend at the precinct run your license plate. That car's registered in Knope County, Texas. Looking at you, young as you are, I'm guessing you're a runaway. Now, if anybody's going to make a call, it's going to be me calling Knope County to see if you drove off with your daddy's car. Or is it just a straight-up stolen car? Maybe there's people looking for you who you don't want to deal with? Am I right?"

There was no way out of the building. All I could do was sit there, surrounded by French and his men.

"Okay, you say I owe you money. How much to get the car back?"

"We can work something out. I'm not unreasonable. I don't expect a kid like you to reach in his pocket and come up with it all at once. Instead, you can do some work for me. I've got a couple of things in mind."

Goddammit. How useless can $25,000 be? No way to use the cash to buy my way out of Frenchie Town without getting robbed or killed. I'd have to play along with these thugs until I figured something out.

"What kind of work?" I asked.

Booker jutted his chin toward the door, and the two guys blocking it moved aside. He started out and motioned for me to follow. We walked to the empty lot next to French's house.

"Meet me in the parking lot behind Tally-Ho at ten tomorrow night," Booker said. "You're gonna help me make some deliveries."

"Deliver what? Where?"

"None of your concern. Just shut up, show up, and do as you're told."

"How much work will it take to get my car back?"

"Stu will decide that." He reached into his front shirt pocket for a Marlboro.

"Fuck if I know what Frenchie wants with a cripple like you. If it was up to me, I'd knock you in the head and tell God you died."

Booker grinned and lit up. Huffed out a wry laugh and blew smoke at his shoes.

"Who knows? Might be he's gonna turn you into a movie star."

I rushed back to St. Empty and clawed my backpack out from behind the refrigerator and started searching for a back way out of the old church. *Movie star?* What the fuck did that mean?

In the darkness of the basement, I groped until I found a single lightbulb that worked. It was enough. There was a door hidden behind a thick stack of long folding-leg tables. I fought off some spiders and knocked the tables aside one by one to get to the door.

There were only two boards nailed across it, both nailed on the inside. One was loose, and I worked it back and forth until it came off. I found a piece of pipe in a dark corner and pried the second board loose, and popped out into the night.

————

I hopped a Metro bus eastbound toward Lodean's place. The driver scowled when I handed her a twenty, but stuffed it in her shirt when I said, "No change." Just after nine, I knocked on Lodean's front door.

"Cowboy? What's going on?" I'd awakened him from a deep sleep in front of the television.

"Is your offer of the little trailer still good?" I asked.

"Sure, sure. Let me get the key."

We walked out to the trailer and he said, "You still don't have your car?"

"French says I owe him money."

"That sleazy damn bastard."

"He wants me to work off what I owe him."

"Oh, no. Hell no. Don't do that."

"I think I'll have to give up on getting the car back."

"I'll drive you around tomorrow and we'll look for it. I know a place or two he might have stashed it."

Lodean opened the padlock on the trailer and handed me the key.

"Stay here as long as you want. The water and electric are all hooked up. Got a full tank of propane too."

"Thank you, Lodean," I said as he was leaving for his house. "I can pay rent."

He didn't speak or look back, but waved a hand in the air, dismissively, as he walked away.

———

I put my pack on the miniature table and rummaged through it for no reason, I guess, other than to remind myself that the money was still there. To feel I had some small measure of control, even if that control was over only a speck of my life, that which fit in a frayed Army surplus backpack.

I counted the cash again and put it in neat stacks and stared at it. I had to face the ugly facts and dip into the money to buy another car. Sacrificing the Lizard seemed the only way to escape Frenchie Town. The thought of French or Booker driving around in Sunshine's car nauseated me. Driving it—or worse—crushing it into a cube of junk. That car had ceased to be inanimate steel and glass and rubber to me, not at that time. That car was Sunny. Truth and reverie made tangible.

———

Sleep refused me, so I started rummaging through the array of drawers and compartments in the trailer to see what kind of stuff Stu French had lost to Lodean: plates and glasses and silverware. Sheets and blankets and towels. Two bottles of Scotch and a bottle of Canadian Club.

In a compartment under the settee, I found a flashlight and a mahogany box full of poker chips with "SAF" inlaid in the wood and several packs of playing cards with the same monogram. In that same compartment, there were two large manila envelopes duct taped to the roof, hidden from view by the poker box.

Each envelope held four reels of 16mm film. I unrolled a few inches of the black-and-white film and held it to the light. A naked girl, nine or ten years old, sitting on a mattress on the floor in the corner of a dark room. A few frames later, a second naked girl appeared and joined the first one on the mattress. They began touching each other. I crammed the film back in the envelope.

The first girl was Mae. A couple of years younger, but definitely Mae.

———

I grabbed a handful of money and the flashlight and locked my backpack in the trailer, then caught the Metro back to Frenchie Town. French's house was dark except for the front porch light. I walked around the entire perimeter of the house, stopping every few feet and listening closely near the basement windows, to see if I could hear the same soft, muffled sounds I'd heard a few weeks earlier. All quiet.

Using the butt of the flashlight, I scraped at the seams between the limestone foundation blocks until a narrow section of mortar crumbled away, leaving a slit. I shined the light through the slit. I couldn't see much, but what I saw set my hair afire. A mattress in one corner of the basement, exactly matching the one in the film.

I grabbed a rock from the flowerbed. Broke the glass in the back door and stomped wild through the house until I found the basement door.

I turned on the lights in the basement. There was the dirty mattress from the film on the floor in one corner, with sheets draped along the walls on either side. An improvised backdrop. Lights on metal stands pointed toward the mattress. A tripod sat between the lamps, but no camera.

I found three wire dog crates placed along the rear wall, lined with blankets. Two of the cages held some ragged stuffed animals and picture books. Candy wrappers. Empty soda bottles. The cages were large enough to crate Great Danes, but they were not used for dogs.

The cages looked empty, but I opened each one anyway to make sure no child lay hidden under the blankets. I didn't find any kids, but I did find one of Mae's psychedelic shoes. The sight of her shoe ignited a rage that pumped through my heart and lungs and throat, and for a moment, I thought the top of my skull would launch into the ceiling of French's depraved hole in the ground.

Keys jangled on the front porch and footsteps entered the house and creaked across the floor above my head. It was Stu French, and he was humming as he came home.

I couldn't go back up the basement stairs and the only other way out was through a locked, steel door in the very back of the basement. I had to stay put and hope he didn't see the broken glass in the kitchen.

French moved from the foyer into the front parlor, still humming.

I searched the basement for a hiding spot and found a closet just beyond the dog cages. Something inside blocked the door, but I pushed until it gave way and stumbled over the obstruction—a canvas duffel stuffed with French Enterprises' softball gear. I pulled the bag clear and quietly lifted out one of the aluminum bats.

I stood there, bat in hand, and realized it wasn't a closet. It was a darkroom with bottles of chemicals and supplies for film development strewn around and long strips of film hanging from the ceiling like stalactites.

He kept humming until a phone rang somewhere in the front of the house.

"Booker?" French said. "Where the hell are you? OK, soon then? How much? Fuck, I didn't pay anywhere near that much for the last kid. OK. OK. Drive around to the basement door in the back when you get here with her. I'll go down and unlock it."

He hung up and walked down the hallway. His footsteps squeaked on the basement stairs, one, two, then he stopped cold for a long while.

What was he doing? Stopping on the steps like that? Holy Fuck.

I'd left the light on in the basement. Shit shit shit. Maybe he'll think *he* left it on.

"Odell," French called out. "You down here?" I heard him ease down the last few steps, heard his loafers scratch across the concrete floor. Another pause.

Each of us stood still as gravestones, me behind the darkroom door, him somewhere in the middle of the basement. Movement again. He was coming my way.

I readied the bat overhead. French bolted through the door with a claw hammer in one hand, his other hand pawing for the light switch. I landed a blow to the side of his head, and he stumbled to the floor, swinging blindly with his hammer and caught me squarely in the ankle, triggering a lightning strike of pain from ankle to groin.

Yet no amount of pain was going to save Stu French. I threw my full strength and weight into the next swing—he was a much easier target now, prone on the floor—and the bat met his skull with a cracking sound that fueled me, an ugly, exultant noise. Another hit, then another, and I no longer felt myself in my body or even in the room; I was working on instinct, pounding, *this is for Mae*, pounding again, *this is for Mae. Oh, Mae, where are you? Where are the others?—yeah, crack, motherfucker, crack.*

Booker would arrive any moment. I kept the bat and limped through staccato jolts of pain upstairs into French's kitchen and grabbed some paper towels. Went to the front hallway and found the telephone. Grabbed a pencil to dial the operator and told her children were being held captive and raped at French's street address. With a paper towel, I wiped the pencil and phone clean of fingerprints, and any door handles I might have touched.

Hobbling out the back door, I wiped my fingerprints and blood off the bat, then wrapped a paper towel around the bat's handle to avoid any more prints and carried it across the street to the softball field, where I leaned it against the backstop in some tall weeds.

It was time to get off the streets before the police arrived. I cut through the shadows back to St. Empty and, before going in, watched as headlights strafed the garage near the back of the house, and a French's Dry Cleaners van pulled up beside the back porch. Booker got out of the van and carried something—or someone—wrapped in a blanket around the corner toward the back entrance to the basement.

Two police cruisers pulled up within minutes. Lights flashed, voices shouted, and trucks came and went through most of the night. At one point, I looked down from St. Empty and saw a policewoman leading a young girl to a cruiser. Later, I saw Booker in handcuffs.

Had killing French shifted anything on karma's scales? Anything at all that I could offer to atone for having killed Wonderful? French would have killed me, so I had little choice. But maybe you don't get karmic credit if you're just acting to save your own ass?

I discovered that it wasn't the killing of French that bothered me. What bothered me was how little remorse I felt after bashing his skull. I was afraid I wouldn't sleep that night, but I was wrong.

I barred the door to St. Empty and slept deeply until sunrise.

Around dawn the next morning, I rode the bus back to Lodean's and took the two envelopes of film, and left before Lodean got up.

I wanted to make sure he'd never be caught with the stuff on his property, and I never told him what I had found. Not knowing Cincinnati, I rode the Metro aimlessly for a couple of hours before spotting a small park perched high on a hill above the Ohio River.

I took all the film off the metal reels and put the film in a trash barrel with some newspaper and set it all ablaze with a cigarette lighter from the little trailer. I stood and watched to make sure the film was completely destroyed. I threw the lighter into the flames.

It was imprinted with "SAF." That stands for Stuart Asshole French.

Chapter 30
Eleanor Rigby

I never made it to Canada.

Three years after killing Stu French, I was twenty-one and still living in St. Empty. According to the newspapers, French's businesses, money, and property were entangled in a Gordian knot of lawsuits and countersuits among the U.S. Justice Department, the State of Ohio, Hamilton County, multiple banks, and each of his two wives.

The local TV news would show a headshot of French sometimes, one with his stupid, toothy grin. The same damn one over and over. Sometimes I had to do a double take, or blink rapidly, to see that it was French I was looking at and not Cecil Bastrop as he appeared in the old family photos Sunny had given me. My brain would occasionally switch the two, and every time I wanted to erase that stupid grin. Just wipe it out. Cut it off, tear it off, blast it off. Something.

Decrepit St. Empty must have been near the bottom of some priority list somewhere because nobody ever told me to move out. I decided free rent was free rent, so why not stay put? And although I hated to turn Lodean down when he again offered the little camper as housing, there was no way I could live in the porn-hole trailer he had lifted from French, after finding those heinous films in there.

Not long after French went down and Booker was arrested, Pinky and Lodean helped me search for the Green Lizard across French's Little Appalachia holdings. We searched used car lots, body shops, scrap yards, truck stops, parking garages, all with no luck, and few people to answer questions since most of his former employees had scurried away into the hills of Kentucky or West Virginia or ran north to Toledo and Detroit.

But one Sunday afternoon, Lodean drove the Lizard up Eastern Avenue and parked it in front of St. Empty. He'd taken a pair of binoculars and climbed the sixty-foot boom of his construction crane to scan the full acreage of French's Salvage and spotted one of her tail fins peeking out between the rusted hulks of two old Texaco tankers, all three vehicles parked against the back fence. Lodean and Pinky cut a Cadillac-sized hole in the sheet metal fence with an acetylene torch and crowbarred the bent fender up off the tire so it would roll. Then they hotwired the old Caddy and drove her right to me.

Lodean never had a clue I was involved in French's death. He hired me to answer phones, handle some bookkeeping, and prepare job-cost estimates. But the real reason he wanted me there was to keep an eye on Ada when he was working in the shop or away on a jobsite, to make sure she had regular meals and got her meds on time. The business office for Keller Welding, Repair, & Steel Erectors was a former sunporch he'd enclosed at his house, so I was never more than a few steps away from Ada in her TV chair.

I made sure St. Empty's utilities got paid every month, and in the best tradition of Sunny swiping Jesus pictures, I stole an official notice of condemnation from a downtown building and posted it to the weighty front doors of the old church, hoping to make my squatter's home irrelevant—if not invisible—to the rest of the world.

I bought a few pieces of second-hand furniture and rugs and moved my bed to the back bedroom overlooking the river. Then I converted my former prison-cell front bedroom into a library. A damn nice library stocked from every used bookstore, flea market, antique store, and library sell-off I passed by or spotted in the local penny rags.

I had decades of international and American novels, histories, biographies, Greek and modern philosophy. The Bible, Quran, Bhagavad-Gita. All of Shakespeare and two dozen poetry anthologies spanning a hundred years and a grab-bag of random almanacs, encyclopedias, and dictionaries.

With my rent-free situation, a shoebox full of Sunny's cash, and a modest paycheck from Keller Welding, I should have been well set. But I still had two big problems no amount of money and shelter could solve: Wonderful Byrd and Mae.

Booker eventually talked in prison, trying to get a better deal. His attorney worked out a trade: the locations of bodies for a few years knocked off his sentence. He'd been convicted on drug, trafficking, and child pornography charges, but the State had insufficient evidence to convict him of killing anybody. He "had a suspicion" as to where French and his toadies "might" have disposed of some kids, once their film careers ended.

There was no avoiding press coverage of the search; it was on the front page of every newspaper and the lead story on TV and radio broadcasts for about a week. At first, it appeared Booker had sent the police on a snipe hunt. The first dig was in a Kentucky tobacco field that sat alongside the Ohio River between Maysville and Vanceburg. That yielded nothing.

There was a limestone cave not far from the tobacco field, and spelunkers wormed through it for days with no luck. Local police with dogs and state troopers from Kentucky and Ohio and neighboring states, along with dozens of volunteers, fanned out a mile or two from the original dig and combed the fields and woods without locating any evidence.

The break came when an eighty-year-old woman named Nina Leigh Kaye—who lived in an isolated nineteenth-century cabin set high on the ridgeline above the Ohio—drove her ATV down a steep dirt road to the river where Kentucky State Troopers stood studying maps.

"They're on Poe Island," she said, pointing upriver, her overlong platinum hair braided and beaded. She wore a poncho pieced together from animal furs and brightly colored scraps of cloth, and every finger sported a ring. They shunned her at first as an eccentric recluse, a distraction to their task.

"Poe Island?" the head trooper laughed out the words. "There's no Ohio River island by that name."

"I don't know what y'all call it, but my mama called it Poe Island. She read us Poe stories and poems when we was kids. Scared us shitless. She feared the river, didn't want us down there. She knew that island being so close to our place would be a draw to us, like a big fantasy castle. So, she told us that's where Poe lived. Told us he was a lunatic and he lived there with all his demon friends, and anybody who showed up there'd never come back. They'd end up trapped in one of his tales. That was her way of keeping us out of the water. Keeping us from trying to swim or float over there. Worked too. Till we was about twelve."

"Ma'am, you must be talking about Heron Island."

"Call it what you want, but from my cabin, I seen lights there at night on and off the past few years. Seen boat lights float up to it. Too dark and too far to see people, but I could hear boat engines and see lights. Then seen lights moving in and out of the trees on the place. I bet anything that's where them little girls are."

Nina Leigh Kaye was right.

The remains of thirteen girls were buried there, aged six to twelve. Some had been dead for years; some were more recent. Mae was one of them. Mae Esa Langley from Cragmont, West Virginia. Her mother sold her to a tall red-headed man in black-rimmed glasses when she was three.

––––––

Two weeks after the bodies were found, I drove Kentucky Highway 8, hugging the Ohio River to Maysville, where I hired a guy named Shel to take me upriver fifteen miles to Heron (Poe) Island on his boat.

"You know that's still a crime scene," he said, "but if you got money to waste, I'll take you. You just taking pictures?"

"No. I want to get off on the island."

"They won't let you do that. There's police tape all over." Shel's disgusted expression was clear. He thought I was either an idiot or a pervert. Maybe both.

"No refunds, understand?"

"Sure. Let's go."

The island looked larger than what I'd seen on TV or in the newspapers. It sat two hundred yards from the Ohio riverbank and at least four hundred yards from the Kentucky side. It was a wedge about a mile long, and the east end was the thick part of the wedge, at about a quarter mile wide. At the wide end stood a pair of fractured, pockmarked limestone towers rising a hundred feet from water level, with trees and bushes poking from between boulders like whiskers. The rest of the place tapered down to a rocky plain just above water level and was covered in thick hardwood forest closely matching the riverbanks on either side. I better understood what Nina Kaye, the poncho woman, had said in her TV interview, how such a place would grab a kid's imagination. It was indeed beautiful—forbidden but just within reach—and vibrated with the promise of magic and dangerous adventure.

There were no other boats about and Shel, while gruffly complaining about getting himself arrested, landed me on the sandy, flat west end. I pushed through thick brush and honeysuckle deep into the woods until I spotted a grotesquely large rectangle of yellow crime-scene tape. No workers were there. The coroners had pulled bodies from several holes in the rocky earth, the graves scattered among old-growth ash, oak, and hemlock. Here and there, muted shafts of sunlight broke through to the forest floor.

I crossed the tape and walked to the middle of this makeshift Poe Island cemetery of unmarked—and now empty—graves. I stood and looked at all the holes in the ground for a long while, then sat on a boulder.

One of these holes had held Mae and maybe others who were caged in French's basement that night I went to his house naked, in desperation, and kicked barefoot on the door. Why didn't I do a better job looking in the basement? There were noises. I heard something. Why didn't I break the glass in the back door and go in *then*, not weeks later? I could have saved them. I was there. Just feet away. Just one rock through one window away.

For the last several weeks, I pushed myself to think about something else. About truth and beauty and peace. About the beauty of trees. Or the graceful, peaceful curves of the Ohio River. I told myself that for every Mae there were thousands—no, millions—of children who are loved and cherished and nurtured into happy adults.

But the internal happy talk never worked. My thoughts always circled back to Poe Island and Mae. Darkness drove out light, and the next news cycle seemed to always deliver another Mae. Another Mae, and I'm back—naked at midnight on French's porch, kicking his door like an imbecile. And there are rocks, rocks, rocks—so many fucking rocks—rocks I don't pick up. Rocks I don't use. Rocks that save no one.

I was consumed by the awfulness of it all. The constant stream of Maes, like an immense dark river, and I no more than a rock island in its current. Impotent to stop the endless shit-colored river from flowing over and around. Rocks are useless. Rivers grind rocks to dust. This is the truth of rocks.

I placed Sunny's shoebox full of Jesuses at my feet. Took a handful. Walked among the holes and scattered them. Some on this one. Some on that one. Some on each and every one.

There were plenty to go around.

Chapter 31
Drive My Car

The morning of my suicide broke as bright and sweet as a schoolgirl's smile.

I sat on the bed and counted the remaining money. Shoebox of cash in hand, I drove to Children's Protective Services and handed the box to the receptionist.

"A donation," I said. "Fifty-one hundred dollars." I turned to leave.

"Wait! Don't you want a receipt?"

———

I drove out Columbia Parkway—Wonderful Byrd riding shotgun and Mae in the backseat—with no particular plan for how to end it, other than I wanted the Lizard and me to go together if possible. Maybe I would find a high bridge somewhere. With enough speed, I could launch us off a high bridge into deep waters. We'd had rain like an incessant toothache all that spring, and all local rivers—The Ohio, The Great Miami, The Little Miami—were above flood stage and disastrously high in some areas.

I drove until the Parkway became Highway 50, and I made a few random turns, but couldn't find a bridge that was tall enough to work. Soon I was out in the country on Round Bottom Road, a narrow two-lane road skirting thickly forested hills.

Railroad tracks ran parallel to Round Bottom, and every mile or two, another country road would cut across my path and across the railroad tracks. That could work. A train.

I spotted the gated entrance to a pasture where two horses grazed, and pulled off Round Bottom and backed the Lizard up against the gate so I could see clearly up and down the tracks. I turned on the radio and waited and listened for a train.

After an hour, I started the Lizard to make sure the radio hadn't drained the battery, and saw a light turn green on one of the train control towers.

There it was, about a half mile away, the single cyclops headlight on the front of a Baltimore & Ohio freighter. With the train maybe a hundred yards out, I drove onto the tracks and killed the Lizard's engine. The radio played on—Jefferson Airplane's "Somebody to Love."

Wonderful sang along with Grace Slick, quietly at first ...

The B&O bore down fast on the passenger side of the Caddy ...

his voice rising the closer the train got ...

I saw the engineer frantically working the controls as the big engine's steel wheels flooded the ditches of Round Bottom Road with sparks and smoke ...

shouted lyrics about truth and lies and love ...

A blur of color and a wall of sound ...

his falsetto piercing and forlorn, cracking in spots ...

A deafening steel howl of death. A calm silent blackness ...

Wonderful's voice fading, fading, gone.

———

I awoke cockeyed and prone on the ground with two beautiful young women. One sat astride my waist, vigorously dry humping me. The other kept kissing me softly and repeatedly. Had I awakened in the middle of a ménage a trois conducted on the floor of a gorgeous green forest beneath a crystalline sky? Shit, Sunny was right all along, and I was a dumbass. There really is a heaven. But how'd I get in?

"He's awake," the humper said. "Check his pulse again."

"Pulse is weak but steady. Forty-five," the kisser said. "He's coming around."

Unfortunately, my senses surged back, and a state of full consciousness brought slashing pain to my head, neck and back. The humper was not humping me at all but straddled my body to put more leverage and muscle into her CPR. And the kisser was no kisser, but working in tandem with the humper, blowing air into my lungs.

The humper was Tess James, and the kisser was Ella Schultz.

They were roommates and best friends and both worked as ER nurses at Christ Hospital in Cincinnati. Tess and Ella were enjoying a day off from work and had turned off Round Bottom onto Tealtown Road on their way to the Cincinnati Nature Center and a day of spring hiking.

They saw the train hit and drag the Lizard down the tracks and then throw it off the twenty-foot-high trestle that crosses above Tealtown Road. The Caddy was bent into a crescent, with its nose and tail essentially pointing in the same direction. But the heavy, solid car had served as my steel cocoon, saving me from fatal—or even very serious—injury.

I had multiple cuts from flying glass and some bad bruises, but no broken bones. When the paramedics arrived and took over for Tess and Ella, they suspected a concussion and told me I would need to spend a night or two in the hospital until everything could be checked out.

"Which hospital?" I heard one of the paramedics ask the other.

"Where do *they* work?" I asked him, pointing at Tess and Ella.

"Take him to Christ," he said over his shoulder to the driver. Then he leaned in close to my face and winked and whispered, "Good choice."

———

I was at Christ Hospital for two days while they checked me head-to-toe for broken bones and various possible internal injuries. Both Tess and Ella stopped by briefly at different times, and while Tess was there, Lodean and Pinky came in.

"Cowboy, you just can't seem to stay out of trouble," Lodean said, grinning and pulling my toe.

"How did you know I was here?"

"I saw your car on the TV," Pinky said. "They been showing pictures of it on the news. It had to be you, an old green Caddy with Texas plates. Them plates are way expired, by the way."

"Bad place for it to conk out on you," Lodean said. Then he spoke to Tess, "He's one damn lucky young man, ain't he?"

"Very damn lucky," Tess said. Pinky was taking full notice of Tess. When he was done staring at her front, he moved around the bed to get a full view of her backside.

"What happened, did it just die on you right there as you was crossing them tracks?" Pinky asked, eyeing Tess's rear.

"Right," I said, "just died on me."

"Man on the news said if that train'd been going any faster, you'd be dead for sure," Pinky said.

"Well, it's good to see you're still in one piece," Tess said. "I've got to get back to work."

Pinky smiled broadly and tipped his cap to Tess as she passed him in the doorway, then he leaned his head out the door and watched her all the way to the elevator.

"Umm mmm," Pinky said once his focus returned to the room.

"I've got to hand it to you, Billy. You been here one day and got a fine little foxy nurse like that visiting with you. How you manage that?"

"Like Lodean said, I'm one very lucky young man."

"I'll tell you what lucky is. Lucky is when she comes back tonight to give you a sponge bath," Pinky grinned and shook his head in mock amazement.

"Boys. Boys," Lodean said. "Listen to me. Pussy makes you crazy. Love makes you sane."

"Ever'body likes to go crazy now and then," Pinky said.

"You going to get yourself into all kinds of trouble one of these days," Lodean said to Pinky. "Listen to me. Stop chasing and start loving."

"How bad is my car?" I asked.

"Bad," Lodean said. "We saw them haul it into the salvage yard over by the shop. It's just a big, twisted piece of iron now."

Fuck. Now I've even killed the Lizard.

"How hard did the flood hit you?" I asked.

"Pretty damn hard. I managed to move all my vehicles and most of my tools to higher ground. The house was flooded up to the second floor, so we lost everything we had in the basement and first floor. Ada and me been staying up at Teasly's place in River Mill. The shop's in really bad shape. Some of the foundation was washed out, and the west end collapsed. French's little trailer was swept plumb away downstream. Nobody's seen it since."

"Fuck that bastard," Pinky said. "They still ain't got no idea who killed him. I bet it was Booker. You know, like they got into some kinda bad argument."

"I'd guess it was the Cleveland Mob. Whoever it was ought to get some kind of damn medal," Lodean said. "I hope they flat-ass get away with it."

Pinky went for coffee, and Lodean looked out the window at the parking lot and said, "You sure you're gonna be OK? You're looking a little down these days."

"I'll be alright," I lied.

"You got anybody you want me to call for you? Some family back home?"

"Not a soul."

Lodean and Pinky were the closest things I had to any family, and that struck me as ridiculous and pathetic, given that I knew so very little about them, and they about me.

"Remember that day you found me hiding behind the door of St. Vitus?"

"Cowboy, no matter how old and senile I might get, I won't never forget that."

"And you walked in and there I stood, total buck-ass naked trying to hold that little pillow over my dick?"

Lodean grabbed a pillow off the bed and held it across his crotch, then laughed and pounded the bed railing.

"I bet you thought I was completely nuts."

Lodean slapped his thigh and leaned backwards laughing.

"I think I might be crazy," I said, with a straight face.

Lodean stopped laughing but still gave me his warm, familiar smile.

"You've never asked me about my arm."

"I figured if you wanted me to know, you'd tell me."

I told him the story of how Cecil killed Lucy and cut me. And I told him about my part in the death of Wonderful Byrd, and how I'd been seeing and hearing him at night in St. Empty. I didn't tell him about killing Stu French.

"Lord God," Lodean said when I finished the story. He shook his head and looked me in the eyes for a long moment.

"I think I'm insane," I said, tearing up. "I mean for real."

He shook his head and put his hand on my knee and said, "You know what I say about crazy? You're just as crazy as you wanna be. And you ain't. And it seems to me you've got some good reasons to keep on living."

I knew then that Lodean had divined the truth about my "accident." He wasn't buying the BS story about the Lizard's engine dying on the tracks in front of an oncoming train. I turned my face away in shame and embarrassment. Wanted to hide under my sheet. What must he think of me now?

"Baby sister Lucy, God bless her, didn't have no choice between living and dying," he said. "Nor did little Mae. And neither did that poor soul Wonderful. But you sure the hell do. *You*." He poked a rough-skinned finger into my chest. "You need a reason to live? Do it for them. Show some respect and love for your sister. Do it 'cause you owe it to that boy who died by your hand. He can't live 'cause of you. Live and do some kinda damn good in the world, alright?"

My only response was an almost whispered "Lucy."

Pinky returned with three coffees, and Lodean thankfully changed the subject. The three of us talked briefly before Lodean announced that they should go and check on the receding waters at his property before dark.

Lodean shook my hand as he was leaving.

"Do me a big favor, will you? I want you to forget about Cecil. Hate don't cure grief. There ain't no use throwing a good man's life down a shithole after a bad one. Jesus will take care of ole Cecil in the end. You forget about him. You hear me?"

I nodded at Lodean. I had the greatest respect for him, but I knew I would have to deal with Cecil myself one day. It couldn't be left up to Jesus. It was far too important for that.

———

I lay awake most of that last night in the hospital, dwelling on what Lodean had said about living for Lucy and Wonderful and Mae. To not disrespect the dead by throwing my own life away. It was worth trying. Live for love. Fight through the pain and live for love.

And it occurred to me that Lennon was wrong when he wrote "All You Need Is Love." It's not. But it may be the *main* thing you need, a happy life being otherwise unobtainable without it, like trying to light a flame without air.

Is there any person, no matter how rich, or powerful, or famous who is truly happy being unloved?

<h1 style="text-align:center">Chapter 32
Another Girl</h1>

The next morning, I was released from Christ Hospital. I no longer had a car or any money, so it seemed like the perfect time to start dating. Besides, I was freshly bathed and shaved, and some candy-stripers had washed my clothes for me overnight, and I was looking as good as it got. Without bus fare, I faced a long walk back to the East End and St. Empty, so instead I took the elevator down to the ER with the hopes of running into Tess or Ella. It was nine o'clock.

By five that afternoon, I'd read fifteen magazines cover to cover and watched dozens of doctors, nurses, and others begin and end their shifts. I decided to give it one more hour, and I was rewarded because at six o'clock, Ella arrived for work.

Both Ella and Tess were bright, vivacious knockouts, but in different ways. To my taste, Ella was the pick. Her personality was more subdued and introspective compared to Tess. She was a bit classier in speech and bearing, whereas Tess was extroverted and flirty. She had a Nordic scrubbed frost-kissed look to her face, framed by long auburn hair worn in a ponytail at work, but flowed free otherwise. Ella's eyes were what wowed you, though. A rare shade of blue, a blue muted by a dark undertone, a shade I called china blue.

Ella was the pick only if you were forced to choose. Honestly, I was perfectly willing to get as close as I could to both of them, because Tess was also hang-tongue gorgeous and fun to be around. When she walked, her short blond hair bounced, every curve strained the seams of anything she wore, even hospital scrubs.

But Tess wasn't on duty, and Ella was, so I watched Ella clock in and disappear into the back trenches of the ER. I hung out in the waiting room near the nurses' station and kept a watchful eye, and tried to think of an excuse to talk to her.

Around eight that night, I spotted Ella talking to a doctor at the nurses' station. Then she went across the hall into the break room. I hurried past the nurses who guarded access to the treatment area and ignored the "Staff Only" sign on the break room door and followed her in. Several people sat drinking coffee or sodas, some talking, some watching television. Ella took a cup and filled it with coffee; that's when I ambushed her.

"Hi," I said.

"Oh," she said. "You shouldn't be in here."

"I wanted to say thank you again for helping me, and also say that I'm really sorry I spoiled your day off."

"No worries. How are you? Your noggin OK?"

"It's fine," I said, "there's not much in there to hurt."

"That's great. Now go before the floor nurse spots you. You don't want to tangle with her."

"To really apologize, I'd like to buy you and Tess a beer somewhere," I said, hoping that my suggestion of including Tess would make it sound more social and less forward.

Ella leaned against the counter, added cream to her coffee, and stirred. She gave me a tiny, almost imperceptible smile—bemused, the way a teacher might look at a third-grader who's just slipped her a love note.

"There's this place called Tusculum Tavern," she said. "We've been hanging out there lately. It's down in the East End."

I must have looked shocked, because when she saw my reaction to "East End," she immediately took an apologetic tone and said, "I know, I know, it's pretty redneck down there, and I wouldn't normally go, but this is a Tess thing. She's kind of a wild child."

"No, it's fine. I live very close by. In the East End."

"Oh, God." Her neck and face flushed. "I'm sorry, I didn't mean to offend you."

"None taken."

"Are you from Kentucky?" she asked.

"Texas," I said. "Why?"

"Your accent. I knew you were from somewhere south."

"Tusculum Tavern sounds great. When?" I said, trying to close the deal.

"Why don't you come by tomorrow night. I can't promise we'll be there because you never know with Tess, but if we see you there, then we'll see you there."

I made the long walk to St. Empty and scoured the place for loose change and found enough to take the bus the next morning out to French's Salvage Yard. The receding flood waters had left the place a muddy, stinking shithole. I told the yardman I wanted to sell the Lizard for scrap, and the two of us waded ankle deep in black, putrid mud out to see the wreck. He told me he'd give me two hundred dollars.

"I'll take it," I said.

"You got a title? Got to have a title or I can't make a deal."

"It's in the trunk with some other stuff I need."

He pried the trunk open with a crowbar. It was like a lunatic's library had exploded in there, with paperback books and dozens of pages of my handwritten summaries of novels and bad poetry and worse song lyrics scattered, clumped and spread in all directions. Boxes of miscellany I'd never bothered to move into St. Empty. I sorted papers until I found the title.

Back in the salvage office, I handed the yardman the title.

"Your name's Sunshine Bastrop?"

"It is," I said. "But everybody calls me Sunny."

"Sign it here," he pointed a muddy finger at a line on the title. "I'll get Irene to notarize it later."

Our business concluded, I waded back out to take one last look at the Green Lizard. She was crushed, gouged, bent nearly double, and packed with broken glass—yet, amazingly, still in one piece, though barely recognizable as a car. I ran my hand along the crumpled roofline and marveled at how Sunshine had managed to reach out from the grave and wrap me in iron and save my sorry ass one last time.

———

I got to the Tusculum Tavern about eight o'clock that night. It was in a Civil War-era two-story brick building. A neon sign hung out front proclaiming "Tusculum Tavern – Since 1910 – A Third Rate Saloon."

Downstairs was a bar and a scattering of tables and pinball machines. Upstairs was another bar and a small, raised stage where a band was setting up their gear. There were almost no tables or chairs upstairs. That space was reserved for a large dance floor ringed by a few pool tables.

Cantilevered out the back of the building from the upstairs bar was an open deck with tables where you could drink and enjoy the view across the Ohio River toward the hills of Kentucky. This part of the neighborhood had suffered only minor flooding. I sat at the upstairs bar and ordered a beer and prayed Tess and Ella would really show up.

It was an eclectic mix that night, hard-bodied ironworkers and bargemen and an off-duty cop or two, mixed in with softer, pudgier Hyde Park and Mariemont boys—mostly accountants and lawyers—who had come slumming in the East End, some of them bringing their pretty, preppie girlfriends (foolishly I thought) because the iron-workers and bargemen immediately targeted the fresh-scrubbed Hyde Park girls, blowing past their boyfriends as if they were invisible. Soon, Tess and Ella arrived and rewrote the laws of gravity in the place.

There might have been women with better bodies, but not many, and none I had seen in real life who equaled Tess's overtly sexual aura. There was something in the way she moved, something in her gait and swing and the tilt of her head and the way her dark eyes lingered on you that seemed to pump up your testosterone and shut down your brain. Tess knew she could be as discriminating as she pleased among the men in the tavern, because there wasn't one there who wouldn't dump his aged grandmother in the snow for a few minutes with her.

I felt guilty for willfully ignoring Lodean's admonishment about seeking pussy simply for pussy's sake, but being within eyesight of Tess had a way of loosening my grip on reason. I thought ceaselessly of the CPR episode next to the railroad tracks, when she straddled me and rhythmically pushed her soft, warm crotch into my waist.

Tess and Ella hit the upstairs bar about ten o'clock, just as the band—Dancin' Hissy—tore into Chicago's "25 or 6 to 4." The girls took up stools on one end of the bar. Although I headed for them immediately, three other guys had already pounced.

"Cowboy!" Tess said when she saw me. Ella gave her a look.

"You made it after all," I said.

"Why are you calling him that?" Ella asked.

"'Cause it's cute. And 'cause that's what his granddad calls him."

"Oh, he's not my granddad," I assumed she was talking about Lodean. "Just a friend."

"I heard you were buying us beers, Cowboy," Tess said.

"Whatever you like," I said.

"Hudys," said Ella.

"Hudys all around," I held up my bottle and tried to catch the bartender's eye as she moved our way.

A ponytailed guy wearing a black wifebeater and mutton chop sideburns asked Tess to dance, and she took a long slug of beer and they hit the floor. Tess danced with wifebeater and then she danced with a guy who could have arrived from court or maybe church, who tossed his suit coat and tie on a pool table.

Tess worked up a thirst dancing and came back to where Ella and I were talking and drank two Hudys and ordered all of us tequila shots, complete with lime and salt. Ella taught me how to do the shots while Tess danced with two of her Hyde Park girlfriends.

"So, you're a long way from home. How did you end up in Cincinnati?" Ella asked.

"Long story," I told her the tale of my derailed attempt to escape East Texas for Canada, leaving out the parts about snake handling, psychosis and homicide. She seemed fascinated with the idea of me living in an old, abandoned church.

"I love your name for it. *St. Empty.*"

"Come by sometime and get the grand tour."

"And why Canada? Ever been there?"

"Never."

"I have. It's overrated."

"I'm from Canada," said an especially handsome guy on the stool next to Ella. "Maybe if you dance with me, you'll develop a better opinion of my homeland."

Fuck. Tess and Ella were dancing with guys who were *not* me while I sat at the bar alone. I ordered another tequila shot and a Hudy and thought about how I was drinking up the last remnants of the Lizard in a failed attempt to get laid.

I watched Tess dance her perfect body across the floor and hop up on one of the pool tables and turn it into her own personal stage. A dozen men gathered around the table as the band played "Jumpin' Jack Flash," and Tess put on a classic go-go dancer show—

minus the tall white boots—but she did have the Goldie Hawn haircut.

I downed another Hudy and stared at Tess, pumped up my nerve and asked myself, what's the worst that could happen? Then paused. Wait, bad question, history has shown my "worst" can be pretty fucking bad. But, if anything could take my mind away from Wonderful and Mae and Stu French for a while, Tess would do nicely indeed. I decided to give it a try.

I ordered two more shots of tequila and walked them over to Tess. Two of her admirers helped her off the pool table, and the band began its first slow song of the night. Tess threw back a shot and I downed the other and said, "Dance with me?"

She put her hands on either side of my neck and pushed her bosom into me and I put my arm around her, and we did a too-many-shots sway across the floor. I had no idea what I was doing since I'd never danced a stroke in my life—if you don't count the Mrs. Santa Claus waltz —but I just moved along, and she followed. Part way through the song, she kissed me lightly, sisterly, on the cheek and pressed her plump shiny lips to my ear and whispered, "Dance with Ella."

So, I did. Dancin' Hissy launched into a cover of Hendrix's "Fire." Ella and I jumped and bumped around the crowded dance floor, and we both laughed at my pitiful white-boy moves. We sat on the deck for a couple of hours after that and talked about anything and everything until two in the morning.

"I better take Tess home before she starts stripping," Ella said. "Let's get back together soon."

"Yes. Soon."

———

The next day, I took the bus downtown and from there got a taxi across the river to Kentucky, where fireworks were legal. I spent more of my quickly dwindling Lizard money and bought a handful of real skyrockets, the big ones like you see Wile E. Coyote using, not those little wimpy bottle rockets, and a small assortment of other fireworks. Back across the bridge, I went into a florist shop downtown Cincy and asked the lady how much to buy the long narrow box like the ones they put roses in.

"You don't want the roses?"

"No ma'am. Just the box."

"Vince. Vince," she shouted over her shoulder to someone in the back room.

"There's a guy out here, says he just wants to buy the box and not the roses."

"Tell him he can't get laid that way," Vince said. "But two dollars if he wants to waste his money."

I put the rockets and fireworks in the box and wrote on the card:

Can I stand next to your fire? – Billy

Then I took the Metro to Christ Hospital and left the box with one of the nurses working the ER desk.

"Give this to Ella tonight."

———

Ella knocked on the door of St. Empty about seven the next evening.

"I thought maybe we could shoot off some fireworks," she said, holding up one of the Wile E. Coyote skyrockets.

"Most definitely," I said. "And later, we can launch that rocket too."

She stepped inside and looked around, both fascinated and repulsed.

"You weren't kidding, this place is weird."

"It's kind of like me. Dark and brooding. Missing some important parts."

She poked her head in every room.

"The best view is out the back," I said.

I followed her down the hall to the bedroom.

"Killer view," she said, looking out the window at the river. "People pay the big bucks up on Mt. Adams to get views like this."

We sat in the bedroom because that was where the best view was, her in a stuffed chair and me on the bed, and watched the boat traffic on the river and talked until dark and drank a bottle of wine.

Soon we were both on my bed. Across the river in Kentucky, bright snaky tongues of lightning licked out from a black-plum sky, distant but moving toward the river. The storm bathed us in staccato bursts of light—momentarily strobing shadows of our naked bodies up the wall and across the ceiling—the storm close enough for light, too far for thunder.

Ella pressed her lips lightly to the scars marking my empty shoulder. It was less a kiss and more a metering, the way some women test a child for fever. I slid my arm across Ella's breasts and down her stomach and back up and around the whole of her body and let the heat from her ignite my bones.

Chapter 33
Get Back

Ten Years Later - 1985

Jay, my and Ella's three-year-old, flew down the stairs on his belly, backwards with tiny legs pointed down. Bump, bump, bump to the bottom. A bizarre but effective method of descending stairs, one of his many lovable quirks. Would I get carpet burns if I tried it? He climbed into my lap with a copy of *Lowly Worm.*

"Read this," he commanded.

Two pages into *Lowly Worm,* Ella answered the telephone. She handed it to me, her voice low and worried, "It's someone named Tyler. From Texas. *Sheriff* Tyler? He says he has information about your father."

The phone felt heavy and dangerous. Loaded. Jay jumped down with his storybook, and I walked out the back door, out into a misty suburban night, taking in the smells of the place: smoke from a neighbor's chimney, wet mulch, Ella's late-season chrysanthemums. I drew a careful breath before speaking.

"Sheriff?" We'd been in touch only a few times since I was waylaid in Cincinnati in the early seventies. He was still alive after all this time. How old was he now? Seventy?

"Hey there, Billy. Listen, I know it's been a while since we've spoken, but something's come up. You still interested in Cecil?"

"Always and forever."

"How soon can you get down to Brownsville?"

"You found him?"

"Bastard moved to Mexico. My contacts say he's in Matamoros."

"I'll be on a morning flight." I could barely speak. "Call you later with the details."

I was too broken up to talk further with my old friend. I didn't want to show him any tears. We had a lot of catching up to do, but I'd save that for our meeting in Texas. He was a good man, a man who kept his word. That night, he reached out halfway across the country to keep a promise he made to a one-armed boy long ago. A promise to help me hunt down my father.

———

"I have to go to Texas," I said to Ella. She'd emerged from a bath and was sitting on our bed wearing an old sweatshirt, brushing her hair, stretching out long coppery strands in measured strokes.

"Billy, please tell me what's going on. Who was that man on the phone? Why do you have to rush off to Texas?" I'd told Ella nothing over the years about Wonderful or French, and very little about Sunny.

"His name's Oren Tyler. He used to be the sheriff of Angelina County."

"That's where you were raised?" Ella was confused about my childhood geography.

"No," she quickly corrected herself. "Angelina is where you lived *before* the accident." She glanced at the empty right sleeve of my T-shirt. How could I expect a Cincinnati girl like Ella to keep straight the pointless differences between backwash Texas towns she'd never seen?

"Korvus is where I grew up. That's where I lived with Aunt Sunshine. Or as she would say, '*Aint*' Sunshine.' Angelina's two hundred miles further south. That's where I lived with my family. Before."

Ella knew my aversion to talking about Texas, and she knew I hadn't been back since I left. All that made talk of my past a dicey thing to bring to bed. Undeterred, she doled out the questions, palm up, as if hand-feeding a skittish pony.

"This man, Tyler, knows where your father is?" She searched for the right tone, chose her words carefully. I could see her thinking, what's this pony going to do? Buck, run or nuzzle?

"He's in Mexico." I struggled to keep my voice even. There was much I'd kept from Ella, betraying her with silence and omission, giving her a hole-ridden, murky backstory over the years. She moved to my side of the bed and leaned against me but still closed in with questions about my expatriate father, the retired sheriff Tyler and my newfound interest in family ties.

"You're planning to see him? You think he *wants* to see you?"

"It's just something I need to do. He abandoned me a long time ago, and I've always promised myself I'd find him. So, I'm going down there. He's not getting any younger. I want to see him before he dies." I'd hoped to leave without lying straight to Ella's face, a hope that faded with each question.

"Shouldn't you call first? Maybe not just show up?"

"He's way out in the boonies. Tyler's tried to call him but can't get through. We have to go in person." The lying had already begun.

"Want me and Jay to go with you?" I knew it was an obligatory offer. She didn't really want to miss work and drag our son to a Mexican border town.

"No. It might turn into an unpleasant meeting. I'm guessing Cecil doesn't care much for kids. Or Yankees."

She was right to be concerned. I didn't know how he'd react, what he might do. Hell, I didn't know what *I* might do.

———

While Ella slept, I sat in a chair by our bedroom window watching clouds float across the face of the moon, like translucent swans lighted from within. How had I ended up with someone as good as her? She had become a critical care nurse at Cincinnati Children's Hospital with a huge gentleness of soul that beamed forth from her, lighting her way through life. She loved, trusted, and soothed me, and sure as hell deserved the truth. I should have told her the risk I was taking. She should've known, but I wasn't strong enough to tell her. I tried to convince myself that lying, in this case, equaled love. Protection.

Watching Ella sleep, I pushed the thought from my mind that I might never see or touch her again. Her body shifted, and I heard a muffled, low moan. Then she laughed in her sleep. If only I could have saved that laugh, that warmth and comfort, and taken it with me. The perfect shield against men like Cecil Bastrop.

The trip was an insane idea. A ridiculous risk.

The November wind picked up and pushed the swans faster across the moon. Rain and sleet ticked at the window, and I recalled a passage from one of my mother's poems:

Another storm rises,
Dark breath blowing
Round shivering stars
And through the moon

In Jay's room, I kissed him goodnight and goodbye, careful not to wake him. He was already dreaming. A menagerie of stuffed animals looked down on me from netting hung above his bed. The rhythm of his breathing transfixed me, and I smiled back into the soft faces of cats, seals, reindeer, cows. A moose. Could they speak to him? Did those benevolent creatures sleep all day, dreaming of Jay? And at night, as he sleeps, do their stories seep into the dreams of their tiny master?

I sat in his room for almost half an hour. To soak him in.

Just in case.

Chapter 34
The Long and Winding Road

Along with a hundred other people, I dropped through the dawning sky toward DFW airport, sealed in the large aluminum body bag of a Boeing 727. The flight was not directly to Brownsville, but to Dallas, so I could rent a car and take a detour—a pilgrimage of sorts—through the Piney Woods region of East Texas, to Korvus.

Once we touched down and began to taxi, a flight attendant spoke on the PA system, her voice too chipper for so early in the morning.

"Welcome to Texas, y'all. I sure hope you brought your passports, 'cause you know what they say. It's like a whole 'nother country down here."

Two hours later, I was at the Peach Ridge Cemetery near Korvus, where I placed a dozen grocery-store flowers on Sunny's grave. I walked a few steps to one of the oldest graves in the cemetery, that of Moses Rose. I dropped a single flower down. Legend had it that Moses Rose was the only man to desert the Alamo when Colonel Travis told his small group of volunteers they were unlikely to survive against the onslaught of Santa Ana's army of thousands.

No one knows how Rose came to be buried there. It's not a source of town pride that the coward of the Alamo lies in their ground. In crowded Peach Ridge Cemetery, every gravesite near him remained empty but one. In a plot unwanted for almost two centuries, Sunshine Pearl Bastrop is the only soul resting next to Rose, the pariah of Texas.

Turner Bastrop lies a hundred yards away in the Bastrop family plot, alongside empty dirt he intended for his children, Sunshine and Cecil. I buried Sunny as far away from Turner as I could. Better for her to rest beside Rose, a disgraced man who wanted to live, than next to another Bastrop who deserved to die.

As for Cecil, I planned to leave his bones to crumble to dust in Mexico.

Ten Hours to Matamoros

There were no commercial flights to Brownsville from the tiny Korvus air strip, so I'd be driving it. Ten hours from the northeast corner of Texas to the southernmost tip. It would give me plenty of time to think about everything I didn't want to think about.

I gassed up the rented Chevy at Bixby Gulf, south of the cemetery, and bought a *Texas Highways and Byways* map, a Dr Pepper, and a jalapeno kolache. In the car, I took a handful of Beatles mixtapes from my duffle bag and placed them on the seat next to me.

I inserted the first cassette and settled in for a long haul. But as the miles clicked off, it got harder and harder to hear guitar and harmonica, French horn and sitar, over the chattering crowd of skeletons I'd brought along for the ride. They just wouldn't stay buried, and were already dancing—rhythmic clack and clatter—through my head.

Eight Hours to Matamoros

I pulled into Ned's Tires & Brakes to have a flat fixed. While I waited, I stared out the grimy window at a highway sign across the street:

Houston Intercontinental Airport
108 Miles

The arrow pointed due south. Brownsville was southwest, but the sign called to me. Practically screamed out to me. I should've turned there and flown home. Forgotten about Tyler and Cecil and Matamoros. Fuck. How could I risk losing Jay and Ella? I could be killed in Mexico, or worse, arrested and sent to prison. Then one day, Jay would sit wondering why his crazy fucking father molders in a Mexican prison. I'd be no better than my own father, in his eyes.

I walked outside to check Ned's progress with the tire. He had his son working with him in the shop, and the kid looked to be about twelve or thirteen, doing the run-and-fetch "gopher" work that kids that age can do. Ned called out for a spiral probe needle, but the boy brought him a split eye. Ned rose from the tire and slapped the boy hard enough to send his Astros cap flying.

"Get your head outta your ass, son. Spiral! Spiral!"

No, I had to keep going. I had to confront Cecil. For Lucy. For myself.

I paid Ned-the-prick and resumed course southwest.

Six Hours to Matamoros

I passed a series of four hand-lettered billboards near the tiny community of Kindred, between Navasota and Brenham. They were patched together from warped, faded plywood and spaced about a half mile apart:

HELL IS EMPTY
AND ALL
THE DEVILS

ARE HERE

The paint was chipped and faint, but still legible.

At Pig Mama's BBQ—attached to a Texaco station—I ordered a chopped brisket sandwich to go. A fiftyish woman with Dracula-black hair—except for a short gray tuft dead center of her forehead—brought me my lunch in a stained brown grocery bag.

"Chips?" she said with a cigarette rasp.

"No chips, but I have a question. Who painted the signs?"

"Signs?"

"The 'Hell is Empty' signs."

"My daddy did. Long ago. God knows why."

"Must have been a Shakespeare fan." I smiled.

"Who?"

"You know, Shakespeare? *The Tempest*, I think? Or could be from *Hamlet*."

"No, them words are from the Good Book. That's all Daddy ever read."

Two Hours to Matamoros

Somewhere between Kingsville and Sarita, I spotted a long stretch of snake carcasses on both sides of the highway, each nailed to a fence post. Nailed through the head and left as fodder for buzzards, hawks, raccoons. Anyone looking for a free meal.

Rattlers, copperheads, cottonmouths. At least a quarter mile of them. I pulled over and got out for a better look. Some were half-eaten. Some half-rotten. The rattles were gone—cut off by collectors —on any rattlesnakes left whole.

A few feet across the barbed wire, I saw a scrawny, juvenile possum looking up at me, partially hidden behind a cholla. Odd to see a possum in the middle of the day, unless it's sick or starving.

The snake hanging closest to me was too putrid to touch, so I walked to the next post and tugged on a fresher one. The body separated from the head after a couple of quick jerks, and I threw it over the fence to within a foot of the possum. The critter stared, motionless.

A car slowed alongside the fencerow, rolled the passenger window down.

"What the hell you doing?" A woman shouted.

"Feeding a possum."

"Weirdo," she said and turned to the driver. "Must be a Yankee." They sped away.

I continued toward Brownsville, through the double row of vipers, thinking about Sunny. Thinking about her final three snakes.

Yea, though I drive through the valley of the shadow of death, I will fear no evil ...

Chapter 35
Tomorrow Never Knows

Brownsville sits where the sharp knife tip of Texas presses into the soft flesh of Mexico, just a few hundred feet across the International Bridge from Matamoros.

I parked my rental at Guzman's Bar Paraíso on the northern edge of town and sat in the car a few minutes before going in, watching fifty-foot palms lean against the night, almost glowing, partly irradiated by the fast-food neon clinging to them, and partly lit by a butter-rum moon.

I crossed the Paleozoic shadows of the palms into Guzman's. Oren Tyler was in animated conversation with a tall, broad-shouldered Hispanic man working the bar, a man whose Mayan ancestors once cut the hearts from virgins, and whose conquistador ancestors brought horses to the New World and used them to slaughter entire civilizations. I figured the man was Guzman, since he acted like he owned the place. There was no mistaking Tyler, although I hadn't seen him in well over a decade.

Tyler had kept most of his hair, grown full of dull gray streaks, and his right forearm still showed the work of a WWII Parisian tattoo artist who once mistranslated Tyler's drunken, slurred request to ink his arm with "Texas," and instead imprinted "XXX" across the forearm of his semi-conscious customer. The old warrior loved the story of how he got "exes" instead of an outline of the Lone Star State, and that was the story that had Guzman laughing so hard he couldn't refill Tyler's shot glass with Wild Turkey without spilling a dollar's worth on the dark walnut bar.

Guzman looked up from wiping the bar and shifted his smile into neutral, glancing first at my pink polo shirt (disbelief), then scanning down my tan chinos (frown) to my white Nikes (disgust). He finished his inspection by looking me in the face with a "die yuppie" scowl, but his eyes were drawn away to my empty right sleeve. The big man threw his mouth open in surprise, almost smiled again, and poked Tyler's shoulder with a rebar finger, signaling the old sheriff to turn around.

Tyler didn't immediately recognize me. Indeed, I didn't recognize myself, fifteen hundred miles from Ella and Jay, standing in a bar with gringo truckers headed north with late-season cabbage and lettuce, and Hispanic laborers and mechanics, many in the country illegally, headed south to families in Tampico and Juarez with enough American dollars to get them through another few months.

This was a place of few colors, brown and browner, Walmart blue jeans and bluer collars. It was a place of mason jars filled with radioactive pequin peppers, the smell of handmade tortillas toasting on scarred black iron, the jukebox sounds of Freddie Fender, high and nasally and monaural. I felt the whole bar staring at me, tired gray eyes squinting through a haze of Camels and Marlboros at the odd vision of an apparently lost yanqui tourist approaching Tyler in the tentative fashion of a newbie anthropologist approaching his first silverback.

As Tyler turned around on his barstool and faced me full on, Freddie and his band ceased in favor of the whining self-pity of George Jones. He instinctively reached his right hand out to me, the way men had been offering their hands to me in friendship or empty protocol all my life. Every time it happened, both parties were embarrassed.

I could only respond with an awkward grabbing of his right hand with my left, a maneuver I'd never managed to impart with the level of masculinity it called for. It always came across more like the furtive touching of lovers rather than the peaceful meeting of men. I grabbed the back of his extended right and managed to work a few fingers into his palm, and he gave them a hard squeeze. I could see his dismay about momentarily forgetting.

"You made a big man, Billy," Tyler said, inspecting me head to shoes, assessing my height and weight, a bit over six feet and two hundred pounds. His eyes lingered a beat at the exaggerated size of my left forearm and bicep, grown large and strong, like the only apple on a tree stripped of all other fruit.

"Don't let me interrupt any lying, now," I tried to catch Guzman's eye with my somewhat forced smile, and although my East Texas accent had faded considerably from extended Cincinnati living, I tried to revive it a little for Guzman's benefit, and to counterbalance my pink polo shirt, which I realized was a particularly bad choice for the trip.

"Guzman, pour this man a Turk," Tyler said.

"No thanks. I am hungry, though. Is there a menu?"

Disgust returned to Guzman's face as he turned and shouted back into the kitchen, "Maggie!" Then he walked to the other end of the bar where two truckers had just settled, engrossed in a football game on a small television wedged in between liquor bottles.

"Are you sure it's him?" I asked Tyler.

"Cecil Bastrop? Damn straight, it's him. I walked right up to him in the Cadillac Bar over in Matamoros two days ago. Not more than five feet away."

"He didn't recognize you?"

"It was crowded as hell. And he was too drunk to care about another old gringo fart like himself walking through the bar."

Maggie delivered two longneck Lone Star beers we hadn't ordered.

"Hey, Billy. There's a new wrinkle we need to discuss."

"Yeah?"

"There's these two kids who might be a problem. The Ruiz brothers."

Tyler filled me in on what he knew. He'd located Cecil largely through Guzman's connections on both sides of the border, and Guzman was convinced the brothers were a potential complication to my plans. They were looking to kill Cecil, and were afraid I'd beat them to it.

According to Guzman, Cecil had been living in Mexico since his release from prison in Texas. He did odd jobs for a few years but ended up working as a coyote for the Gulf Cartel. Their network used old gasoline tanker trucks with false bottoms to smuggle drugs and people—both cartel soldiers and civilians—across.

A year earlier, Cecil's tanker broke down alongside Highway 77 outside San Benito. He abandoned the truck in the South Texas sun with a dozen people locked in the bottom. Three people died. Two of the dead were the mother and sister of Jesús and Angel Ruiz.

"Guzman's sweet on a Ruiz cousin who settled in Brownsville a few years back," Tyler said. "His honey told him what happened, and he told me. She says the brothers will be here tomorrow or the next day. Nobody was expecting them until next week."

"Can we talk to them?" I asked with an edge of panic. "Come to some agreement? Explain who I am, that I need to see him first?"

"No. They ain't gonna talk. I tried that already. We gotta beat 'em there or you'll be visiting a corpse. Right now, we got the advantage. I know his address and the brothers don't. Not yet anyway. We go tonight and then get you out of town."

Tyler took a long guzzle from his beer and laid a five-dollar bill on the bar.

"You gotta understand how important honor is to these boys," he continued. "They're beyond dirt poor, but between honor and money, they don't give a rat's ass about money. Nothing's more important than honor. Nothing. They've spent over a year tracking him down, and they're hellbent. They won't let the murder of their mother and sister go unanswered. It's unthinkable."

"Seven years is what's unthinkable," I said. "Obscene. Seven years is all the time Cecil spent in the pen."

"Billy, we've got a lot of law in this country, but we got piss poor little justice. Let's move over to a table where we can talk."

Tyler led me to a table near a storage closet where we couldn't be easily overheard.

"Now, all bullshit aside, son, are you sure you want to go through with this?"

"I'm sure. I can't sleep otherwise."

"You haven't seen him in over twenty-five years. There's no telling what you'll do. He's your daddy, all said and done. And there's sure as hell no telling what he will do. You got to be ready for anything. You bust in on him in the middle of the night, he's liable to shoot you before you can get a light on."

The whole misadventure had sounded good in my head, but shit was getting real. I was flooded with visions of Jay and Ella in a future without me, my fly-swarmed body rotting in a dumpster for weeks. I held my breath and averted my eyes from Tyler and called on every speck of will I had to shut down a tremble.

"I've got to do it. Put it all to rest."

"What are you carrying?"

"Huh?"

"Your gun."

"I don't have a gun."

"Mercy Jesus. Didn't you hear me say he's a driver for the Gulf Cartel? You better have some protection. No problem, I got a spare or two in my truck."

"Sheriff, you've done more than enough, and I'm very grateful. You got me this far. I don't want to tangle you up in this anymore.

There's no reason for you to risk prison or worse for me. Just give me his address, and you can head back north to Angelina."

"Now what kind of Texan would I be if I let a guy from Cincinnati—wearing a pink shirt no less—sneak into fucking Mexico and wreak havoc alone? Where's the fun in that?"

"When do we go?" I asked.

"Two a.m."

————

We shared a room, there being only one room available at the first motel we tried, and I was too tired and Tyler too drunk to look elsewhere. Tyler conked out immediately, but between the sheriff's snoring and the roar of interstate traffic just yards from our door, I lay awake. Headlights strafed through a slit in the curtain, and I was transported back to my little bedroom in Sunny's house, age four, right after my amputation.

Sleep was a terrible struggle after I lost my arm. It got worse when I moved in with Sunny, because I could still feel the damn thing, especially at night. It burned, it itched. It was there and it wasn't. Woozy from blood loss, I lay in bed, amazed and terrified at the incessant thunder of U.S. 271 traffic vibrating her house. Eighteen wheelers—laden with chickens or pulp wood or iron drilling pipe—rushed constant as heartbeats through daylight and darkness. They ran hot all the time but went full batshit reckless after sunset. It seemed the trucks rocketed directly at me, ground-hugging Detroit comets, headlights burning through the window shade. Sometimes two at once, shaking my teeth, driving bass into my diaphragm, lights stabbing into all corners of the room, painting a dance troupe of jittery Doppler-effect shadows across the walls and ceiling: the outline of a chair, distorted chest-of-drawers, exaggerated hat rack, little boy sitting up, malevolent clump of sheets, partially open door, roll of bandages, bottle of rubbing alcohol thrusting three feet high, little boy lying down, tree limbs morphing into machetes.

. . .

Barking dogs awakened me. Despite Tyler's snoring and the traffic, I must have slept some after all. For a disconcerted moment, I stroked the motel sheets, reaching for Ella in a bed that was too small and too hard and smelled of too many people to be my own.

I heard running water and the sharp coughing of Oren Tyler. I turned on a light and sat on the edge of my bed, pulling on my pants and watching him prep for our mission.

He lifted a handgun harness from his suitcase and looped it around his midsection over the top of a T-shirt, positioned so the gun —a snub-nosed .38 revolver—rode in the small of his back. He buttoned his shirt over the rig. His shirt was split in the back, so only the short handle of the pistol protruded, but his jacket covered it.

Tyler retrieved a 9mm Beretta from the nightstand and slipped it into the right-hand pocket of his leather bomber jacket. Next came an over-under double-barreled derringer, probably a .22. He put a hollow point bullet in the breach of each barrel and strapped the derringer above his left ankle, high enough to be covered by the top of his cowboy boot. The other boot did not go unarmed. He took a four-inch dagger from his shaving kit, withdrew it from an ornate dark leather scabbard, and held it up to the lamp. He grinned proudly.

"Got this in Sicily. Palermo, I think it was."

He sat on the twin bed across from me and shaved a half inch or so of silver hair from his upper forearm with the dagger, then pitched it on the bedcovers next to my leg, handle first. As Tyler pulled on his boots, I picked up the knife. It was no piece of junk, and very old. Real silver with bas relief snakes and a death's head decorating the handle.

"Nice," I said, coming fully awake and realizing where I was.

Tyler reached into a scratched and gouged leather suitcase and handed me an old police model .38 Colt revolver, and I tucked it in my belt against my belly, the cold barrel pointing at my nether region.

"Watch it, it's loaded," he said. "And very simple to use. Just point and shoot. But not at the head. Too easy to miss. Always point at the chest."

"I want to confront Cecil alone," I told Tyler.

"You sure about that?"

"I'm sure. Just him and me."

"I respect that. He's your dragon. But you still better have me nearby as backup. Stand watch outside while y'all 'talk'."

Chapter 36
All Things Must Pass

Tyler drove his truck ten miles west of Brownsville and turned south onto a caliche road toward the Rio Grande.

I fished around in my coat pocket for the frayed silk Shiva, the one Veda gave me in kindness so long ago, that day I got my first arm. The truck rocked and bounced on the rough road and the moon rose behind us. I closed my eyes and caressed the silk.

> *I am become Shiva*
> *I am become Shiva, Lord of Arms*
> *I am become Shiva, Lord of The Circle*
> *I am become Death, Destroyer of Worlds*

Within a few miles, a dirt road crossed the caliche, and there was a Jeep waiting for us at the intersection. The Jeep had a driver and a man riding shotgun—and holding a shotgun—and he was wearing a U.S. Border Patrol uniform.

"Pay the man," Tyler said.

I handed the border patrolman five hundred dollars, a quarter of Ella's and my entire savings account. They drove us off-road to the river where a man stood on a small wooden raft, holding a long pole. It looked to be less than two hundred feet over into Mexico across shallow water.

The raft quickly delivered us across the river, where another Jeep was waiting. In twenty minutes, the driver stopped on a narrow street somewhere on the western side of Matamoras. It was three a.m.

"He lives there," Tyler said and pointed to a second-floor apartment above a first-floor tobacco shop. A narrow metal staircase led up to the apartment. The driver put his hand out to me, and I parted with another five hundred dollars, apparently the going rate for tight-lipped services at that hour. He stuffed the bills in his jacket and rolled away as soon as our feet touched the street.

At the base of the stairs, Tyler pulled his Beretta 9mm and chambered a round.

"I'll be right here," he said. "Go tend to business."

I climbed toward an amber porchlight at the top of the staircase and kicked the door, hoping it was cheap and the framing would splinter. The frame cracked but held, and I worried because I'd already made enough noise to wake anyone inside.

Another kick and another and the door opened two inches but was caught by a security chain. Panicked, and expecting someone to shoot through the door, I stepped back and threw my shoulder and full two-hundred-pound weight into the chain and it popped loose.

Inside, I paused and drew the .38 and stood still for a full five seconds, looking around and letting my eyes adjust to the darkness. Not a sound anywhere. If someone heard me—and how could they not—they were hiding and ready.

Then I heard a staggered, arrhythmic snore.

In the bedroom, pale light filtered in from a three-quarter moon. I hovered for a moment over the sleeping man's bed. He was wearing black sweatpants and no shirt. There was a lamp on the nightstand—minus its shade—and I flicked it on.

"Hey," I said, gun pointed at him. Nothing. "Hey!" Nothing. "HEY!" I poked his ribs with the Colt and stepped back. The snoring stopped, and he rolled toward me and shaded his eyes from the harshness of the bare lightbulb.

"Shit!" he shouted and rolled to the far side of the bed, pawing at the nightstand drawer.

"Up! Up!" My gun shook. It was heavier than I expected.

I marched him into the living room—away from the bedroom where there were likely weapons—and flipped a light switch. A ceiling fan moaned to life, *thwap, thwap, thwap,* it's overhead bulbs bright enough to do surgery.

God, he looked so much older than I'd pictured him. His movements stiff and unsure, stutter-stepping and stooped and bow-legged, wincing and squinting against the overbright light. He was pale as bone with creped and sagging skin on his neck and arms and chest.

"Who the fuck are you? What do you want?" His words were weak, phlegmy. He coughed, trying to clear the croak from his voice.

"You work for Fuentes?" he asked. "Did Fuentes send you? Tell him I got his money."

"Take off your pants."

He snapped his head toward me, no longer squinting against the light, and snorted a half-laugh.

"Go fuck yourself."

I rammed the pistol to his forehead. He dropped his sweatpants around his ankles.

"Spread your legs."

"Are you kidding me?"

I pointed the gun at his dick. He spread his legs as far apart as he could manage, shaking.

I saw a long, wide crescent scar near the top of his inner thigh. Jagged and coarse. There was no doubt it was him. I'd finally found Cecil Bastrop, and despite a lifetime of thinking about that moment, I wasn't prepared for the shredding inside my skull and the explosive rush in my chest. Spikes of emotion jutted out in all directions: Rage. Exhilaration. Terror. Dread.

I aimed the gun back at this face. I'd caught the white whale, but had no idea what to do with it.

"Sunny told me about that scar. When the boar got you as a kid."

"Sunshine?" He exhaled the word slowly and rubbed one hand across his face. He took his time examining me, eyes tracing the lines of my face, my hair, my missing arm.

"Oh, dear Jesus. No! It ain't you!" He shook his head but kept bloodshot eyes locked on me.

"Yeah, me. Back from the dead. Pull your damn pants up."

"How is Sunshine?" Cecil struggled with his pants, stumbled a step backwards toward the couch.

"Dead. Fifteen years."

"Shit." He bowed his head, stroked his hands on his thighs. "She raised you?"

"Shut your fucking mouth. Like you care … ."

"Did y'all live in Papa's old house … ."

"What do you care? Never a word from you. Never a goddamn word. Now you want to know stuff? You destroyed all our lives. All of them. Mama, Lucy, me. Sunny too."

"I knew you lived, but not till later. After they arrested me."

"Do you have any fucking idea what my life was like? Look at this," I pointed the gun at my empty sleeve.

"Just fucking look at this, you worthless, damn piece of shit. Look at me. Look how you fucking wrecked me." Despite my best intentions, I cracked. The tears came and I let them and the Colt's grip felt good in my hand and I pointed the barrel back at his face.

"I need to tell you something," he said. "I want you to know this. I didn't aim to cut you that night. I swatted that blade at you. Sideways. Just trying to knock you down. Stop you from running away."

"But you did try to drown us, motherfucker. Both of us."

"I thought y'all was dead by then. I guess that's what I thought. Hell, who knows what I was thinking? I was mostly *not* thinking."

"A baby, goddamn it." I pushed the gun against his skull, a little too hard. The force tottered him backwards, and he flopped onto the couch.

"Lucy ... Lucy ... ," I said and followed him as he fell back, trying to keep the pistol pressed to his temple. Snot filled my nose and I blinked away tears, and the spike within me that was rage said: *Pull the trigger. Just pull the damn trigger.*

"I can see you come here to harelip the devil. I sure deserve it."

I regained my composure, but still a string of snot dripped off my nose and into his lap. My hand sweated around the grip of Tyler's gun, and I told myself to lessen the death hold I had on the thing. Relax the muscles a bit before my hand cramped.

"Did you ever think about us?" I heard myself ask and was shocked by my own words, words I never planned to say.

"Sure. Many times. Thought about you. Thought about Lucy. Spent hours in the pen thinking about her. Mostly about the night she was born, and I held her that first time. Before then, I'd never thought about having a baby girl, but Sunshine was there, and she was the one who put the baby girl in my arms. I walked baby girl down that hospital hallway when she didn't yet have a name. Just walked up and down while Sunshine stood in the door to your mama's room and watched us, and I looked down that long hall at Sunshine, and I knew all that'd happened to her. I knew how our sorry papa hurt her so deep and so harsh that such a hurt as that has no real name, evil as it is. I whispered over and over to baby girl, 'I'm taking care of you, you can depend on that. Ain't nobody hurting you. Nobody never. 'Cause I'll kill 'em.'" He jabbed an index finger toward me to punctuate his words.

"And here you stand with a gun to my head. Why don't you go ahead and pull that trigger, fulfill that promise I made? Make it a full circle."

I thumb cocked the Colt.

"Gwon," he said. "Hell, you'll be doing me a favor. I got stomach cancer. Done spread all over. So, make up your mind. Kiss me or kill me."

I tightened my grip on the revolver but couldn't shake the feeling of being watched, watched by those only I could see, the long train of haints I was doomed to drag with me to my end of days. I looked into Sunny's eyes. I saw my mother, Julia, and Lucy—and Mae too—but most of all, there was Wonderful. Crying on the floor as the Lobos lunged and ripped. Looking to me for help. Looking in the wrong place.

They were all watching, and as I watched myself, it became clear that I was not where I thought I was. I wasn't standing in a shabby apartment on a back street in Mexico, looming over a demon. I stood over a fragile and wasted man, cornered by a wolf of his own making, reminding me too, too much of Wonderful Byrd sprawled on that piss-soaked floor. It didn't feel like a moment of triumph and justice. It felt like just another bull-in-the-ring.

I eased the hammer down and bent and looked Cecil Bastrop in the eyes. Looked as deeply as I could into the fount of my afflictions.

"You are my father, but I am not your son. I won't do what you would do."

———

How do you know what the right thing is? Is there even such a thing as the right thing? There are actions in life that seem clearly wrong, but to me, knowing the "right" decision is more difficult. These thoughts circled my head the next day as I sat in the Valley Sky Bar at the Brownsville/South Padre airport, waiting for my flight home to Cincinnati.

I sipped a lukewarm beer and tried to read a potboiler novel, but couldn't concentrate for more than two minutes, so I switched to watching a TV dangling from the ceiling above the bartender's head. A show about unsolved crimes, the usual litany of cold case kidnappings, heists and murders.

I didn't put a bullet in Cecil's head. Was that the right thing? Would it have been wrong to punish him a second time, with a death sentence no less—the State of Texas had already punished him with a prison sentence—for the crimes against Lucy and me?

And what about his role in the horrible deaths of those people he was driving across the border? Leaving them trapped in the bottom of a steel tanker to roast to death in the Texas sun. It seemed right that there should be some justice for that. It seemed right that their deaths should not become another cold case.

I found a pay phone and called Bar Paraíso and gave Guzman Cecil's address.

"In case you know somebody who needs it," I said.

I said I killed three men. Cecil Bastrop was number three. He didn't die by my hand, true enough.

But I sent the reapers to his door.

———

I didn't expect to sleep on the flight home, but stress and exhaustion and the drone of the jet knocked me out, and I dreamt of water.

I stood on a narrow stretch of sand on the edge of broad, calm waters. Maybe it was a lake, maybe a river. In front of me was the water, and behind me an impenetrable thicket, black and thorny and tall as a man, running as far inland as I could see. Across the water was the sandy bank of an island where the land was green and forested and edged with tall limestone outcroppings.

A woman stood on the island—a welcoming, benevolent figure— waving her arms and pointing at something, pointing at a small, crude raft near where I was. The raft was attached to a rope and rigged to pulleys on both sides of the water. Pulling the rope would send the raft back and forth across the divide.

There was rustling in the thicket behind me, and a little girl pushed out through the bramble. Lucy, two years old. She ran to me, calling my name, and hugged my neck. I wrapped my arm around her and kissed her chubby cheeks.

"I never forgot you," I said.

"I know."

I lifted her onto the raft and grabbed the rope, not knowing if I could pull it with one arm or not. But before I could send her across, there was more movement in the brush, someone else pushing through. Another child? Mae?

A boy stepped out, about nine years old. Shoeless. Bruised. Wearing dirty bib overalls and no shirt.

"What's this place?" he asked.

"I don't really know," I said. "But you're okay. Get on this raft here. You see that woman over there? She's waiting for you."

He waded into the water and climbed on the raft with Lucy.

"What's your name?" I asked.

"Cecil," he said. "Cecil Bastrop."

What else could I do?

I pulled the rope. It was a strain, and the raft barely moved with each pull, but I kept at it. Put all my weight into it and pulled and pulled and ...

I bolted upright in a cold sweat and cried out, panting.

"Sir, are you alright?" a flight attendant asked. "You don't look well. Can I get you something? Aspirin, maybe?"

"Yes. And water, please."

The pilot announced our final approach to Cincinnati, and I looked through snow flurries at the blurred lights of the runway. I closed my eyes and surrendered to the float, that magical sense of controlled falling, and dropped homeward from a cold, dark sky.

Chapter 37
Baby You're a Rich Man

Ella and Jay are going to the Christmas Eve service tonight at River Mill Methodist, a church they've attended on and off for the past six months. They want me to go. I've never been to a Christmas church service.

On previous Sundays, I've stayed behind and built a fire or made chili and generally lain about, sometimes reading or listening to music, sometimes staring into the frozen woods behind our house, looking for nothing in particular in the fractal beauty of their twisted black limbs.

"We need to be there by seven," Ella shouts up the stairs. "Do you need help with your tie?"

"No. I can manage."

I'm not wearing a tie. Nice slacks and a jacket will be good enough. I open the drawer to get my dress belt, a drawer where I also keep random stuff that has no other logical home. Sunny's shoebox is in there, something I salvaged from the trunk of the Lizard after my botched suicide. There's one lone, crumpled, paper Jesus left in the box alongside my silk Shiva. And the two yellowed newspaper clippings about Cecil's trial. To these things I add another brief newspaper article—a recent one, an article in Spanish that Sheriff Tyler mailed to me—reporting the discovery of Cecil Bastrop's body in his Matamoros apartment. Three bullet wounds to the head.

My prosthetic arm lies on the bed next to my clothes, and I fumble to untangle the harness. It brings the image of a dead, beached squid to mind, with finger tentacles trailing behind it.

The damn thing's a denial and always has been. A euphemism. Like seating mannequins around a dining table and calling them Mama and Lucy and Daddy. You can do it, but it's not Thanksgiving. I put the prosthesis back in the closet. Way back. I'll agree to go to church, but I won't bear my own cross.

"Where your arm?" Jay asks.

"I put it away, sweetie."

"Why you not wear it?"

"It's too cold, and we have to wear big coats tonight. It's too much trouble."

"Too much trouble," Jay repeats. He notices the snow has resumed, coming down in ever-thickening crystal waves.

"Look, look! Snowman coming down!" Snowman is Jay-speak for snow.

———

There's a placard in the church foyer announcing that the service will be a children's service tonight.

"Oh, well. Jay will be thrilled," I say, secretly pleased. I might actually enjoy a children's service.

"Sure, he will. But I was really looking forward to something traditional," Ella says, not hiding any of her disappointment.

We make our way to a pew at the front of the sanctuary and take our seats. There's an opening prayer, then the choir sings "Joy To The World."

I sing along and make goofy faces at Jay, who is wedged between Ella and me. Ella gives me a "stop that" look halfway through the song, and I momentarily stop the goofy faces, then resume as soon as she looks away. Jay cackles.

The pastor tells us we are in for a special treat. A couple from Prague who specialize in administering the Gospels to children will conduct the service. And they have some very special friends with them. As the pastor says this, two men bring out a marionette stage and set it up in front of the pulpit.

The Czech couple, dressed head-to-foot in black, take their positions behind the stage and the show begins. There's a wooden Mary and Joseph and an innkeeper and donkeys and camels and cows and sheep, all beautifully carved and painted, all masterfully manipulated on their strings by the people from Prague. I smile at their menagerie. Not a single snake in sight.

The most impressive thing the Czechs wield are the angels, a veritable flock of them painted gold and silver and fitted with silk gossamer wings. The whole flock hangs from strings in a single rig of sticks, all maneuvered with a long pole. They fly in unison when a puppeteer sways the pole.

When the narrator gets to the part of the story where the birth of Jesus is announced to the world, she quotes from the Book of Luke:

'And suddenly there was with the angel a multitude of the heavenly host praising God, and saying, Glory to God in the highest, and on earth peace, good will toward men.'

On this cue, the puppeteer swoops the flock of angels back and forth across the Bethlehem sky to illustrate the "multitude of the heavenly host." After a swoop or two, something snaps in the rigging of strings, and several angels crash to the hardwood floor, body parts bouncing and scattering not far from us.

Jay launches out of the pew and across to the little stage, where he grabs a loose puppet piece and starts running back toward me. I glance over at Ella. She slaps her hands over her face, peeking through fingers at Jay sprinting toward me. What's going through his peanut head? Maybe he thinks this is the planned, dramatic end to the Jesus puppet show, where everybody gets a souvenir? Maybe he doesn't realize the story is not over, and the unexpected dismember-ment of characters in the middle of the act is spoiling the solemnity of the occasion.

"Here, Daddy! You need this!" Jay thrusts a smooth, Czech-carved puppet arm into my hand and then leans against my knee.

"This," he says. Points at it and fidgets with his clip-on reindeer bowtie.

If Brother Granger were here, I could finally give him an answer. I do believe in something. I believe loving Jay and Ella is my only reli-gion. I believe, if not in the perfection of messiahs, then in the power of circles. In a great circle of rope that moves a little ferry across still waters to Heron Island. Or maybe it's Poe Island. Who knows?

I scoop Jay into the crook of my arm and pull him into me like a little piece of truth. Then the three of us settle in, anxious to see how the story ends.

Acknowledgments

I must first thank my wife, Donna Berry Roberts, for always being my first reader and for her love, support, and immense patience in listening to me cuss, thrash, howl, cry and sing glory halleluiahs during the decades-long creation of this book.

Heartfelt thanks to our sons, Mark and Adam Roberts, and to our daughters-in-law, Madeliene and Kendra Roberts, for providing wise counsel for my art and nourishing love for my soul.

Thank you to Mrs. Betty Lunsford, my Honors English teacher senior year in high school, for indulging my request to add creative writing to her lesson plans (much to the dismay of my classmates), and for slipping me a couple of banned novels to further stoke my interest in fiction. Wish you were still with us to sneak this book to the right someone because I'm sure it'll be banned somewhere.

Gratitude to my star editor John Matthew Fox who provided expert developmental editing, coaching, and advice, and told me the hard truths about early drafts of this book, allowing me to improve it immensely.

I must send a salute to my cross-country Zoom-powered writers' group. The time and effort these talented writers put into reviewing and critiquing my work is greatly appreciated. By name, they are:
- Mary Hester
- Jasper Rine
- Mike Saeugling

Many years ago, I was fortunate enough to have met—and received some brief but invaluable long-distance mentoring from—

Gail Galloway Adams (West Virginia University) and Chuck Kinder (University of Pittsburgh), both writers and fiction educators. Gail Adams put many hours into reading and critiquing a very raw first draft of this novel, and I greatly appreciate that selfless, unpaid act, and for the fact she miraculously saw enough good things in it to encourage me to keep writing. I owe much gratitude to Chuck Kinder for convincing me I wasn't wasting my time pursuing writing, and for teaching me my mantra: *Fiction is Trouble*. May he rest in peace.

Also, a long, long time ago in a galaxy far away, several friends and colleagues read and provided feedback on early chapters and were kind enough to not tell me how ugly my baby probably was at the time. I want to offer thanks to those kind souls. Some are no longer with us, and some names have changed, but in the time capsule of my mind they are: Jim and Jennifer Russell, Lisa and Rick Spaulding, and Mary Ann Schmidt. All good friends, all great lovers of literary fiction.

A final thank you goes to John Jarrett at Silent Clamor Press for seeing the potential in this novel, and for publishing it, and to Fatima Hassan for her expert editorial eye and insights. I'll be forever grateful.

Also by Jim Roberts

A Foreword Reviews 2024 Book of the Year Finalist, Short Story Category

Jim Roberts' debut collection of short fiction delves into the relationships between fathers and their children: the good, the bad, and the awful. These nine stories open a window into the most primal elements of the human condition–childhood and parenting.

"The stories collected in *Of Fathers & Gods* excel at walking the thin line between the profane and profound. In doing so, they resonate with veracity, empathy, and meaning, proffering insights into the mess of human existence." -N.T. McQueen/Foreword Reviews

Buy from Amazon.com, Bookshop.org, Barnesandnoble.com and many others.

About the Author

Jim Roberts is the author of the short story collection *Of Fathers & Gods* (Belle Point Press, 2024). The collection was named a finalist by *Foreword Reviews* for an INDIE 2024 Book of the Year Award. He has also been nominated for a Pushcart Prize and twice named to the finalist list for the Screencraft Cinematic Short Story Award. His work has appeared in Prime Number Magazine, Rappahannock Review, Reckon Review, Snake Nation Review, Flash Fiction Magazine, and ArLiJo-The Arlington Literary Journal. Roberts grew up in rural East Texas and currently splits his time between Ohio and Texas.

And Your Byrd Can Sing is his debut novel.

BOOK CLUB DISCUSSION GUIDE and SPECIAL OFFERS

Visit **jimrobertsfiction.com** to download your free *And Your Byrd Can Sing* <u>Book Club Discussion Guide</u> and access other special offers and additional free content

---

A Request from the Author to Readers:

If you enjoyed *And Your Byrd Can Sing*, please leave a review on Goodreads or Amazon or another book review platform. It's free to do, and very much helps your favorite authors.

Thank you for reading!

Jim Roberts

At Silent Clamor Press, we seek to illuminate the human experience with excitement, elegance, and unflinching honesty. If this work has resonated with you—offering a profound journey or a new way of seeing the world—consider sharing your reflections with others. Your voice enriches the ongoing conversation that keeps literature vital and transformative.